# THE JAWS OF REVENGE

A John Deacon Action Adventure

# Mike Boshier

Also by Mike Boshier

High Seas Hijack

Terror of the Innocent

Crossing a Line

# VIP Reader's Mailing List

To join our VIP Readers Mailing List and receive updates about new books and freebies, please go to the end section of this book.

Copyright © 2017 Mike Boshier
All rights reserved.
ISBN: 978-0-473-40024-8
www.mikeboshier.com

# Acknowledgements

Special thanks to my wife and daughters without whose support this book would not have been possible and to a great friend and excellent guitarist, Pete Cook.

**If you liked reading this book, please leave feedback on whatever system you purchased this from.**

Check out the rear pages of this book for details of other releases, information and free stuff.

# 1

**1683 A.D.**

Stretching his back, the farmer wiped the sweat from his eyes with his sleeve and fanned his leathery face with his hat. He was already tired, and it wasn't even lunchtime, but the days were long. He rented just over a fiftieth of a Labor, or about three acres, from the church; growing corn and vegetables as well as some fruit and olive trees in the steep, rocky soil. He also owned almost fifty chickens, some sheep and goats, and two old donkeys. He wasn't rich - between the church's annual rent and their ten per cent tithe, little was left each month - but he worked hard as his father and grandfather had before him, and the harvest this year was good. Soon he would have enough money to buy the bright yellow material his wife so wanted for a new dress to wear to church each Sunday.

It was one of his goats giving him concern now. He could hear its frightened bleating, but couldn't see it. Grabbing his scythe, he scrambled up the rocky terrain, not willing to lose a goat to one of the packs of roaming wild dogs. The bleating was coming from behind a gorse bush. Pulling some of it aside, he found a small fissure behind a large boulder. He was sure it had moved since he had last been up here, possibly when the earth rumbled and moved again last night. There had been large eruptions many years before he was born and again six years ago when hot lava had spewed from the land. Everyone had prayed for forgiveness from the volcano demon, Guajato, but still many people had died. Rocks and boulders had rolled down the mountainside carving new paths, killing and destroying in their way. The town on the other side of the mountain had been severely damaged, with almost a hundred people killed, but his small farm had escaped the worst. One wall had partly collapsed trapping and injuring his wife, not seriously – just bruising and cuts – and he'd soon repaired the damage, but he and his family still prayed their thanks to God every day.

He could hear the goat's cries clearer as he slid in behind the boulder. It had stuck its head through a small gap and was trapped by its horns in some undergrowth. Cursing the animal, the farmer pulled and twisted its neck until it was free and ran off. Sitting down to rest in the shade for a few minutes, he realised the small gap opened into a larger tunnel previously blocked by the boulder. Looking in, he could see nothing after a few feet, but an acrid smell stung his nose and made his eyes water. As he walked back down the hill, he decided he would return later with his son and torches.

He loved his wife. She'd been the prettiest girl in the village when he'd married her, and age had still not taken its toll. She knew her duties and had provided him four children, two daughters, and two sons. The eldest son had died soon after birth, but his remaining son was seven and would grow to be a fine man, but the boy was still too young to work hard. Unfortunately, daughters do not help much in the fields, which was why he was always tired. His daughters had inherited their mother's good looks and were also reaching puberty – a fact not unnoticed by the local village boys. Even more reasons to keep an old farmer tired.

Lunch was a simple meal of corn, olive oil, bread, and water, but the break re-energised him. Bringing his son and two lit torches, they climbed back up the steep hillside to the entrance. The smell didn't seem as strong now, and their torches burned brightly in the entrance.

Slowly moving inside, the torchlight showed a long tunnel broken and disjointed but possible to just pass through. The sides were damp with water oozing from within the rocks. By turning sideways, they could gain access through the narrowest parts. About three hundred yards in, the tunnel opened out into some small caverns, some with more small tunnels leading off them. They were deep within the mountain by now, and his son was trembling.

'Papa, the monster will get us,' he said.

'Shush, don't worry, my son. There is nothing here to hurt you. Don't worry,' he said, also trying to hide his own fears.

The noise of water running was louder here. It was coming through the very rocks themselves, running down the walls, and then seeping through cracks in the floor.

'Madre de Dios,' he whispered. 'It's hot!'

'What Papa? What is hot?'

'The water, my son. The water coming out of the rocks is hot. Here, feel it yourself.'

'Papa, I am scared. I want to go back to Mama.'

'No. We have come this far, we will continue. Come,' he said, moving further along a smaller tunnel.

After a few more hundred metres this became a dead-end, but the temperature had risen. The air was thick with moisture and hard to breathe. The farmer gripped the clay of the walls in the tunnel and the clay crumbled under his hand, near-boiling water flowing over his fingers and burning his skin, but the walls at the tunnel end were different. Harder and dry. And even hotter.

With the torches flickering and sputtering in the damp atmosphere, and guiding his son by the shoulder, as they turned to leave there was a sudden strange groaning wail. His blood ran icy cold in his veins, and he felt his heart stop. The boy burst into tears and gripped his father's legs. Hearts pounding, they moved fast back towards the entrance, gasping the clean mountain air as they stumbled out the entrance.

Dusk comes early at these latitudes. Sitting around the table eating their meal that night, the son was speaking of his bravery.

'We were inside the monster mountain, and I was fighting the monsters. They were attacking us, and Papa and I would have died if not for my bravery,' he said.

'Don't be silly, little brother,' his sister said. 'There are no monsters in the mountain.'

'There was, there was, wasn't there, Papa? It roared at us, and we had to run.'

'Something roared, my child, but I don't know what. You keep away from there. We leave the monster alone, and perhaps it will leave us alone,' he said.

Three months later the attackers came. The church bells echoed off the mountainside. This was the warning call, the call-to-arms, but it was too late.

The villagers rallied quickly with pitchforks and stakes, ready to defend. Those attacking aimed and fired. The front rank of villagers fell quickly to musket and sword; blood, flesh and brain matter flowing over the cobbles. The villagers fought as best they could but had no chance against the experience and weapons of the attackers. The remaining villagers fell back, many making for the hills willing to leave everything behind, anything to get away. As he turned to run something struck the farmer's head, and he collapsed as darkness enveloped him.

The farmer slowly awoke, lying amongst the dead and injured. His head throbbed, and blood masked his eyes. A musket ball had creased his skull, ripping flesh and he had fallen at the early attack. He'd been lucky – many had been hacked to death. Some had fallen on top and covered him – the attackers had thought him already dead. Struggling to his feet, he gagged on the coppery smell of blood and flesh covering him. It was dark and silent. How long had he been there? The battle had moved on, and the villagers had lost.

Stumbling across the fields back to his house, he could see a light. Peering in through the window, he saw his wife, partly naked, lying on the floor. A knife was jutting from her chest, blood and semen still leaking down her thighs. With a low cry, he crawled in and held her still warm body, begging God for her life back. Elsewhere his farm was a wreck. Food and anything of value gone.

Holding her cooling body close, the sudden gentle creak of a footstep near the door turned his blood to ice, and his limbs locked solid.

'Mama, Mama,' his son cried. 'Mama.'

Scrambling to his feet, the farmer saw the priest holding his son.

'Father, you are safe,' he said. 'What has happened? Where is the rest of my family?'

'My son,' the priest replied, 'it is God's will you live. I thought you were dead. They were here and raped your wife. Some of them have taken your daughters. Their fate will not be good, I fear. I saw your son running away and managed to catch him.'

The son rushed towards his mother, but the farmer grabbed him first.

'No, son. There is nothing for you to see here. Come away,' he said.

'Mama, Mama,' he screamed.

'Quiet boy,' the priest said, 'they are still close.'

But the boy's screams had been heard in the still night, and the farmer could see the distant torches stop, then start back towards the house.

'Quickly,' the farmer said. 'Get to the tunnel. We will be safe there.'

'But what of the monster?' the boy cried.

'Better a monster than a sword.'

Grabbing a discarded axe, a torch and flint, slipping and falling, the farmer dragged the priest and his son uphill in the dark to the boulder.

'Quick, get inside and keep quiet. If they catch us we are dead,' he said.

Scrambling in through the opening, the farmer pulled the gorse into the entrance behind them, further hiding them from view, as the three of them cowered against the wet walls in the dark.

'Madre di Dios,' the priest whispered. 'The ground. It feels like it's vibrating. Can you feel it, my son? It is starting again!'

They could hear the men close by, searching, but the opening was easily defendable. A loom of yellow light appeared slowly followed by a lit torch and an outstretched arm through the gap. A fierce swing of the axe and with a sickening thump the severed arm fell from the elbow, sparks dancing as the torch bounced on the floor. Before the attacker could raise a scream, the farmer swung again viciously at the neck, almost severing the head from the shoulders. With the body wedged there, it was nearly impossible for more attacks.

Passing the fallen torch to the priest, the farmer shooed him and his son further up into the tunnel, and they waited. After what seemed an eternity, broken only by the sound of the boy gently sobbing, and with a faint groaning seeming to come from the very earth itself, the farmer moved quietly back nearer the entrance to see what was happening. The faint vibration below the farmer's feet suddenly increased and threw him backwards to the ground. The noise deafened him – a deep-throated roaring as the earth shook and with a louder roar and a violent shake, the rocks and boulders in the entrance roof collapsed, further sealing the tunnel and crushing and trapping the farmer.

When at last it stopped, and with ears ringing and dust in their eyes, the boy and the priest stumbled back down to the tunnel entrance before gagging at the sight. Barely breathing through his collapsed lungs, and with white splintered bone jutting from his shattered limbs, the farmer knew the end was close.

Looking into the priest's eyes, the farmer gasped, 'F...Father, please take care of my son. I beg you in God's name to save him.'

'My son,' the old priest replied, taking the boy's and the farmer's hands. 'The entrance is blocked, and there seems no other way out. I think we will all be sitting at God's feet shortly,' he said, as another groaning wail came from further in the tunnel.

# 2

## 2010, Madrid, Spain

Fawaz Aziz Al Farah slid the ceramic knife back into its sheath and slipped it into his rucksack. He wouldn't be killing tonight. He'd chosen a ceramic blade so that the metal detectors at various locations around the city wouldn't detect it. You even went through metal detectors at the museum and art galleries now, he thought. He hadn't needed it yet, but it paid not to get over-confident. He hurried back from the Tetuan district to where he was meeting Rachel at a small pavement café in Colmenarejo.

'Baby, you're late,' Rachel said, as he swung in by her and sat down heavily. 'Where have you been?'

'I am sorry to have kept you waiting my love. I have been very busy with my studies,' he replied. 'Are you ready to order?'

'I already have,' she said. 'I've also ordered some wine for me and mineral water for you.'

He smiled and took her hand. 'So, my little one, did you get the diary today?' he said.

'I sure did. Senora Valdez kept her promise. She even copied it for me, as it's too rare to be allowed out. The Senora also copied all the local maps as well as some other paperwork she found. She was wonderful and I thanked her by buying her some flowers.'

The waiter arrived, placed their meal of paella on the table, and started to serve her. As usual, the waiter was flirting with his eyes at her, but tonight she only had eyes for the man she knew as Manuel Garibaldi.

Rachel Sanchez was twenty-three, and a Spanish-American descendant from Phoenix Arizona. She was two years into her double Master's Degrees of Geology and Volcanology and having decided to become a student at the Carlos III University of Madrid, was enjoying life. It was the start of the weekend, the weather was mild, she was enjoying her new boyfriend's company, and she could relax all weekend.

They had met just a few weeks ago. She had been rushing to a lesson on campus when he had bumped into her and knocked them both flying. Apologising profusely, he had helped her pick up her fallen books and insisted he meet her that evening to buy her a drink as an apology. He was good looking – a little older and darker-skinned than her light Mediterranean colouring, but handsome with it. She'd accepted his apology and hurried off to her lesson.

When she had met him later, he handed back to her a book. He had apologised again and said that he had picked it up that morning by mistake. He'd said he was in Madrid studying law, had quickly read her book that afternoon and was keen to discuss it with her. It was a book on earthquakes and volcanoes, and they had talked about it until late. He seemed to also share her love of her studies.

Since then, they had rarely been apart.

'Manuel, you seem little distant tonight. Is everything OK?' she asked.

'It is nothing. I am a little tired, that is all. It has been a busy week,' he said, realising he'd been lost in thought. Weeks previously, he had overheard Rachel discussing the possibility of the East Coast of America being severely damaged by events beyond its control. He'd eavesdropped as she chatted with friends at a nearby café. Her voice was typically American - quite loud and clear

9

and easily listened to by anyone who cared – while she discussed the planned thesis she was working on. She'd been slightly drunk, and he had found it easy to follow her and her friends home to see where she lived.

Years before, the message had come from the Imams and had been clear. 'Collect information, anything that could damage the Great or Little Satan and feed it back'. It was easily understood and complied with. Anything useful was collected, from where American and British tourists gathered and ate, to sightings of embassy staff. Don't decide whether you think it is useful, just gather the data, and feed it back they'd been told.

Fawaz Aziz had done just that. He had been instructed by his Imam to obtain train timetables. Three weeks' later, he'd been ordered to take a dummy run. Two weeks' after, on the morning of March 11th, 2004, Moroccan, Syrian and Algerian brothers had detonated bombs on the rush-hour commuter trains entering Madrid. One-hundred-and-ninety-one people had died and almost two thousand were wounded.

He had rejoiced that day.

His latest mission had developed after he'd fed back Rachel's overheard conversation. The message had come back two days' later. 'Obtain further. Investigate. Leave no trace'.

He had spent a number of days following Rachel and understanding her routine, chosen a suitable name, and then accidentally bumped into her one afternoon three weeks' ago.

Taking a mouthful of bread, Fawaz asked, 'So Rachel, why is the diary so important?'

'Well, a lot of the notes I have are about earth tremors in and around the Canary Islands. As you know, overall it is presently the second most active volcanic region in the world,' she said. 'But the diary is fascinating. It's about a mountain and pirates,' she said.

'What? Pirates? No, I don't believe you,' he said.

'It's true. Let's finish our food, and I will show you back at my apartment.'

Later that evening sat in her apartment, her with a glass of Cava, him with mineral water, they both looked through the paperwork and the copy of the diary.

'So, tell me about this mountain and the pirates?'

Over the next two days, Rachel told the person she knew as Manuel Garibaldi everything about her thesis, the diary and the maps.

A week later, Rachel awoke one morning to an empty apartment. The man she knew as Manuel was gone, along with the copies of her maps, paperwork, and laptop.

And the diary.

# 3

## 2012, Swat Valley, Hindu Kush Region, Afghanistan

He shifted his aim fractionally, moving an elbow for better comfort, as he focussed on the target. The weapon was held tightly down on his backpack for support as he took first pull on the trigger.

'Hooyah, John. Do it and let's go home,' he imagined Bryant saying.

'OK,' he muttered to no one in particular.

He thought of Bryant and how they'd joined the Navy together, gone through BUDs training in the same team, and completed numerous successful missions together. He'd been promoted faster than Bryant, but they'd remained close friends anyway. Heck, he'd even been Bryant's best man at his wedding. Until last week when an IED had detonated under the lead Humvee on a dirt track a few kilometres east of Barge-e Matal in a scrubby dirty village too small for its own name.

Deacon had been in the front seat next to the driver following in the tracks of the lead vehicle. The lead vehicle was always the riskiest, always the first to be targeted. That's why you changed places every thirty minutes or so – no one wanted to be lead. Deacon and Bryant's vehicles had swapped positions only minutes before. Rounding the corner the shock wave of the blast hit them before the sight of the explosion could register. The force of the explosion blew the front wheels completely off the lead Humvee and flipped it in the air. Like a scene from a bad movie, Deacon could see what was happening before his body could react. The Humvee turned upside down and landed on its back, snapping the roof gunner in half. A severed hand slapped against Deacon's polycarbonate windshield, and blood splattered and obscured his view.

Reacting by instinct, Deacon yelled to evac and cover the perimeter – a favourite trick of the Taliban was to place snipers close to pick off would-be rescuers.

Three SEALs had died that day. Bryant and the driver, both being in the front, hadn't stood a chance. Neither had the roof gunner. Two others in the rear survived, but their injuries were enough to move them out of the service. It had been a bad day. Whatever explosives had been used appeared far more deadly than before.

Rushing forward, his ears still ringing from the blast, Deacon knew he was too late. Bryant's legs had gone, and the explosion had blown his protective vest off. His stomach had split open with the air blast, and intestines and gore were splattered around his dead friend's head. Fighting back the bile that rose in his throat, Deacon said a silent prayer for his fallen comrade.

Reinforcements arrived twenty minutes later, and the hunt for the bomb makers had begun. Local villagers were 'persuaded' to give names and their whereabouts. It didn't take long. Eventually, two names came to the forefront. Abdul Masarweh and Mohammed al Durbani.

<>< ><>

Exhaling his breath, he gently pulled the trigger. The kick punched into his shoulder. It was a feeling he still enjoyed. Looking through the Leupold riflescope he adjusted his aim fractionally and less than a second after the first, the rifle coughed again and a second silenced round was on its way. The metal-jacketed rounds, travelling at a little under three thousand feet per second, took over a second to reach their targets. At almost nine thousand feet of altitude, the air was noticeably thinner with less resistance making the rounds travel further and drop less. Deacon had already mentally adjusted for this and recalibrated the 'scope. At that distance both targets were showing through the riflescope together – it was only a fraction of a degree difference for the crosshairs to cover one or the other. The first chest exploded into pink mist, and the body snapped forward. A heartbeat later, before the second target could react, the second round entered target two's back just a fraction left of centre. Even if not killed outright, in the mountains and without full medical treatment both would be dead within minutes. Two body shots. Two kills close to maximum range. He'd always been a good shot. Not quite as good as Bryant, but still pretty good. That was why he'd earned 2nd Place Honour Man at SEAL Sniper School.

Sliding his 6-foot-2 frame back down off the boulder, O-3 Lieutenant John Patrick Deacon, US Navy SEAL Team Three, smiled at his colleague, brushed dirt off his backpack, and repacked his MK11 rifle. For normal trekking he carried his standard M4A1 assault rifle, along with a Sig-Sauer 9mm pistol in a hip holster and a Ka-bar combat knife, the sniper rifle being too fine an instrument to risk damage in normal use.

'Charlie Base, this is Bravo Green. Mission accomplished. Request exfil,' his colleague radioed.

'Bravo Green, this is Charlie Base. Understood. Exfil Tango Foxtrot at 13:10 Zulu,' came the near-instant reply.

With his sniper's rifle secured, the two of them commenced down the valley to the RV position, weapons primed. They hadn't seen any other insurgents close by, but you couldn't afford to relax.

John and his four-man squad had tracked these targets for four days after the Predator drone had lost them in the many valleys of the Hindu Kush Mountains. Whether they were al-Qaeda or Taliban didn't matter. They'd crossed the border back into Pakistan trying to evade capture, but Deacon had sought and received authority to go after them. But quietly, he'd been told. Don't create any sort of incident. Find them, capture or kill them, and get out were his orders. And it was down to good old-fashioned tracking skills that they had come across them earlier. He'd wanted to catch and interrogate them, find where the explosives had come from, where they'd got the plans for the new bomb, but what with the terrain and the weather they'd managed to keep just far enough ahead. John had split his team into two trying to get in front of them, but they'd always managed to keep just out of reach and were close to safety near to a large village in the Kalash valley, but Deacon was determined not to let that happen. Now they were on their way to paradise to meet their virgins. Job done, he thought.

The Sea Hawk helicopter came in low and fast. John lit his IR Strobe on his jacket to help guide the pilot in. Textbook pickup, they were on their way within moments, heading over to pick up their colleagues before heading back towards the border minutes later. None of them trusted the Pakistan forces anymore. They had lots of talk but limited action. Some of the foot soldiers seemed OK, but you couldn't tell with the officers. Meant to be on the same side, yet the West was supposed to believe the Pakistani's didn't know Bin Laden was living in their own fucking back yard and had been for years, Deacon thought. Now they only dealt with the Pakistani's at arm's length. As long an arm as possible, he thought.

The adrenaline that had sustained them for the last four days was spent. Immense tiredness overcame them, and they slumped in the rear of the craft, accepting water and high energy bars from a crew member. Each lost within their own thoughts, they dozed. They'd all lost comrades in the past, but it was still hard to take. Deacon sighed. Whoever said revenge wasn't sweet was wrong; he smiled wryly, his mind wandering.

Not many SEALs are married – the life of any soldier, let alone a Special Forces SEAL, doesn't bode well for married life. Always away training or deployed, having to keep secrets from their partners, constantly facing danger, spending more time with your comrades than loved ones. No, long-term relationships are hard to hold down when you are a member of the greatest fighting force on earth, he reasoned. However, some did choose the married way. Bryant had with Alex, and they'd made a great couple. They even had a child on the way. Deacon was a brave warrior, but two things scared him; snakes and now having to tell his best friend's wife she had suddenly become a widowed mother-to-be. The last thing Alex had said to him before they'd deployed was to look after Bryant for her and bring him home safely. He'd failed. Bryant was going home, but instead of proudly walking off the ramp, he'd be in a body bag. Deacon would never know what to say to her. Never a coward, but he was thankful that that duty would fall to the C.O.

As his eyelids drooped, he thought again of how fucked up this region of the world was and what little he knew about it.

*Peshawar, in the north-west frontier region of Pakistan, with a population over three million, is the provincial capital of one of the most dangerous areas in the world. Most locals don't know if they are Afghanis or Pakistanis – blood mixes easily in these*

regions and borders only matter on paper. Many don't care. What does unite them though is being Pashtuns.

Pashtuns are the largest ethnic group in the region. They have ruled the region for over 300 years. All local leaders and most government roles are held by Pashtuns. They are tough, fierce, and loyal. Rarely beaten in combat, the last conqueror was Genghis Khan. The Mujahideen, trained and supplied by the CIA, who fought and defeated the Soviets in the 1980s were mostly Pashtuns. Strict followers of the Sunni Muslim sect, they defend their way of life fiercely, rejecting Western ways and thoughts. The entire region is off-limits to outsiders.

Peshawar has for centuries been the 'Gateway to Afghanistan' situated, as it is, on the only through route to the Khyber Pass, the famous road that cuts through the mountains and connects the two countries.

To the north of Peshawar lies the Swat Valley, a 150-mile, steep-sided, range of high mountains running north to south. This is deep Pashtun country, largely inaccessible, defiant to the Pakistan central government, and home to many of Osama bin Laden's al-Qaeda training camps, where modern-day jihadists live and train.

Peshawar is a city caught in a time warp. Ancient meets modern. A city where the pulsing blood of fanatical Islamic warriors fights against cell phone usage, where horse and carts compete with modern vehicles for road access. However, what is a common thread across the region is hatred for the West, and Americans in particular. Once, the locals had seen America as the saviour, back when the fight was against the Soviets or the USSR, as it was known back then. The Soviets were fighting alongside and supporting the Marxist-Leninist government of Afghanistan against the Afghan Mujahideen in the Afghan Civil War. With the Cold War still active, the West supported anyone opposing the USSR, and the Mujahideen were supplied with weapons and training from the US and UK. Saudi Arabia helped foot the bill. When the USSR, realising they were in a no-win situation, pulled out their troops during the late 1980s, it left massive destruction in its wake. The prolonged Soviet conflict had left Afghanistan ranked 170 out of 174 of the poorest, least developed countries in the world.

A mistake made, though, was the US lack of interest in reconstructing Afghanistan after the Soviets withdrew. They chose to hand over interest in the country to their allies, namely Saudi Arabia and Pakistan. But, that was before the vacuum left when the Soviet withdrawal was replaced by factions loyal elsewhere. Pakistan quickly took advantage of these changes and forged relationships with local warlords and the Taliban. A young Osama bin Laden then brought money and wisdom to the turmoil in the early days of al-Qaeda. What he preached made sense to young men who had known nothing except fighting all their lives. His words had fallen on eager ears. And eager bodies willing to fight for a cause. Any cause. As long as they believed it, they were ready to die for it.

Al-Qaeda became a state within Afghanistan, the 'Islamic Emirate of Afghanistan', between 1996 and 2001 and joined forces with the Taliban against the ruling government. During 2001, of almost fifty thousand Pakistani, Taliban and al-Qaeda forces fighting the Afghan government, less than fifteen thousand were actually Afghans.

After the al-Qaeda organised September 11, 2001, 'Twin Towers' attacks on the US, and the Taliban refusal to hand over bin Laden and disband the al-Qaeda bases, Operation 'Enduring Freedom' was launched by the US and UK. This invasion by Western armies into Afghanistan fuelled the hatred and comradeship of the Taliban and al-Qaeda forces against intervention from the West and led to frequent and on-going insurgent attacks against the western armed services.

Osama bin Laden, the founder and head of al-Qaeda, was eventually killed in Abbottabad, Pakistan on May 2, 2011, by a team of US Navy SEALs. The operation code-named 'Operation Neptune Spear'.

# 4

## Peshawar, Pakistan

Colonel Bahrawar Tarkani of the Pakistan Army was at his local Peshawar headquarters when the phone rang. Corporal Rawani took the call.

'Colonel, it appears the Americans have again entered Pakistan territory,' he said. 'Our local Army units have advised that a team of four, possibly six, have assassinated two heroic Taliban fighters west of Karakul. An American Sea Hawk helicopter crossed our border to rescue them.'

The Colonel swung around, raised his fist high as if to strike, and shouted, 'Who? Who has been killed? Give me their names... Quickly, you fool!'

The Corporal stuttered, 'Abdul Masarweh and —'

'al Durbani? Was the other person Mohammed al Durbani?' the Colonel screamed.

'Y...yes sir.'

Unable to control his fury, the Colonel drove his fist into the Corporal's face, breaking his nose and blinding him with his ring. He hit him over and over again, trying to drive his anger away.

'By all that is true, and in the name of Allah the Greatest, I will seek revenge,' the Colonel seethed, fist clenched. 'You Americans think you own the world. You burn our Qur'an, your soldiers piss on our dead, you murder our border soldiers and our children with your drones. You ignore our borders, and now you have murdered my nephew. In the name of Allah the compassionate and the merciful, I vow, YOU WILL PAY

19

FOR THIS! As Allah is my witness, you will pay, Insha'Allah!'

Two weeks later, Colonel Tarkani had decided on his revenge. It would take just over two months to implement.

# 5

## Kandahar, Afghanistan

Deacon cast a slow look towards the farm, the electronics in his night-vision goggles amplifying what little starlight there was and giving the landscape a ghostly green hue. Everything was dark, and even infrared wasn't showing any heat sources or movement at this time of the morning. Intelligence had determined this to be a 'place of interest' so the order had come down to investigate.

They'd been dropped off by silenced helicopter over three miles away as even reduced engine noise would still travel far in the dead of night. There was no moon, so they'd managed to move quickly, stopping regularly and scanning the area with infrared and night-vision goggles. A Predator drone, flying at a little over fourteen thousand feet, also had the area under surveillance and Deacon was in constant radio contact with the pilot, located at Creech AFB, Nevada.

His team of six had already paired off into the regular attack formation and were approaching the darkened farm from three directions. The sudden barking of a dog broke the silence and Deacon and his colleague dropped lower to the ground behind a makeshift stonewall. Petty Officer Ramirez peered around the edge of the wall and uttered, 'Shit, it's loose,' as the dog raced towards them, teeth bared. With little other choice Ramirez aimed and fired and, with a soft cough, the silenced round hit the dog in its chest and blew its spine apart.

Within moments, voices were heard, and seconds later, the air erupted in AK-47 gunfire as the sleeping guards came quickly awake and fired at shadows.

'Well, I guess they know we're here now,' Ramirez muttered, as bullets splattered the ground close to where he lay.

Peering around the other end of the low wall towards the farmhouse Deacon could see two of his men approaching it from the left side.

'Alpha, get in close. Bravo, Charlie, lay down covering fire,' Deacon radioed, as he started firing towards the windows.

Alpha team moved quickly towards both corners of the building and as near to the open windows as possible while hidden from the occupant's view. On the count of three, both SEALs tossed fragmentation grenades through the open windows and ducked back down. The twin blasts came seconds apart, the force collapsing one wall and partly lifting the roof. Other explosives within the room began to detonate, and a can of something highly inflammable exploded.

Deacon and his men raced towards the building kicked the severely damaged door open and went in firing. Two of the occupants, clothes ablaze, started firing but both fell quickly to the targeted rounds from Deacon and his men.

The fire had quickly spread, and the walls and ceiling were burning so Deacon and his men grabbed what paperwork and items they could find and quickly retreated.

Within minutes, the building was completely engulfed before the fire eventually died down an hour or so later.

Deacon and his men combed through the charred remains before calling in air support for the lift back to base.

# 6

## Bagram Air Base, Central Afghanistan

Deacon was breathing hard. Born and raised in Norfolk, Virginia in 1981, his life had always centred around the Navy. His mother was an accountant, his father a US Navy attack submarine commander, both now retired. The middle of three children, both sisters were happily married with the elder having two young boys who adored their adventurous uncle. Tall and muscular he'd always been incredibly fit, playing American football at college and in the High School swimming team. Graduating Columbia University with degrees in Political Science and Mechanical Engineering, he'd chosen the Navy specifically with the SEALs in mind. He'd finished high in each of the rankings, particularly well in swimming and unarmed combat. He had a wry sense of humour, was equally at ease talking with an Admiral or a canteen worker, was always willing to push himself to extremes and was 100% dependable.

At a little over six foot tall and with short dark hair, he'd never considered himself particularly good looking, especially with the scar across his chin - the result of falling off a motorbike he'd been trying to repair when he was 15, but women didn't seem to agree. Slightly rugged and with dark brown eyes, he always found it easy to have a lady on his arm when it suited. Still keen on fitness, every morning, where possible, he would rerun the initial SEAL endurance test; a five-hundred-yard swim, followed by forty-two push-ups, fifty-six press-ups, six dead-hang pull-ups, before finishing with a ten-mile run. However, stationed at Bagram for the past four months, he was a little too far from the beach for the swim, he mused, but he would keep to the others. Now, increasing his speed to push himself to the limit on the last mile, he thought of the meeting later today with Patrick Hythe.

Patrick Hythe was a Major in the British SAS. They'd met and worked together a little over four years ago on a joint operation in Iraq. Insurgents had been placing numerous IEDs on roads just north of Basra, and it was during a joint US/UK operation to remove the threat that they'd met. Hythe was a few years older than Deacon, slightly smaller in build, but with a razor-sharp mind. He was one of the best field planners Deacon had ever met. He also had a black sense of humour, as many warriors do, and, unusually for a Brit, enjoyed genuine Kentucky Bourbon. They had become friends even though the traditional inter-service rivalry continued. The SAS regularly taunted they were better trained than SEALs, better disciplined and better soldiers; and, strangely enough, the SEALs taunted the exact opposite. In practice, SAS and SEALs often share training at their UK or US bases, and any rivalry is usually forgotten about over a couple of beers in the mess.

Deacon's group was due to rotate out back to the US on four weeks' leave and training tonight, and the bosses had decided the Brits could take over. Deacons job today was to brief Hythe on the latest field intel and on the latest IEDs discovered.

A Humvee was fast approaching, and he slowed for its arrival. Hythe was in the passenger seat.

'John,' Hythe said, 'I believe we are scheduled to meet.'

'Patrick, it's nice to see you again,' Deacon replied, shaking hands. 'You're early. Let me get showered and we can meet at my CO's office in fifteen,' indicating to the driver to give them a lift back to the barracks.

Approaching the barracks, Deacon sprang out of the slowing vehicle and jogged to the showers. Twelve minutes later, washed and dressed in clean fatigues, Deacon knocked and entered his CO's office.

'Lieutenant, you know Major Hythe, I believe. Please use this time today to bring the Major up to speed, particularly on the effectiveness of the latest IEDs you've found.'

'Sir!' Deacon replied. 'Major, I have a room set down the hall, and my team are waiting,' Deacon said, holding the door open for his friend to lead.

As one, Deacon's men stood to attention and saluted as Hythe entered. After brief introductions, the men took their seats, while Deacon's master chief petty officer remained standing and said, 'Major. In a raid two days ago near Kandahar we uncovered remnants of a design for an improved IED. What our experts noticed first was the use of a higher power explosive substance, almost as powerful as C4, and secondly, the inclusion of hardened ceramic bearings. Combined with an improved remote control, we believe this to be a deadly addition to their arsenal and is similar to what hit us a few weeks ago up near Barge-e Matal.'

'It was certainly something bigger that hit us back then, Major,' another colleague said, rising from his chair. 'Normally a Humvee gets tossed, and a wheel may be wrecked, but what hit us then just chewed through the floor. It just ate through the anti-blast screening. Those in it never stood a chance.'

'The raid two days ago was intelligence-led,' Deacon said. 'We attacked a farm after a tip-off. A fire started which destroyed virtually everything, but we managed to capture some paperwork intact. Part of one page showed details of a remote transmitter with a range of almost two miles. It's commercially available and used in remote-controlled aircraft design for aeroplane enthusiasts and is available virtually anywhere in Europe. It's encrypted and built in Taiwan. Papers also mentioned an improved explosive compound being used in the IED and that tests had shown a much higher explosive blast. They are also packing the explosives with ceramic bearings that conventional metal detectors won't detect, but significantly increase the damage radius,' Deacon continued. 'We also captured some of the explosives and ball bearings. We've sent them to the Joint Weapons Intelligence Division (JWID) here at Bagram and are waiting for their feedback.

'The only other reference in the documents is to who appears to be the designer. We don't know who he is or where he's from. But he seems to be head and shoulders better than who's been designing them before and appears to be finding new, improved ways of making their stuff better,' Deacon continued.

The meeting continued for another hour as Deacon and his men passed over all relevant information they'd gleaned during their tour. All the information would have been disseminated officially and passed down, but direct transfer between the troops had shown time and again to be the most efficient method.

# 7

## 6 Weeks Later, Peshawar, Pakistan

From a distance of just a few feet away, the truck looked like it would break down at any moment. The paint was peeling, the wings and tailgate were dented and the signs on the sides old and faded. The engine blew black clouds of unburnt diesel and smoke and ran with a loud knocking sound. The driver and mate wore old clothes and had their windows open to fit in with the surroundings. To all extent, it fitted in perfectly with all the other dented, faded and broken trucks in Peshawar.

But a closer examination would show new tyres painted to look old, uprated suspension, and a well-tuned engine with protective steel around the block. The black clouds and smoke came from a carefully placed container spraying diesel directly into the end of the exhaust pipe; the sound of the smooth running of the engine masked by small loudspeakers playing engine noise. Sub-machine guns were stored under the dash, just out of sight. This was no ordinary local vehicle. This was one of a fleet of transit vehicles used by Pakistan's Strategic Plans Division (SPD), the people tasked with guarding and transporting Pakistan's nuclear weapons.

Pakistan had long boasted their multiple nuclear weapons were protected by the same sort of three-tier national command security authority as in the US. Most of the larger conventional bomb weapons were stored at the Kamra Air Weapons Complex, inside the Pakistan Ordnance Factories at Wah, Islamabad, in what was called 'screwdriver ready' status meaning they could be

27

deployed within hours. Previously this had been true, but after the US-led raid that killed Osama bin Laden in May 2011, along with the lack of involvement of Pakistan troops and the lack of sharing of intelligence information from the US, relations between the US and Pakistan had cooled. This had fuelled and increased the Islamabad led governments' longstanding fears Washington might try to dismantle or steal the country's nuclear arsenal. As a result, Islamabad set up a further group, the SPD, led by retired General Khalid Rasami, who operated under the overall command of the Army Strategic Forces Command, the force responsible for training, deployment and activation of Pakistan's nuclear missiles. Rasami expanded the SPD's efforts to disperse components and sensitive materials to different facilities to keep the location of nuclear weapons and components hidden from the US spy agencies. But instead of transporting all the nuclear warheads in armoured, well-defended, but easily-observed convoys as done previously, he began a low-key approach of moving some of the smaller weapons in doctored low-security, innocent-looking, vans on congested roads to hide them from US spy agencies and blend in with the background.

It had proved to be an effective method of hiding something in plain sight, with the movement plans only being distributed to a restricted list of senior commanders.

As local commander, Colonel Bahrawar Tarkani's name was fifth on the list.

At a junction up ahead in front of the Mosque of Mahabat Khan, a horse reared causing its cart to tip, and over twenty crates of oranges spilled onto the road. The bus behind stopped and hit its horn, while pedestrians and children alike rushed to pick up the fallen fruit. Two motorcycles approached from the rear, one on either side of the SPD truck. As they passed the rear, both pillion passengers tossed teargas grenades under the truck. Passing the front, they both fired their suppressed weapons into the cab, killing the driver and seriously wounding the guard. Two more motorcycles approached from the rear and as the rear doors were opened to allow fresh air in, the drivers and pillion passengers opened fire with their weapons. Eyes streaming and coughing, the occupants stood no chance. Within seconds it was over. The fallen oranges disappeared, the bus pulled away, and the four pillion passengers, two in the front cab, two in the rear space, drove the truck off while flanked by four motorcycle outriders. The two in the rear disabled the inbuilt GPS tracking devices while the front passenger finished off the guard with a shot to the back of his head.

The crowd of people again took possession of the road with two of them picking up the remnants of the teargas canisters. Four children scoured the area retrieving the spent brass cartridges and scuffing the dirt with their shoes to cover any spilled blood.

Within fifteen minutes the truck and its contents were hidden deep within the Old City of Peshawar, well beyond the reach of the just-arriving Pakistan Security forces.

# 8

## Islamabad, Pakistan

Professor Yousef Rashid sat drinking his mid-morning coffee, the bright sun reflecting from the window in the courtyard and half-blinding him. He heard a faint scraping noise behind and, as he turned to look, felt a hand placed on his shoulder. He also tensed as he felt something small and round press into his left kidney.

'Professor,' the voice said. 'Put down your coffee cup and walk with me. If you struggle or make a noise, you will not see your family again. If you do anything other than what I am telling you, you will not see your family again. Am I making myself clear? If you don't obey me exactly, you will not see your family again.'

As he rose unsteadily from his chair, the object was pushed further into his kidney making him flinch.

'Professor,' the voice said again, 'we already have your family. If you do not walk out of here with me within the next minute, your daughter will be shot first. Do you need me to tell you what we will do to your sons and wife?'

As they exited the courtyard, a dark coloured SUV pulled up, and the side door slid open. As the Professor was manhandled in through the side door, he could see the terrified eyes of his wife staring back at him.

Three days later a burned-out car was found in a back alley with a body inside, also burned. Fingerprint recognition was unavailable because of the intensity of the fire. The wristwatch was identified as the same Professor Yousef Rashid wore, as was a wedding ring. After removing the body, Police also found the remains and melted fragments of a driver licence with Professor Rashid's name on it in a leather wallet which had partially survived the flames and heat. Also found were two bullet holes in the head of the body, one through the temple, the other the mouth, completely shattering the jaw, making dental record checking unlikely.

# 9

## Dubai

Looking out over the water while thinking of the ladies' volleyball match at the beach club this afternoon, Shane Walker slowly sipped his coffee. It had just the right amount of sugar and was unusually hot – a nice change from the lukewarm brown stuff the machines in the Consulate usually produced. The noon 'Adhan' call to prayer echoed across Dubai Creek. The minaret speakers screeching out the tinny muezzin's announcement. Within a few minutes, the full 'Iqama' would be given, and the few Emiratee's employed within the building would also begin their prayer. Walker had never understood why the mighty US of A had to employ local cleaners and doormen in their Embassies and Consulates throughout the world. How could they ensure nothing sensitive was ever overheard? How could they keep the place 100 per cent secure when you had bloody Arabs walking around the place, he thought. Stuff the politics, he decided, security is what counts.

Although carrying the rank of Captain, this was to cover his official assignment as Military Attaché within the embassy as CIA agents don't hold military rank. Turning his chair back away from the bullet-proof window, his fingers moved over the keyboard. Every day, as head of the CIA within the Dubai Consulate General, he completed a daily intelligence briefing, along with his thoughts and comments before passing it up the line to the Embassy in Abu Dhabi. Today's was a bit more detailed than most.

He'd received a report from one of his sources in Islamabad, the SPD in Peshawar had called in reinforcements from Islamabad and was running an exercise. This, on its own, wasn't particularly unusual, but normally his source, a Government official easily corrupted by the lure of money, was aware of planned exercises weeks in advance, and this time he'd been caught on the hop. Almost as if it was a reactive versus planned event, Shane thought. What was more worrying, though, was security at Pakistan's ordnance factories and military bases had also reportedly been stepped up and they were almost in lock-down mode. Walker had been in contact with key government officials at Pakistan's Inter-Services Intelligence Agency but had received bland answers, ranging from a training exercise to an unscheduled security review. The message that had been re-iterated numerous times was there was nothing to worry about. Walker, however, had been in this business long enough to know when people told him not to worry he usually did the exact opposite. Instructing his source in Islamabad to keep his ears open and feed anything back, Walker examined two newspaper reports he'd been sent.

Both were small reports almost hidden on pages fifteen and twenty, respectively. The first detailed the possible kidnapping of Professor Yousef Rashid, one of Pakistan's top weapons scientists, which might account for the sudden increase in security, but the other detailed finding the Professor's body a few days later after an unsuccessful robbery attempt. It stated forensic examination had confirmed the remains found were the Professor's and the case had been classified as a mugging-robbery gone wrong and was now closed.

The US had installed powerful ground and satellite surveillance equipment monitoring the area from Peshawar to the north of the upper Swat Valley and could intercept almost any telephone, mobile phone or radio call within the region. Although Pakistan was officially an ally of the US, voice and data traffic was continuously intercepted and passed back to Fort Meade, Maryland, where it would be merged with other Echelon data. Walker noted there had been a significant increase in 'chatter' in the past week in the region, but the encryptions levels were very high with some more advanced methods of encryption being used.

Locally, Walker also had access to human intelligence or 'Humint' resources throughout the UAE, and something was different in the Deira region of Dubai city, he thought. There seemed to be increased tension in the air – nothing to put his finger on, just a feeling on the street, but something had changed recently. Had the professor been simply robbed and murdered or was something more dangerous occurring, he wondered. He made sure to include this at the top of his report before hitting the Send key while sipping his coffee as his thoughts again turned to the ladies' volleyball match this afternoon.

# 10

## South West Pakistan

The Balochistan Plateau region in the south-west of Pakistan is one of the most sparsely populated provinces in the country. To the north, it borders Afghanistan, south the Arabian Sea, and to the west, Iran. Being located so close to Afghanistan, many of the locals living in this barren, desolate land support the Taliban. Even those that do not would rarely oppose them – revenge attacks on a family buys loyalty. This south-western border of Pakistan closest to the Gulf of Oman and the Arabian Sea has for generations been the routes for smugglers. In the past, this was people trafficking, drugs, weapons, copper and gemstones. Nothing much has changed over the centuries, and the old, well-worn tracks and passages still reverberate to camel and donkey caravan trains. Smuggling something into, or out of, Pakistan is child's play to men born in these lands.

The small team of twelve camels and donkeys slowly swayed as they negotiated the rough terrain. Travelling silently, you couldn't hear them from more than ten feet away, apart from an occasional wheeze from an animal. On paper, one minute they were inside the land called Pakistan, the next moment in Iran, but to these hardened mountain men, it was just one hill and valley after another. By dawn, they approached a small rough track, wider than the one they were on and able to take a truck. Four armed men were waiting for them and between them, they unloaded one of the sturdiest camels. The container was just over six feet long and two feet in

35

diameter. Weighing almost four-hundred pounds, it took three of them to comfortably lift it onto the waiting truck, to the relief of the camel. A few words, the handing over of some rubies, and the truck was again on its way. The camel train had hardly stopped – that is the way business is done by the mountain men.

A few miles further on the truck stopped, and the men got out. It took them moments only to don their uniforms, re-join the truck and head for Zahedan. Within minutes, they were joined by two truckloads of Pasdaran Guards and three armoured support vehicles.

At the same time and three-hundred-miles south of there, a grain and vegetable truck slowly meandered along the M8 before joining the N10. Hidden under crates of fruit and sacks of grain was an identical container. The truck, with four guards, weapons hidden, headed for Gwadar on the northern shore of the Arabian Sea.

At the port, the truck approached a dhow unloading on the quayside. The Captain, Mustafa Karam, welcomed his visitors on board before calling for the customary serving of sweet tea.

The lead driver pulled a small leather pouch from his pocket and tipped the contents into Karam's hand. Toying with one between his finger and thumb, he held it aloft against the dhow's flag. His weather-beaten face cracked into a smile as he saw the red of the ruby matched the deep red of the UAE flag of Dubai. The goods would be loaded within the hour, and Karam would be on his way again.

<><><>

In the seventeen hours it took to deliver the first package to Parchin Military Complex, just outside of Tehran, and for Captain Karam to finish loading his dhow and set sail, al-Qaeda became a nuclear weapons terrorist group with two 20KT nuclear weapons safely out of the country.

# 11

## Three Weeks Later - Helmand Province, Afghanistan

Sergeant Stan Dougherty of the Light Dragoons was the first to see the faint small dust cloud fine on the horizon. Standing in the .50 cal roof gunner position in the lead vehicle while scanning the horizon with his binoculars, the jostling of his Jackal 2 light armoured vehicle added to the dust being kicked up and the lenses needed cleaning every few minutes. It wasn't the easiest way to check for the enemy. With the setting sun low in the sky and glaring in his eyes he wasn't even sure if it was his imagination. The terrain of this part of Helmand Province was rocky, dry and dusty. Often, small dust devils would swirl and rise in the heat and then disappear just as fast. On every excursion, time was wasted investigating each one, but you never took chances – the one time you ignored the signs could be the one time the dust was kicked up by enemy insurgents.

His Lieutenant agreed that Dougherty takes his four-man team and investigate.

As they approached, the dust cloud had disappeared, further adding to his idea it was his imagination. Stopping and dismounting, Dougherty relinquished his gunnery position to a young private and climbed out followed by a colleague. Walking around they could see footmarks in the dirt. As he keyed his microphone switch, he heard the tell-tale whine of a bullet and the thud as it hit. The warm blood spraying on his face mixing with the dust already caked was followed a fraction of a second later with his realisation that the blood wasn't his. As he dived for cover, multiple AK-47's opened up firing in his direction. He keyed his microphone and shouted, 'Alpha 1, Alpha 3 under attack. Man down. I say again, Alpha 3 und–.'

There is an old soldier's saying that you never hear the one that kills you. Stan Dougherty, had he lived, could have confirmed that saying. He never heard the bullet approaching, nor felt it explode against his forehead. He never felt his brains blow out the back of his Kevlar helmet, nor the second bullet hit him in the mouth. He did see a bright flash of light, and then the face of his wife as his body collapsed under him. Had the muscles in his face still worked, he might even have managed to smile.

The young gunnery private was quick off the mark. The Browning .50 cal was already cocked, and he returned fire within a half-second of seeing his colleagues hit, but he had no target to engage. These Afghans were using better-than-normal camouflage and with the setting sun in his eyes, he had trouble seeing where to aim. Not realising they were already outflanked, the driver spun the wheel and reversed, thereby exposing both their flanks. The next fusillade tore into their sides, and they died where they were.

Six minutes later, with the dark evening fast approaching, the Lieutenant led the charge in his armoured Land Rover and second Jackal 2, but by the time they got there, the enemy had disappeared.

Scanning the area with night vision and infrared heat-detecting binoculars showed just empty desert.

# 12

## Bagram Air Base, Afghanistan

Deacon and his team had returned to base from a routine patrol when his CO called him into his office. Since returning from leave almost two months' ago, he and his teams daily challenges had been routine. They had been out on numerous patrol missions, but nothing beyond the ordinary duties of his colleagues in green.

Ten minutes later, Deacon was briefing his men. 'We're flying down to Bastion to meet up with the Brits. This is a joint operation with us, the British Marines, and the Welsh Guards. A group of insurgents shot up a British sneak-and-peak patrol and killed four of them. By the time their support arrived, there was nothing to be found. It looks like the insurgents have got something happening in the north of Kandahar. This operation is to find, intercept and engage them. Two UAV's are already covering the area. We will be under the overall command of Colonel Baxter of the Welsh Guards. Our C-130 departs in thirty minutes,' he said.

Amidst groans of about working with the Brits and being under their command, the squad quickly assembled their required weapons and jogged to the waiting aircraft.

Exiting the loading ramp at Bastion, they were met and taken to a briefing hut. Colonel Baxter opened the session by introducing himself.

'Gentlemen,' he said. 'Briefly, a British recon patrol was ambushed yesterday about forty kilometres north of here and four killed. Unfortunately, by the time reinforcements arrived, the insurgents had vanished. But expended cartridges would suggest between fifteen and twenty of them. We've found no trace, but a UAV has picked up movement a few kilometres east of there. The terrain is not good for us - lots of rocks and gullies. Captain Fields will go through the finer details, but this is a joint British / US mission, and we will go in heavy. The mission is to seek, engage and destroy the enemy. Close air support is available as needed.'

After an extensive briefing Deacon and his men, along with most of the Marines, made their way to the airfield where they boarded two Sea Hawk and four Black Hawk 'copters. The remaining Marines, along with the Welsh Guards, boarded six Warrior infantry vehicles that left immediately. The airborne groups would over-fly, outflank and cut off the insurgents while the land-based contingent would bring up the rear.

The Sea Hawk's real-time video feeds showed little life as they approached the area the UAV had previously scanned. Coming into land Deacon thought he could see some darker shapes against the rough terrain, but then he and his men were down. As they exited and took standard defensive procedures behind rocks and in gullies, the rhythmic 'chug' of AK-47's on automatic fire came through loud and clear. With bullets striking the fuselages, the 'copters quickly rose and moved out of range, but stayed close enough to offer support when needed.

Deacon realised that the dark shapes he had seen as they were landing had been the insurgents, but he couldn't understand why the infra-red cameras weren't detecting them. Deacon estimated there were about thirty insurgents who would become trapped as the land vehicles came up behind them.

The firefight was vicious and lasted longer than expected. As the vehicles approached, the insurgents began firing RPG's. Three struck one of the Warriors, one exploding near its cannon, while the others exploded against the ceramic armour plating. Flames enveloped it as the shouts and screams of the men trapped inside drowned the cheers of the Taliban. Under extensive supportive covering fire, all but two of the soldiers managed to escape the burning Warrior. While members of the assault team reached them with medical aid, the other Warrior's opened up with their 30mm cannons. For the next ten minutes it became a fierce battle with neither side willing to lose ground, but eventually, the stronger firepower of the coalition forces, supported by the Black Hawks, began to take effect. They managed to slowly advance, with machine guns and grenade launchers gradually taking their toll as the insurgents fell back, many wounded and falling to the concentrated gunfire. Quite a number managed to escape, hiding, then escaping down through the gullies, but Deacon and three of his men chased after one small three-man group, determined to try to capture them dead or alive.

Coming around a blind corner in the gulley, Deacon felt the 'snick' of a bullet pull at his battledress. The bullet had hit one of his shoulder straps, severing it completely. An inch lower and he would have lost his collarbone. Two inches to the right and he would have lost his throat. Diving for cover Deacon heard the grunt from one of his men. His colleague, following with his rifle held to his eye, had been hit by fragments of metal and plastic exploding in his face as his rifle sights were hit by the bullet that had just missed Deacon. Half-blinded by the blood running down his forehead, they scrambled for cover as Deacon, and one of his men quickly applied a field dressing while the remaining SEAL gave covering fire. After satisfying himself that his man was safe from excessive blood loss, Deacon and his two other colleagues re-engaged the enemy, throwing two fragmentation grenades along the gulley and attacking while the blast was still echoing.

Two Taliban died in the blast and Deacon managed to hit the other as he tried to escape. After, walking amongst the dead, Deacon was confused. The Taliban had fought almost to the last man and had fought hard. Over twenty-five of them in total were dead or dying, and the coalition had taken a heavy toll as well, with three dead and almost a dozen wounded. Why, Deacon wondered, had they fought so hard. The Taliban's tactics were always hit and run. What was so important that so many men were willing to die, he wondered.

Bending over one of the corpses, he could see a plastic-based material. Picking it up, he saw it was thin and felt lightweight. Shaking it out, it became an eight-foot by four-foot plastic-lined sheet, albeit this one pockmarked by bullet holes and shrapnel. The inside surface was a light grey colour, while the outside was covered in a harder wearing camouflage material. This was what they had been hiding beneath – these were the darker objects he had seen as they'd come into land. Gathering a few of them up, he bundled them together, determined to pass them to the JWID for analysis.

# 13

## Tehran

It was not usual for Rear-Admiral Ahmad al-Jalil Behbahan of the Islamic Republic of Iran Navy to be nervous, but today was not an ordinary day.

The Ministry of Intelligence and Security (MOIS) is the post-revolutionary successor to the SAVAK secret police and primary intelligence agency of the Islamic Republic of Iran. The very buildings and security around MOIS are designed to instil terror in the public. Answerable directly to the Supreme Leader, many have been taken in for 'questioning', few ever return.

Unlike the public, Rear-Admiral Behbahan had no need to be nervous of the environment, but it was always prudent to be cautious when meeting with the Supreme Leader.

'Oh, mighty exalted leader, I am humbled in your presence. I am honoured, Excellency, for you wanting to see me,' Behbahan said.

'Admiral,' the Supreme Leader replied, 'your communication interests me. Have you brought him with you?'

'Yes, Excellency. Shall I have him brought in now?'

'No, not yet. First I wish you tell me some more about him.'

'As you wish, Excellency.

'Saif Mohammed Khan, born in 1968, from Iranian parents both living in the US in New York. The parents were trusted sleeper agents for many years. Their cover was their rug and carpet import business and their restaurant in New York. Their cover was perfect. Their son, though, was taken with the western ways. He changed his name to Steve Caan to be more American and became a typical American youth. He joined the US Navy from school in '87. Their security never detected his parents' allegiance to us, most likely due to their ineptitude. Rising to the role of Lieutenant on the USS Sides, specialising in intelligence and surface warfare, he became an excellent planner and tactician. He was very highly rated within the US Navy and was heavily involved in setting up Navy tactics and in planning Special Forces incursions etc.'

'So,' the Supreme Leader asked, 'he is an American spy? How can we trust him?'

'Oh exalted Excellency,' Behbahan said, 'he is now a true Muslim and a true believer. He is one of our best planners in causing harm to America and one of our most faithful long-term servants.'

'Go on,' the Supreme Leader said.

'As you know, your Excellency, in 1988 our airliner, Flight 655, was shot down by the murderous American dogs. The US Vincennes shot it down, killing all 290 passengers and crew. The US never admitted responsibility or apologised to Iran, merely later 'expressing regret' for miss-identifying it as an attacking Iranian fighter, and paid some compensation to the victims' families. However, the mighty US has never formally apologised. Instead, President Reagan presented the captain of Vincennes with a medal for his actions. On that day, Saif says, he began to change, finally seeing the US as the aggressor, and started to read the Qur'an in private. He became devout but kept this very well hidden. He discussed his feelings with his father when on leave, and he was introduced to their contacts who disclosed their work with us. His local Imam told him to remain

45

acting as a normal American, still drinking alcohol, to fit in with the crowd, stating that Allah will forgive him due to his services to all Muslims. He was to continue as before, but to pass information back through his parents, but not to do anything to make the Americans suspicious. I think he thought of it as a game, but he worked for us aboard the USS Sides for another five years before a further security review, where his promotion was blocked due to having Iranian parents. In 1996 there was a large spy case in America when a former National Security Agency spy was arrested. Although nothing to do with Saif, we felt we had pushed him as far as was workable and wanted him out. Also, America was rechecking yet again everyone's security clearances, and there was a chance he would be found out.'

'Was he ever detected?' the Supreme Leader asked.

'No, your Excellency. Never,' Behbahan said. 'He left their Navy in late 1996 and travelled to Dubai. There he was met by representatives of my Department and a new mission planned. This was at our early stages of supporting al-Qaeda. We wanted him to work with them. We believed him to be a true Muslim and by now devoutly anti-American, but knowing what Bin Laden was planning for New York, we thought to let them take the risk. He was met by Taliban forces in Gwadar, and we let it be known that we thought he might be a possible US spy, but if not, could be a valuable asset to al-Qaeda. He was held and beaten but, however hard they tried, they couldn't break him. He was transferred to al-Qaeda, and he was further interrogated, but never once faltered. After meeting with 'The Sheik', who eventually believed him to be a true convert, he was permitted to work with Mohamed Daoud Al-Owhali, one of the four al-Qaeda members involved in the 1998 US embassy bombings in Nairobi. His planning and organisation skills became

46

imperative and, as you know, the attack was successful. Unfortunately, a stupid error by Al-Owhali soon after ensured Al-Owhali's arrest who then provided names and location details of his three companions. They were arrested and tortured, but under a directive from Bin Laden, Saif's name was never released by any of the bombers. Saif then worked with local Taliban and al-Qaeda within Pakistan in the Hindu Kush region.

'Having proved his worth, he was promoted within al-Qaeda at Bin Laden's command and began to work with senior al-Qaeda members. Together they planned the USS Cole attack in Aden in 2000, which killed 17 US sailors and wounded almost 40 more.'

Halting the discussion to drink sweet tea together and sharing Baghlava biscuit cakes, the Supreme Leader quickly read the briefing Behbahan had sent him.

'So Admiral, Saif had built up a reputation with al-Qaeda?' the Supreme Leader said.

'Yes, your esteemed Excellency. And not just al-Qaeda. He has offered assistance to multiple militant groups such as Hamas, Hizballah, Harakat-al-Falastini, and various groups in Yemen and Somalia, including al-Shabaab. Although not directly involved in the twin towers attacks, knowledge of the security measures and the security levels at American airports helped bin Laden in planning it. But unfortunately, American peasants reacted against anyone they considered 'foreign'. His parents were attacked by a US White Supremacists group, and his mother raped. The father was beaten and suffered a heart attack and stroke, and their family restaurant and shop was burned down. But all this has done is further reinforced his belief that the US is the enemy and is the greatest aggressor to Islam.

'After the West joined together and invaded Afghanistan, we brought him back here to protect our

47

asset, and he now resides in Bandar Abbas and works with the IRIN and IRGC in strategy, tactics and planning.' Behbahan said.

'Very impressive, Admiral,' the Supreme Leader said. 'Please fetch this remarkable man to me. We have kept him waiting long enough.'

# 14

## Tehran

Saif Mohammed Khan walked in behind the Rear-Admiral. The Pasdaran, the regime's Praetorian Guard, stopped him again. These guards, the elitist of the elite of Iran's Islamic Revolutionary Guards Corps (IRGC), had all sworn an oath of loyalty to the Supreme Leader. For the fifth time that day, he was frisked and electronically wanded, but allowed to proceed. With two of the fiercest guards he had ever seen standing just to his shoulders, he approached and bowed before his leader.

'Salaam alaikum, Oh, mighty exalted leader, I am humbled in your presence and honoured your Excellency,' Khan said.

'Wa alaikum al salaam,' came the reply. 'I have heard many good things about you. Come and sit and tell me what you do to make the mighty Americans fear us.'

'Excellency, it is my greatest honour to serve you. I believe Admiral Behbahan will have already provided you information of my past. Since moving back to Iran in 2005, I have been working closely with both Navies providing technical advice and information on American systems, rules of engagement, and special operations. In particular, I have worked closely with Commander Jahangir, of Kilo submarine 'Yunes' to give as much information about offshore methods of US Navy operations. I've also worked with Captain Al Hassan, commander of the Fast Attack Inshore Patrol boat 'Daeva' of the IRGC about inshore work to defeat US raids.

'I also spend my time working with senior members of MOIS in intelligence planning and formulating various ways and methods of harming the US and the West. A lot of these plans are current, but some are put into mothballs until the right time, such as an outside world event, or the need for more advanced weapons. One of my recent projects has been in using thermal 'heat blankets' used to retain body heat by mountaineers etc. I thought that if they can reflect body heat and not allow any out, perhaps they could be used to hide soldiers from thermal image cameras.'

'And do they work?'

'Yes, Excellency. Extremely well. The standard version is shiny and very flimsy. But working with a Chinese manufacturer, we have designed them to make them almost invisible to heat cameras and by camouflaging them as well, hides the wearer from the naked eye, as well as making them much harder wearing for the battlefield. General Ratoosh in the Artesh is trialling them with his men, and some of the Taliban have already started using them. Less than a week ago a team of fighters shot up a British Army team. When the British reinforcements arrived, our brave soldiers were still close but covered with the blankets and invisible to the naked eye. Even though the British used their infrared and night-vision glasses, they were not found. They seem very successful, and Hamas are interested in using them to breach the Israeli border.

'My last project before that was to come up with a more efficient build of IEDs. From working with the IRIN and the Artesh, we found a higher-performing explosive by using Navy artillery shell propellant. Combining this with ceramic ball bearings, we managed to build far more efficient explosive devices which are almost impossible to detect with conventional means. Not only has this design been passed to the Taliban for use in Afghanistan, but we have also created and tested a bomb vest which passes regular airport X-ray scanners. That design is also on its way to our Hamas brothers,' Saif said.

Taking a moment to sip his tea, the Supreme Leader seemed heavy in thought. Finally, he said, 'I have heard reports from Afghanistan that this IED and the heat blankets are indeed effective. Allah has smiled on you with his good fortune. However, the reason I had you brought here is more to do with a plan you previously supplied to MOIS. This was a plan to hurt American with no comeback on us. It started in Madrid, I think.'

'Yes, your Excellency,' Saif replied. 'This was the plan I called 'The Jaws of Allah' for want of a better name.'

'Indeed,' the Leader agreed. 'Tell me more about it.'

The Supreme Leader, along with Rear-Admiral Behbahan, listened carefully while Saif explained his plan in detail.

'It is an interesting concept,' the Leader said after, 'but why would al-Qaeda waste two nuclear devices on this when they could detonate them instead somewhere such as New York or Washington? Surely that would benefit their cause more?'

'Excellency, I agree that setting off major explosions somewhere like New York or Washington would have a significant impact on America's fear of terrorism, but I believe may present more problems for a number of reasons. First, unless massive bombs were used, in the region of several megatons, the death toll would not actually be that high. A 20 kiloton device would maybe give a hundred-and-fifty to two-hundred thousand dead, compared with over ten million dead plus the extra advantage of totally wrecked cities with my plan. Secondly, imports into America are extremely tightly monitored and controlled – they X-ray containers and have radiation sensors at all their cargo points. It would be very hard guaranteeing actually getting the devices in place without being found out, and if anything pointed at Iran, it would be the equivalent of a declaration of nuclear war against America, a war we couldn't win. Thirdly, al-Qaeda cannot do this alone – they need our assistance, but again we have to be careful not to be seen to be involved, and four--.'

'Are you suggesting we act like cowards behind the coattails of al-Qaeda?' the Leader interrupted, his voice growing louder with anger.

'No, no, your Excellency. Forgive me, I have not made myself clear. My concern is that America is just waiting for an excuse to declare war on us. With a conventional war, and with the might of our Muslim brothers behind us, America would soon realise that we are not as easy a prey as Iraq was. But if they found us trying to smuggle nuclear weapons into America, or even suspected us, that may be their excuse for nuclear retaliation of which we cannot win. I don't think just damaging one or two American cities will be enough to make the mighty US back down. But I think killing ten million Americans and wrecking twenty or so cities at once may do so.'

Sipping his tea, the Leader considered these comments before instructing Saif to continue.

'Excellency, the fourth point I was going to make is that with any nuclear explosion experts can determine from the radiation debris and fallout where the bomb was made. This would be easy for them to do in Washington or Manhattan, but if the debris was spread thousands of kilometres away, under thousands of metres of water and they didn't even know it was a nuclear explosion ... ,' Saif continued.

Making some notes in the documents, the Leader smiled slightly to himself. Looking at Saif, he said, 'Mmm, you make some good points, but I grow weary, my son. My bones are old, and I grow tired easily nowadays. You are correct in that the reason this plan was mothballed was that al-Qaeda and we didn't possess suitable weapons. But the circumstances have now changed. Circumstances that make your plan both attractive and possible.'

Waving the guards to escort Saif out, the Supreme Leader continued, 'The Admiral will contact you again shortly, but you will speak of this to no one. Do I make myself clear? No one!

# 15

## Two weeks later, Bandar Abbas Naval Base, Iran

Rear-Admiral Behbahan smiled warmly at his guest, Admiral Zhang of the People's Republic of China.

'Salaam alaikum. It is good to see you again, my friend,' Behbahan said.

'Wa alaikum al salaam. The pleasure is all mine, Admiral,' Zhang replied. 'It has been too long. You are well? And your sons?'

'They are well, Insha'Allah, and yours?' Behbahan said to Zhang's nodding. 'Come, I have a tour of our facilities arranged.'

Stepping down from the dock into the cockpit of the small launch, Behbahan spoke briefly in Farsi to the Midshipman in charge of the launch. Zhang took the offered cup of sweet tea from the tea boy while the two Able Seamen untied the craft. They ventured out near to the breakwater around Bandar Abbas harbour before coming in close to one of the concrete piers, where two submarines were moored.

'This is the last Kilo 'Noor' to have been upgraded,' Behbahan said. 'Your team has been extremely helpful. We have also finished the upgrade to our oldest Kilo, 'Tareq'. She is the one moored in front. We upgraded the weapons and electronics systems, fitted the latest Chinese sonar, replaced the original six-blade propeller with a newer, quieter anti-cavitation seven-blade version, and replaced and improved some of the acoustic tiles on the hulls. We are currently in the middle of a similar upgrade to our third sub, 'Yunes'. She is over in the dry dock. We will visit her shortly. She will be finished within two months, and then, when all three are completed, we shall have something to make the infidel Americans think twice about. Insha'Allah.

'And my people have been useful?' Zhang asked.

'Very much so, Admiral. Their knowledge of the sonar system is very extensive. Not just in its use, but in the various ways a Kilo can avoid detection. You have how many now?'

'Twelve Kilos out of a total of sixty-four submarines,' Zhang said. 'They vary in age but are all being upgraded to latest specifications. As you know, they are some of the quietest craft around, almost as quiet as our latest Yuan class designed and built by the People's Republic of China.'

'So what will your fleet consist of?' Behbahan asked.

'Of conventional attack submarines we will phase out the older Ming and Romeo class, and concentrate on the Yuan, Song and Kilo class,' Zhang said. 'We also have the option to purchase the latest advanced Amur class from Russia. However, we are also rapidly expanding our nuclear attack and ballistic submarine force. We plan to have approximately six SSBNs within the next few years.'

'By the Prophet, that is a feat even Allah would praise,' Behbahan said. 'The Americans shall come to know the wrath of a mighty and powerful China in the Pacific. When our Muslim brothers unite, and the cursed Americans and their British puppies are thrown back into the Persian Gulf to feed the sharks, we will guard the mighty nations of Islam, and you will defend the mighty East, Insha'Allah.'

Zhang cast his eyes around and, squinting in the harsh midday sun, thought about the forthcoming conflicts. The only thing stopping China taking command of Asia and the Pacific now was America's weapons supremacy and their carrier battle groups. Let the Middle East make the first move and suffer the possible wrath of the mighty Americans, Zhang thought. If the plan worked, America would be brought to its knees. If it failed, it would not be China's problem. With China's projected growth of military bases in the Spratly Islands over the next five years and with the hopeful damage shortly inflicted to the America Pacific Fleet, China could sit back and wait for its righteous return to world leader status. But anyway his Navy would be able to prod and probe the Americans, he thought, just to annoy and antagonise them and keep them in check. The American carrier battle groups are formidable foes, but even an animal as powerful as a lion becomes prey as it ages. A clan of Hyenas can bring down the biggest and fiercest lion if they work together. Soon, the time would come to teach America they are no longer the only superpower, he thought.

'Admiral,' Behbahan said, disrupting his thoughts. 'If you are ready, we shall now go and see the work on 'Yunes',' as the launch cut across the water to the dry dock.

At almost seventy-four metres length and ten metres beam, Kilos are by no means the largest submarines in service, but Zhang still felt a shiver as he ran his hand along the smooth rubberised hull of this 2,300-ton predator.

'Admiral,' Behbahan said, 'your support in these upgrades has been essential. Without you supplying your skilled people to assist, I am sure we would still be working on Tareq.'

'My dear Behbahan, a strong Iran is a powerful friend to have. Our two countries have many areas in common. Our Government decided wisely to assist the Islamic

Republic of Iran with defence technologies and weapons systems. We have invested billions of dollars in your oil and gas production. Iran supplies us with almost fifty per cent of all our oil. We depend on your country for our oil, and you rely on us for our money. It is in both our interests that Iran can defend itself against the imperialist Americans. That is why we have also been helping you with your weapons programs and nuclear research at Parchin.'

'Admiral,' Behbahan said, 'the nuclear project at Parchin has been a great success. Only a very few senior people know, but soon we will have enough enriched uranium to build our fifth warhead. We have copied the design of the warhead in your Chang Feng cruise missile, and we are currently working on fitting the warheads to missiles. We are also examining a weapon stolen from Pakistan and are sharing the data with you. Your technical people are working closely with ours, and the centrifuges you have secretly provided are working day and night. Our Supreme Leader has decreed we shall have our first launchable weapon actually ready for launch within three months. All that is in heaven and earth gives glory to Allah. He is the Mighty, the Wise One, Insha'Allah. We are in agreement. America has become too big and demanding. Daily they taunt and threaten us. Their ships and aircraft fly right to our borders, often over. They fly their cursed unmanned spy drones over our land. They bully us and anyone who opposes them. The infidels need to be brought to their knees.'

'My friend,' Zhang replied. 'We also feel as you do. The mighty US also continually taunt us along our borders. They help protect the devil island of Taiwan, while their submarines and aircraft peck at our borders. They have plans to utilise bases in Australia, and they are also in talks with the Philippine government to open a US base in the Philippine-occupied areas of the Spratly Islands. The People's Republic of China considers the entire Pacific west of the International Date Line as 'China' sea, as well as what is called the South and the East China Sea. The Philippine Sea is our backyard, not the Americans. We WILL get them out of there. Soon they will see we have not been sleeping. Our new fighter planes, submarines and missiles will keep the Americans away. We will push them back to their sunny island of Hawaii and make them grow pineapples. Soon, we will operate with impunity in the western Pacific, the Indian Ocean, and beyond. They taunt and ridicule us now, but their days of power are numbered – we are the new superpower in Asia – as they will wake up one morning and discover!'

'Behbahan,' Zhang said, finishing his coffee. 'This evening has been most welcome, and the food was excellent.'

'My dear Zhang, you are my honoured guest. My home is your home, Insha'Allah,' he replied. 'Let us now discuss the reason for your visit. Come. Let us move to a quieter room and I will tell you my thoughts.'

# 16

## One week later, Tehran

The abrupt ring of the telephone made him jump. It had been a good dream, too, he thought, trying to come to terms with it being only four-thirty in the morning. She was pretty, shapely, and just undoing her blouse, he thought, as he quickly rubbed his face and picked up the handset. The terseness of the caller left no doubt it was an official call. He waited as instructed for the connection to be made.

'Salaam alaikum,' the Admiral said.

'Wa alaikum al salaam, Excellency,' Saif replied. 'It is a pleasure to hear from you.'

'A car will be waiting for you in fifteen minutes. You will come to my office immediately,' the Admiral said as he hung up.

Quickly showering and shaving, Saif was just finishing dressing when a heavy beating of his door started. The Pasdaran were a law unto themselves. There was no small talk so Saif couldn't tell the nature of the meeting. Arriving at the Navy yard, Saif was escorted to the Admiral's offices, but it was not suggested he sat, so he stood waiting for the Admiral to join.

As the Admiral entered with a smile on his face, Saif felt himself visibly relax. The smile meant if not good, at least not bad news. He realised then that the phone call had been the good news, allowing him time to get dressed for the meeting. Had he been out of favour, then the door would simply have been kicked down by the Pasdaran.

Taking a seat as offered by the Admiral, Saif waited for the meeting to commence.

'Khan, the Council has approved your plan with a few stipulations. I know when you first presented your ideas to me, I had you meet with the various heads of departments here at the University, to check if your ideas would work.'

'Yes, Excellency,' Saif said. 'I met with the professors of structural engineering, fluid dynamics, geology, and earthquake and volcanology research. I explained carefully what I had planned and showed them the maps and discussed my theories. I asked if they thought it was feasible and what amount of force would be needed. It took them over a week, but they all agreed anything over 15 kilotons would have the desired effect, but the locations of the devices are crucial. Using topology maps, they positioned them for maximum effect. They were all in agreement as to location and very strict on the exact positioning of the devices.'

'Mmmm, good,' Behbahan replied, 'I have since met with those same professors and let them know we will be implementing the plan shortly. I also explained to them our Supreme Leader's interest in the success of the plan and what would happen to them and their families if their workings were wrong. They have all stuck with their original recommendations to you but again insisted on the device positioning.

'I have also met with and gained the support from the People's Liberation Army Navy of China to assist in the Pacific plan.' Behbahan continued. 'Secondly, we are already in possession of one of the two stolen Pakistani nuclear weapons. The Supreme Leader in his wisdom had already agreed with senior members of The Base our support in their struggle, in exchange for them allowing our experts to disassemble and then rebuild one of their stolen weapons. I am happy to report, Insha'Allah, this has all been approved. The significance of your planned date will cause further panic amongst the weak Americans. You made a good case, and within a few days, you can start proceeding with your plan. Ten million US dollars has been placed in a Swiss account for you to use as required.'

'As to the stipulations,' the Admiral continued, 'the Council have decreed that you must take all measures to ensure we are isolated from this attack. It is imperative Iran cannot be seen to have sanctioned or assisted al-Qaeda with this. Until we have more nuclear weapons built and ready, we cannot take on America's forces. However, this project has the overall approval of the Council. We will offer you whatever support you need, and your involvement in the success of this project will be well remembered, Insha'Allah.'

'Thank you, Excellency,' Saif said. 'All of the believers who will be helping me are from Hamas. They think I am Palestinian. There will be no comeback here.'

The meeting continued another hour where specifics were discussed before Saif rose to leave. 'If it is Allah's will, it shall be done, Excellency,' he said.

'It is Allah's will,' came the reply.

# 17

## Virginia, USA

Susan Draymore was experiencing just an ordinary day at the National Counterterrorism Centre (NCTC) in Liberty Crossing, Virginia. Her role was to review the data being entered into the Terrorist Identities Datamart Environment (TIDE). That data was then re-examined and data-mined to connect the dots to other names and identities. If that process yielded additional results, the information would be passed to the Terrorist Screening Centre (TSC) and also to the Terrorist Identities Group (TIG), both in an adjoining building. Each day, hundreds of names were added to the list and usually passed to the FBI's terrorist watch list, or even onto their no-fly list used by airports to ensure safe travel.

Today was slightly different, though. This alert had come in from an illegal NSA hack into the facial camera and immigration system used in Dubai Airport. Although not real-time, the NCTC ran passenger images from the cameras through facial recognition software as Dubai is one of the world's busiest airport hubs.

Her screen flashed red as a positive identification had just occurred. The slightly noisy image of a middle-aged man appeared on her screen, along with a 14 point verification table. The human face has approximately 80 nodal points, but only between 14 and 22 are required *for* verification.

On further examination, Susan saw that this person was listed not as an actual terrorist, but as a person the US was interested in when he travelled. His name was

Professor Yousef Rashid, and he was a senior weapons physicist at the Pakistan Atomic Energy Commission, but that didn't tie up with his passport he had used to gain access to Dubai. It wasn't forged, it was a genuine passport but showed a different name.

As normal protocol instructed, Sarah included it within her regular daily report to her manager, which was then uploaded to Washington.

# 18

## Washington, USA

Lieutenant Mitchell Stringer, known as 'Mitch' to his friends, was an O2 Junior Grade officer in Naval Intelligence. He'd enlisted after graduating summa cum laude from Columbia University where he'd also met Deacon. They'd hit it off together and had become good friends. Both had intended on joining the Navy and, after graduating, had enlisted with Deacon applying to the SEALs and Stringer applying directly to Naval Intelligence. Since then they'd regularly kept in contact often sharing information when they could.

Stringer was friendly, extremely intelligent, and had a knack for finding needles in haystacks. He also had the ability to speak of technical details clearly with senior officers and had already been earmarked for fast-track promotion.

He was a keen dinghy sailor and had met his fiancée, Helen, at the sailing clubhouse in Alexandria. Both had stood there a little embarrassed, having arrived with friends, but then a smile had broken the ice and things just moved forward from there. Helen was an accountant at a law firm in the city, and they had recently moved into a two-bedroom apartment in the trendy Adams Morgan area of DC.

Stringer had been taken under the personal wing of Admiral Douglas Eugene Carter, the tough ex-Carrier Battle Group Commander who occupied the Chief of Naval Operations chair in the Pentagon. Soon after he had joined Naval Intelligence, Stringer had made a presentation to some senior officers, including Admiral Carter. His ability to explain a technical matter clearly, without being intimidated by the audience or condescending with his knowledge, had found a soft spot in the Admiral's tough exterior. The Admiral had a well-known reputation of not suffering fools lightly and of demanding his subordinates come to the point quickly. Time was too precious to waste with waffle, and word padding, he always said. 'Tell me what you are going to tell me, and tell it to me quickly' was his motto, and Stringer's fresh-faced approach had gone down well with him. Too many people in Washington were too interested in playing politics, the Admiral always said, and because he didn't, Stringer stood out from the crowd.

Stringer was on the receiving list of various daily and weekly reports from the NSA in Fort Meade. Raw intelligence is accumulated at NSA Headquarters, Fort Meade, from various sources and processed. Reports from this data are also further processed, and results passed to the relevant government agencies and departments.

However, since 9/11, and the emphasis on more sharing of data and closer interworking between agencies, the raw data is also passed on to the relevant departments and agencies for their own specialists to examine. Stringer worked in one such department within the Chief of Naval Operations. As with many government departments, there was still a significant amount of internal politics involved and reports would often take days or even weeks to be passed around.

The ringing phone broke through her dreams she realised, slowly coming awake. Extending a hand, she pulled the handset off the cradle.

'Hullo?' she murmured, still trying to wake up.

'Helen? Helen, it's Shane. In Dubai, Helen. You awake?'

'Yeah, Shane. W...what time is it?'

'Midday here. It must be about 04:00 with you. Sorry to wake you but I need to speak with Mitch pretty urgently.'

'Yeah, OK. I'll wake him. The calls are always for him, but he's such a damned heavy sleeper. Can you hear him snoring?'

'Yeah, honey, I can. Hey, sorry for waking you. I am back in DC in a few weeks. How's about we all go out for dinner one night?'

'You're on!' she said as she tried pummelling Mitch awake. 'Mitch, wake up, it's Shane for you. Wake UP!'

Smiling sheepishly, he took the phone from her while rubbing his eyes with his other hand.

'Shane, hang on a mo,' he said as he leant over and kissed Helen. 'Go back to sleep hon, I'll take this in the other room.'

Pulling on his dressing gown and trying to find his slippers, he stumbled into the study.

'Shane, my man. You better have a good reason for calling me at this goddam hour?'

'Mitch, you need to go secure.'

Mitch entered his personal ID number into the STE secure telephone equipment on his desk. Three seconds later both Mitch and Shane heard the familiar 'double-beep' confirming the line was now encrypted.

'You wanted to know news about that dead Pakistani scientist. Yousef Rashid. Well, I just got a report that NCTC saw him arrive in Dubai yesterday. They got a 75 per cent probability hit, although he's travelling on false plates. Any idea what's going on?'

'Shane, you've lost me. Start again.'

66

'Mitch. Wake up, man. Rub your eyes or whatever else you gotta do. Now listen. Remember this Rashid guy was murdered in a failed robbery seven or so weeks ago, according to the local Pakistan police? Well NCTC has picked him up entering Dubai on a different name. He scored 14 points but under a different name.'

'Yeah, I remember. But why would ISI and PAEC in Islamabad lie about him being killed?'

'Mitch, my man, that's your job to determine. Security in Pakistan has been uprated since he was murdered, and my sources said it is just standard procedure because of his security clearance, although they have said officially it was just a mugging.'

'So how do you know about this in Dubai before me?'

''Cus you're in bed playing with yourself, and I'm working,' Shane said, laughing. 'Seriously, it just came over the wire to the Embassy, and I thought you'd like to know.'

'OK, thanks, pal. Do me a favour? Keep me updated if you hear more locally? You know how long it sometimes takes for data to get passed around.'

'Will do, pal. Now get back to bed with your gorgeous gal before I come over there and whisk her away from you, you bum.'

'Yeah, like I'm worried now. Thanks, and keep in touch, pal,' Mitch said, finishing the call.

Too awake to get back to sleep, Mitch sat there thinking. The two of them had met when he had first moved into intelligence. They had gotten on well together and regularly kept in touch. Anything to do the Middle East region, naval practice, weapons, or anything remotely similar, was of interest to Stringer. The fact that a known weapons scientist was stated officially as dead by the Pakistan police from a robbery made so-so reading. More interesting was that the face of a dead man might be somewhere he wasn't expected to be, and possibly travelling on a fake passport made the hairs on the back of his neck bristle.

Maybe the attack on the Professor wasn't as clear-cut as had been portrayed. Perhaps there'd been an insurgent attempt to kidnap or kill this weapons scientist, he thought. That would explain the sudden increase in security and activity in Pakistan. It was also possible that the person detected entering Dubai yesterday was just similar looking to the professor, as the face detection had only picked up 14 of the 22 nodal points and that it was just a coincidence.

But, Stringer didn't like coincidences. Something was going on, and he wanted to know what.

# 19

## Madrid, Spain

Fawaz Aziz Al Farah had decided to use one of his other names for this latest task. Previously he'd visited cemeteries in various towns and viewed gravestones until he found ones of male children who'd died soon after birth. It had been simple to apply for, and obtain, a replacement birth certificate in that child's name. The secret was in choosing children who would have been roughly his age now, had they lived. All he'd needed to do was apply in person at the local town hall stating he'd lost his original birth certificate. The officials would always provide a new one. With a valid birth certificate, it was just a paper exercise to get both an ID card and a driver's licence issued under that same name.

He had over a dozen identities to use when it suited. For this mission, he'd chosen the name of Arturo Guttierez, a child of six months who'd died of cot death in Toledo twenty-six years ago.

It had been easy. Rosa Valdez was a forty-eight-year-old spinster. She was reasonable looking, and not too overweight. She was the senior administrator in the property division of the Spanish church in Madrid and was enjoying life. Fawaz had always found older women easier to seduce and bed. His dark, brooding looks made them melt; a few choice words and a clumsy, inexperienced manner and they all wanted to mother him.

She had met Arturo just a few weeks ago. He had arrived at her office seeking some information and had accidentally knocked a coffee cup over, spilling it on her

69

blouse. She had cursed him and tried to sponge it off, complaining that he'd ruined her top, but between his embarrassment and profuse apologies, he had insisted he meet her that evening to buy her a drink as an apology. He was good looking, maybe twenty-six or twenty-eight, a little darker skinned than her, and handsome with it, but apparently shy. She'd accepted his apology and agreed to meet him that evening.

When she had met him later, he was carrying flowers, and their romance had started. That first evening he had bought her a meal they had talked until late. He also shared her love of her art and music. Since then, they had rarely been apart.

She'd had a couple of lovers over the years but never found one to spend her life with. She was quite opinionated and forceful in the relationship – not something most Spanish men liked – but Arturo was shy with women, and she revelled in showing her experience and bossing him about. He, in turn, was an eager pupil, also trying to please and happy to be dominated by her.

Fawaz / Arturo's latest mission had come from his Imam again. He'd been instructed to rent an old farmhouse, pay in cash, and get all copies of any paperwork. Befriend the woman, Rosa Valdez, who could help. Seduce her, befriend her, whatever. Just get it done and report back. As to the woman use her then discard her.

What really annoyed him about her, what really grated, was her demands. She was always in the right, he in the wrong. She demanded sex when she wanted, and he would have no choice. No wonder she has never married, he thought, she needs a lapdog, not a partner. Even the thought of having sex with her revolted him; her old tired body against his firm physique. Muslim women do not prostitute themselves like this, he thought. Good Muslim women do not act like whores and tarts.

Arriving at her apartment, Fawaz asked, 'Did you manage to finalise the paperwork today?'

'Yes, I did. It is all legal now. You have now rented the farmhouse just south of Jedey and all land around it for twelve months. Here is all the countersigned paperwork.'

He read through the text quickly. It all seemed in order and entirely legal. He now was the only renter, as instructed.

'So why do you want this farmhouse for a year. What are you going to use it for?'

'Rosa, it is as I said before. I want to write, and I need somewhere peaceful to do it. This place will be perfect. My little house of solitude.'

'Well, I won't be happy losing you to that place. I will want you to come back every month to see me,' she pouted. Leaning over and kissing him, she pushed her hand down the front of his trousers as she placed his hand on her breast. 'Come on, get it hard,' she said, 'I'd be better off with a vibrator than that fat slug. You'd better make me come, not like last time. Come on!' she said, taking his hand away and pulling him towards the stairs.

The following week friends of Rosa called the local police after failing to reach her by phone. Forcing an entry, the Sergeant found her apartment empty. Her clothes were gone, along with all her personal items. The Sergeant checked hospitals, but she had disappeared. After six weeks he listed her as 'Missing - location unknown'.

Her body was never found.

# 20

## Qom, Iran

Professor Rashid was unaware that his picture had been taken when he'd arrived in Dubai a week ago. He was currently heading over seven hundred miles away to Qom, Iran. After his pick-up in Islamabad, he and his family had been taken to a remote farmhouse. It had been made very clear to him if he failed to obey orders exactly he would never see his family again. To remove any doubt, his wife's left ear was served to him on a plate. Obey, and he would be paid well and live happily. Disobey, and he would continue receiving bits of his wife, followed by bits of his daughter and then his sons.

Arriving at Dubai International Airport a week ago on a charter flight from Karachi, he spent the next few days purchasing and testing what he needed. Five days later he had joined a small freighter dhow in Dubai Creek, his hair colour and thick chin beard lightened to a grey more in keeping with his fellow seafarers. Travelling alongside microwaves, fridges and vacuum cleaners, he blended perfectly into the dusty, dark recesses of the sun-bleached craft. For centuries, Dubai had been the centre for water-borne traffic into and out of the Gulf. Recent man-made borders cannot change what is in the blood of trading seafarers. This dhow was one of many that made the twice-weekly voyage across the Straits of Hormuz from Dubai to the ports and harbours along the southern Iranian countryside. His was destined for Bandar Abbas and would bring fruits, wheat, nuts and grains back in return.

Professor Rashid was a devout Pashtun and an avid supporter of the Taliban and al-Qaeda, although he had always found it wise to keep his feelings to himself. Promotion and success within the Pakistan Atomic Energy Commission relied, as in many organisations worldwide, on 'playing the game'. These had been Rashid's principles, and they had worked successfully for him for many years, to fit in, to not make waves, and to go along with the crowd. He was a Muslim, but like many, would choose the rules he enforced. Pork was banned, but alcohol depended on his mood, extramarital sex likewise.

Rashid was one of the few senior engineers at PAEC who could bypass the arming codes and reconfigure the detonation systems of Pakistan's nuclear weapons – after all, he had been paramount in their design. With the promise of two million US dollars in a Swiss bank account in his name, and that no more harm would come to his family, he was eager to continue his work. The kidnapping in Islamabad had been quick and efficient. In fact, no one noticed and being a Friday afternoon he hadn't been noticed missing until the following Monday when he failed to turn up at work. By that time he and his family had been separated, and he'd been instructed what he had to do and that he'd see his family again when it was all over.

His dhow's arrival in Bandar Abbas was met by Saif and two guards. After a brief but customary Muslim greeting the guards had taken his bags and escorted him and Saif aboard the waiting Islamic Revolutionary Guards Corp Mi-17 helicopter. Instead of jump seats for troops, this Russian-made transport craft was fitted for VIP travel, with comfortable seating, increased soundproofing, and fold-down work tables, making Rashid think this was a senior officers' personal craft.

73

Two thousand feet below the landscape whisked by, grey and broken, with stony hills and crags rising from the barren terrain. There was little sign of man-made life, occasionally a dirt track came into view or a small group of Bedouin tents – their owners scratching a living in the harsh countryside, trying to exist alongside its raw beauty.

Even with the added soundproofing discussion was awkward, so Rashid allowed his eyelids to close. Three hours later, they arrived at Qom's nuclear facility. Rashid's first thoughts were how little showed above ground. The helicopter touched down and then rose again moments after Rashid and his colleagues had climbed down. The area seemed empty apart from one small white-painted building apparently on its own. As he walked towards the entrance, he could see other camouflaged fortifications nearby, and the long shadows of anti-aircraft guns and missiles trained to the sky were reflected on the ground from the setting sun.

Entering the building, it became evident that this was not as deserted as it first looked. He was X-rayed, and fingerprints were taken, along with an iris scan. His pass was red with the words 'Escort at all times' clearly written in Farsi, and he was assigned two guards. High-speed elevators took Rashid, Saif and the two guards down to level seventeen. Rashid noticed there were at least a further dozen levels lower. Exiting into the bright, hygienic passage reminiscent of a clinical ward, they were led to a small electric train. Climbing on, they were transported many kilometres through dark tunnels until arriving at a larger cavern where Saif announced they would stay until his current work was completed.

'My dear Rashid. This is where you will eat, sleep and live until you have completed your task,' Saif said.

'Not tonight,' Rashid replied. 'I have been travelling for almost twenty hours. I want to rest, and I want a meal. Our work will start tomorrow.'

'As you request, my friend. Come, let me show you to your room. When you are ready to eat knock on your door, and the guard will take you for food. Tomorrow we will commence.'

With that Saif walked him to his room and then closed and locked the door behind him. Through the small glass partition, Rashid could see the guard standing outside. Lying on the bed, Rashid felt his eyelids close – it had been a longer day than he remembered.

# 21

Following a brief breakfast, Rashid was eager to start work. In one of the adjoining workshops, by mid-morning he had already stripped down and removed the main components from the weapon's outer casing. The casing was almost six-foot-long and two foot in diameter, but most of that was protection for attaching it to a missile or for dropping from an aircraft. That wasn't required now, and so the actual bomb components took up a little over half that space.

'Professor,' Saif asked, 'What about the PAL? Tell me how will you overcome this?'

'That is why you need me. Although all US nuclear weapons contain a PAL, a device called a Permissive Action Link to prevent unauthorised arming or detonation of a nuclear weapon, we in Pakistan never followed suit. America did offer us the same technology once they realised we had our own nuclear weapons, but then their Congress blocked it for legal reasons. We, however, would not have accepted it. We do not fully trust the US, and it is likely they would have kept a secret override function, or 'kill-switch', thereby sabotaging our capability. Instead, we designed our own systems. Or, more importantly, I designed most of our systems. I designed them. I built them. I know how they work. I can override them.

'As instructed, in Dubai I purchased the components I need from various computer and electrical shops. I never used the same shop more than once and paid for everything in cash. I have brought here with me what is needed,' Rashid continued. 'As you commanded, all you will need to do is enter your unique code, set the timer, and enter your code again to fully arm it.'

The original timer mechanism was somewhat crude and based on an altimeter design – the weapon being designed to detonate five seconds after descending to a set altitude. Rashid removed these mechanisms and discarded them. The plan now to fit the latest timer electronics accurate to tenths of a second to the weapons existing sophisticated electronics. A simple hour:minute:second:day:month:year display, a long-life battery, a processor card and keypad, and a trigger card interfacing to the remaining electronics was all that was needed.

Working with Iranian scientists, he helped them split down, examine and photograph every single component. The Iranians were actually far more advanced in nuclear weapons design than the West gave them credit for. Three Chinese nuclear scientists were also working with the Iranians, and the Chinese seemed very interested in understanding the build quality and design of this weapon from Pakistan.

After four days of detailed breakdown, examination, and testing, it came time to re-assemble the device with the new control mechanisms. After checking, double-checking and triple-checking everything, Rashid began to place the device inside polyurethane protective foam cut-outs within a large Pelicase container.

This container was slightly different though than those commercially available in that it had a thin interior wall of lead throughout the case. The lead would stop normal amounts of radiation penetrating the casing. This was important because many ports and airports now used simple handheld Dosimeter Anti-radiation Detectors to check for varying radiation levels. Locking the two combination padlocks on the Pelicase, the entire ensemble was then placed inside a commercial steel tool chest container. Locking the two padlocks on the outside of this, Saif turned to Rashid and said, 'One down, one to go.'

# 22

## Dubai

Two days' later, the Iran Air flight from Tehran to Dubai brought Yousef Rashid back into the waiting camera lens hacked by the American NSA. This time the alert sounded quicker and was escalated to both Susan Draymore's desk and to her manager. Calling her manager over, she said to him, 'Look at his picture. He has lightened his hair and lightened and changed the shape of his beard to alter his facial shape. I don't think I would have recognised him had it not been for the recognition software.' Looking at his picture, they both agreed this was something Fort Meade needed to know about.

# 23

## The Pentagon, Washington

Lieutenant Mitchell 'Mitch' Stringer slowly sipped his coffee as he sat down in his swivel chair. His laptop was still booting up and running through the security firewall checks when an attractive female secretary brought in the latest daily reports. Scanning through them briefly, Mitch would usually quickly review each one to gain an overall view of what was happening, before reading each in detail. He was thirteen reports down when he saw an estimate that Professor Yousef Rashid had been possibly detected arriving in Dubai again fourteen hours ago.

Slamming his coffee down, he rushed past the startled secretary towards the secure offices of Admiral Douglas Carter.

<><><>

That evening Mitch and Helen met Shane at their favourite Italian restaurant, La Casa, in downtown Washington. Shane had arrived directly from Dubai that morning and was in town for three days of meetings. After the usual hugs and kisses had been exchanged, they sat down at a quiet corner table to enjoy each other's company and some of the best pasta in all of the US.

'So Shane, what's the latest gossip out there in desert land?'

'Well, some more information has come to light since we last talked,' Shane said. 'There is definitely something planned. Don't know what and it's hard to put my finger on it but there is a tension in the air that wasn't there a few weeks ago. Walking around, even in a coffee shop, as soon as the locals realise you're American, it's as if they know something's going to happen. But I don't know what. Maybe it's just me. Maybe I'm sensing something that isn't really there, but I don't think so.'

'What about anything tangible?' Mitch asked.

'Now that, my good old buddy, is where it gets interesting. All this is in my reports, but I know how long they often take to get to you if they ever get there. Reports are coming from Afghanistan that al-Qaeda and or the Taliban have found a new, more powerful explosive, which is alarming on its own. But reports have filtered through that a Palestinian named Saif has been helping them design this. We got informants trying to find out more, but this Saif guy seems like a ghost. Quite a few have heard of him, but no one admits to actually having met him.

'Other news is that Admiral Zhang has been meeting with old Behbahan in Bandar Abbas recently. Not sure why, though. We know China supports Iran and have injected hundreds of millions or maybe even billions of dollars into their oil and gas facilities in return for a large percentage of their supply. Still, I think there's more to it than that.'

'What do you mean? What more do you think there is?' Mitch asked.

'We think China is helping Iran upgrade their three Kilos,' Shane said. 'All three needed a fair bit of maintenance and weren't even seaworthy, but two of them have spent the last few months in dry-dock, and one of those has now just come back from local sea trials. The third one is already in dry-dock, and we now estimate she will be completed within two or three months. This is far quicker than we expected and we only found out through local gossip. Three active Kilos in the Gulf could be trouble.'

'Shit. Does the Admiral know?' Mitch asked.

'Boys, I know you're talking all manly stuff, and I don't mean to interrupt but what's a Kilo?' Helen asked.

'Sorry babe, not meaning to bore you,' Mitch said, 'they are Russian built extremely quiet diesel-powered submarines. The Ruskies have sold a lot off over the last fifteen years when trying to raise money. Some are fairly old now and need refits, but they're extremely quiet and near impossible to detect if manned by a good crew. Iran has three and isn't much of a worry due to lack of maintenance, but if they have upgraded them all ...,'

'Yeah, Mitch. He does as of earlier this afternoon. Part of the reason for me being here now is to present these latest facts to him,' Shane said.

'Then that,' Mitch said, 'is the reason he's called a meeting for tomorrow at 08:00 with myself and some of my colleagues. Anything else I should know? Any more juicy tidbits?'

'Well, just finishing up about this. We don't know what China is getting in return for helping Iran do this, apart from oil, and we don't know why Zhang was in Bandar,' Shane said.

'China has a dozen Kilos, and they have heavily modified them and upgraded them with all their latest weapons and sonar. We are having trouble monitoring them out east, so if these Iranian ones are modified to the same level, it will cause a problem. Not actually within the Persian Gulf as it's too shallow, but the waters of the Gulf of Oman out past the Straits of Hormuz gets pretty deep. They'd be deadly there. It wouldn't take much for Iran to disrupt shipping. Just the threat would be enough,' Mitch said. 'But I wonder what's in it for China?'

The waiter arrived then with their meals, and another couple came and sat at a nearby table, so the conversation was turned to that of three friends dining together for the first time in months.

# 24

## Dubai

The Professor was looking forward to this aspect of the project. Qom had been okay, and the people had been friendly, but it was not the sort of place to relax in. Here would take less time. He had to again dismantle and strip down all the components from the missile casing. He removed and discarded the antiquated timer mechanism and tested the system against the latest components. But this device wasn't ready to be completed and set active yet. It had a journey to complete first. Making sure it was totally safe and disassembled; he placed the main chamber in a lead-lined box and placed all the components within the polyurethane protective foam cut-outs within a large polypropylene Pelicase container.

Finishing the packing, he knew it would be almost twenty days before he would get to open the case again. He spent the rest of the day on his laptop designing a fibreglass waterproof container with exterior shackle points to encompass the entire container. He uploaded this design to the 'cloud' and emailed the link to a name he'd been given.

That evening, Professor Yousef Rashid enjoyed dinner and Arabian belly dancing at a private club function in Deira. Using a disposable mobile phone, he called a specific number in Peshawar. His wife answered quietly. She and the children were still under guard but were well. He confirmed he would be with them in a few weeks and hung up. Settling down to another glass of cheap whisky, he motioned the belly dancer to join him at his private table. Tonight he would allow his less strict disciplines to take over.

The following morning he wore cheap local dockworker clothing and climbed aboard the waiting dhow. Merging in as one of the local Dhow's crew he watched the small crane lift the bundled group of boxes and place them in the hold.

Thirty minutes later the Captain ordered the lines cast off and the dhow headed out of Dubai creek and turned towards the Straits of Hormuz.

Nine hours later shortly after sundown, the captain of the Desert Pride a 26,000 tonne Singapore registered Chinese-owned LPG carrier radioed the Oman Traffic Separation Scheme control desk covering the Straits of Hormuz. He told them he was temporarily slowing its speed eastbound due to a blocked inlet valve. Fourteen minutes later, the Desert Pride radioed again to state the problem had been fixed, and they were returning to normal speed. The operator on the control desk made a note of the message which was also recorded for back-up and went back to reading an old edition of Playboy.

What both the operator and the extensive radar covering the Straits of Hormuz had failed to notice was a dhow exiting the shelter of the islands. It approached the port side of the Desert Pride, pulling alongside for a few minutes, just long enough to transfer a passenger and a package before continuing its journey to Bandar Abbas.

# 25

## Cyprus

British Army sergeant, Bill Thompson, a signals expert from the Lancashire Fusiliers was just finishing his shift at the British Intelligence listening post in Dhekelia, Cyprus. Most fibre connections between Europe, Asia and the Middle East connected through the Cyprus hub. It was planned that way by the telecom providers to make servicing and maintenance easy. Also made easy was the ability of British Intelligence to tap unobserved into these connections. In theory, all telephone calls, satellite messages, fax and data transmissions would transit through this hub. Also, this site housed some of the UK's most sophisticated and sensitive radio detection equipment.

Although a lot of radio transmissions were fully encrypted using the latest DVP double-DES encryption, voice traffic from or to a cellular phone is still relatively easy to detect.

Tuning to one particular cellular call at random in Tehran, Sgt Thompson was surprised to hear phrases in a very localised Pashto dialect that he couldn't translate. Playing the recorded message over again and again, the only phrase the sergeant thought he identified was 'jaws'.

His report, along with the digital recording was transmitted to Government Communications (GCHQ) in Cheltenham, Gloucestershire, for more detailed analysis and translation.

GCHQ is the jewel in the crown of Britain's espionage industry, identified as Britain's equivalent of the NSA.

Both the NSA and GCHQ work closely together and share information.

Within three hours of the data arriving, it was on its way to the National Security Agency in Fort Meade, Maryland.

# 26

## Qom, Iran

Climbing quickly into the passenger seat, Saif nodded to the driver to begin. The unmarked hard-sided truck moved out of the compound, then turned and headed up Route 7 towards Tehran. Saif blew out a long-held breath and looked at the map. The route was about one hundred kilometres north towards Tehran, then west onto Route 2 to Qazvin, and on towards Tabriz. Then turn towards Lake Urmia and on towards the Turkish border. He estimated it would take about twelve hours driving in total, and he would need to share the driving, but they should be there just before nightfall.

The journey was uneventful, boring even. They stopped three times to allow the team of four in the rear to get out and stretch and also for food and drink, but the only slight delay was traffic in Tehran, and they quickly made up lost time.

Pulling into the compound near Dustan late in the evening, the courier was waiting. He had a string of donkeys and most were already loaded. These mountain men have allegiances to their tribes and history, not to man-made borders. Many were blood brothers. Here, locals spoke a local dialect not understood in Iran or Turkey.

The steel tool chest container wrapped in sacking was manhandled from the truck. Now the heavier armoured casing had been removed from the contents it was light enough for two men to hold. The donkey chosen twitched and tried to move away from the added weight, but a sharp stroke of a cane across its rump from the pack leader quickly subdued the animal. A balancing load was placed on the animal's other flank, and then both packages were tied off tightly. A few words, handshakes and a wave and, with a parting 'Insha'Allah' the donkey train was off. As he watched them move away, Saif hoped the next stage of his plan would run as smoothly as it had so far. He planned to meet up again with his package in three weeks.

It was only four miles to the border, but the terrain was uphill and rocky and would take the sure-footed animals three hours to reach. This was a well-trodden path and the ghosts of countless past smugglers hung in the air. At one stage an animal stumbled and brayed loudly, its cries echoing in the still night, but the pack leader quickly stroked the animal and quietened it. These were cruel men living in a harsh environment, but they loved their animals, relying on them often for life or death. Stopping in a small depression within sight of the border fence, the pack leader sent his young boy on ahead to scout the land. Border patrols were few and far between – even the border fencing was mostly broken and run down, but it always paid to be careful. The Turkish Land Forces, or Türk Kara Kuvvetleri, were responsible for patrolling their side of the border. They were well known for their corruption and bribe-taking. Sometimes they wanted more than just bribes, and quite a few smugglers were known to have been shot at by the border guards, their bodies left for the wild dogs and their goods stolen. In particular, the flesh trade made this even worse. Girls as young as nine were often smuggled eastwards, to be sold as slaves, but the guards would rape them first. That was their 'ten per cent commission' they would say. If you argued, you would find yourself staring down the barrel of a rifle. Occasionally a trigger would be pulled. Everything has a price and sex was still one of the most commonly traded items. But this pack leader had been carefully trained by his father and his father before him – don't mix commodities. Smuggle girls, yes, but always be willing to trade them – cleaned up, you still had them to be sold later. Or smuggle goods. This training had stood the test of time in an area where time and politics meant nothing. Sure, the leader now had access to a television and used a mobile phone, but his actions and way of life hadn't changed for centuries. Plus sometimes if one of the girls were particularly attractive, he would keep her and use her for a while before passing her on. He was a businessman but liked his pleasure too.

His son reported back all was clear, and the donkey train continued. Within moments they were over the man-made border and two hours later arrived at their destination. The pack leader greeted his brother, the women brought food, and the men sat around a fire to discuss business. The price for delivery of the steel chest had already been agreed, and within hours it had been transported to the next village.

With over ninety-nine per cent population being faithful to Islam, there was no issue in finding like-minded supporters to help.

One week later it arrived, still in its sacking cloth, at a warehouse on the outskirts of Mersin where it would stay under armed guard for almost two weeks.

# 27

## California

Deacon and his team cheered as the C130 touched down in Coronado. They had just completed another three-month tour and were now on leave and extended training. This tour had been better than the last. They hadn't lost anyone, just a couple wounded, but it felt good to be able to relax. On his previous visit home, shortly after Bryant's death, Deacon had visited a heavily pregnant Alex. Unsure of what to say or do he had just stood there tears in his eyes. Over the next couple of days, they had cried together, remembered together until finally laughed together. Alex didn't blame John - she knew how dangerous their jobs were and knew John would have willingly given his own life to save Bryant. John had promised he would always be there for her, always have a shoulder for her to cry on, and always be the best friend she could ever want. There would never be anything romantic between them - John looked on her as a younger sister, and she on him as an older brother, but they could always rely on each other. Alex had surprised him by saying she and Bryant had previously discussed and agreed to ask him to be the baby's godparent. Although Bryant was now gone, she would still like John to do this for them. More tears had flowed that evening. John had promised to be there for both of them and would be back as soon as possible.

Collecting his truck from the long-term parking on the base, he smiled at the thought of seeing them again. Alex had given birth to a healthy boy six weeks previously, and John couldn't wait to see her and baby Bryant David Schaeffer. Diverting to a local mall, Deacon found the biggest teddy bear and had a blue ribbon tied around its neck.

Arriving at Alex's house, John hid behind the teddy and rang the doorbell. Alex's face lit up in surprise as she opened the door.

'John, you're earlier than I expected. And who's this fine looking fellow?'

'This,' John said, 'is Big 'ol Ted. And I think a young man might be wanting to say 'Hullo' to him,' hugging Alex as he did so.

Deacon spent the next few days reminiscing, enjoying life and getting to know his godson, oblivious to the task that lay ahead.

# 28

## Shanghai

Professor Rashid was still enjoying himself but was bored. The Desert Pride had journeyed south out of the Straits of Hormuz into the Gulf of Oman. It had then set course south-east until passing Sri Lanka, where it steered almost due east before turning south-east again through the Malacca Straits. That was the nearest it got to land before turning north-east into the South China Sea, travelling inside the Straits of Taiwan to the Shanghai Terminal, Shanghai.

The trip had taken over seventeen days, and Rashid had found the trip incredibly boring. Fluent in English, he had read all the available paperbacks on the ship, regularly walked, and then jogged around the deck. Unable to smoke due to the explosion hazard, he had even managed to beat his 30-a-day habit, but the days were long and he often just sat for hours thinking of his future. The Chinese crew had been instructed to ignore him, and his only point-of-contact was the Captain. He had all his meals delivered to his cabin and had begun feeling more and more isolated.

However, his family would be safe; he would be rich beyond his wildest dreams, and all he had to do were two more simple jobs. Then he would be free to leave to be reunited with his family.

As the Desert Pride tied up at the LNG terminal, Rashid arranged for his cargo to be removed. An unmarked white van was waiting along with the ubiquitous Chinese guards and officials. His passport was checked but not stamped, and he was taken with his cargo and armed guards to a machine factory over an hour away.

Captain Ning Twai was waiting for him when he disembarked the van.

'I am here to assist you,' Twai said. 'We have engineers here available. I will translate your instructions. You are to position your cargo to escape any radiation detection devices. I have one of the latest here. Until your cargo passes this test, you will have failed. Do you understand?'

Rashid extended his hand towards Captain Twai, but the gesture was not returned. Rashid had forgotten the Chinese dislike of Pakistan to almost the same level of hatred it directed towards Taiwan.

Gathering his thoughts, Rashid replied, 'I understand, Captain. I know what I need to do. You have my word it shall be done quickly.' With that, Rashid walked towards the other waiting helpers and the yellow machine.

Running his hands over the faded yellow paint on its arms, interspaced by lines of rust, Rashid smiled. He was an engineer at heart and still liked things mechanical. What remained of the glass screens were cracked and opaque, and the black paint had faded to a murky grey. To say this machine had known better times was an understatement, he thought. But it had been born from necessity and looked to have done its job well. Now it needed fixing. Well, not now actually, he thought. Soon, but it needs some help first.

The Caterpillar D6-4R bulldozer was first produced in 1941, and this was one of the earliest. Over seventy years old and still a looker, he thought. The design hadn't changed much over the years in bulldozers. Newer ones had more powerful engines so could accommodate extra drive trains and devices, but the early models just did what they were designed for. Moving earth and moving it well. So well built and reliable were they that some Caterpillar dealers would fix any problems on 'dozers between forty and sixty years old at half price. Anything older than sixty years was fixed up and refurbished for free, as long as the dealer could hold on to it for up a year for marketing purposes.

This septuagenarian beauty was destined for complete refurbishment at Hawaii Heavy Diggers Inc, and would then tour the islands.

But not yet.

Most people assume a nuclear bomb to be large, but they are mistaken. Both Russia and America designed and built small tactical nuclear bombs to fit into suitcases. Most weight with an atomic bomb is taken up in surrounding protective metal, either to protect it in flight if attached to a missile, or heavier steel to protect it when being fired as a shell or dropped like a bomb. However, the core components of this stolen nuclear device were neither very large or heavy. But unless completely protected by lead, or something similar, was liable to be detected with radiation Geiger counters.

Captain Twai removed a Geiger counter from its protective case and pointed it at the lead-lined Pelicase. The reading wasn't significant, but clearly detectable. Walking outside the warehouse, with Rashid in tow, Twai scanned his detector towards where they had been stood. Even from over one hundred feet and through the brick and metal cladding of the warehouse, the radiation emanating from the case was still discernible to trigger the detectors audible clicks.

Walking back to the bulldozer, Rashid asked Twai to request the men take the engine covers off.

The exposed engine was solid with rust, just as expected. By using hydraulic wrenches, Twai's men carefully removed the main cylinder head, exposing the pistons and the main cylinder block. Removing the oil sump, Rashid instructed one of the engineers to cut through the crankshaft at each end with a plasma torch. With the main crankshaft now isolated at both ends, the four pistons were now only held in position by rust. Repeated blows from a sledgehammer and a wedge gradually forced the rusted pistons down within their piston sleeves, eventually crashing to the floor still connected together on the now shortened crankshaft. The cylinder block was now empty of pistons, and Rashid marked a line all the way around the top approximately three centimetres in from the edges. This was the new guideline.

The Chinese engineers used plasma torches and angle grinders to slowly cut the metal away from the inside, slowly hollowing out the cylinder block. It was a backbreaking and dirty process, but eventually, the hollowed-out cylinder block began to take shape. Modern engines are built of aluminium with steel sleeves for the pistons. But engines built in the 1940s were all cast iron. Using the angle grinder to remove the final sharp internal edges, Rashid looked down and smiled at his new rectangular cast-iron container. When space was enough, Rashid asked the engineer, through Twai, to weld a bottom sheet of cast iron in position, effectively making a small sarcophagus, and then placed half-inch sheets of lead on the sides and bottom, and across one corner making a separate compartment. Between the shielding of both the lead and the cast iron, very few atoms of radiation would escape.

Donning his protective suit, Rashid removed the uranium and conventional explosives from the steel tool case. They were currently isolated from each other and perfectly safe. Disconnected and unarmed, the uranium just emitted background radiation.

Within an hour, Rashid had finished his part of the work. All the components were placed inside the lead-lined sarcophagus before another sheet of lead-lined cast iron was welded in place on top. Finally, the previously removed oil sump cover and cylinder head were also refitted and welded into place. Walking outside with Twai, no level of radiation could be detected through the outer wall. Even walking back inside and standing less than ten feet away, Twai's detector failed to register a reading which brought a smile to Twai's face.

The only remaining issues now were the new scratches and weld marks around the engine bay area. Firstly, the engineers carefully painted around and over the marks and scratches with a fast-drying paint to simulate rust. Secondly, once dry, they positioned two hose pipes, both spraying seawater onto the 'dozer engine bay for 12 hours. Leaving the building under armed guard, Rashid bade goodbye to the two engineers and followed Captain Twai to the waiting vehicle. Twai escorted him to Army barracks where Rashid would stay for two days.

Forty-eight hours later, Twai walked with Rashid back to the bulldozer. The water had been turned off and Rashid, even looking carefully, could see no trace of the previous tool work. The corrosive saltwater had quickly added to the rust and covered what had been done. Only very detailed inspection would detect the slight addition of two sheets of cast iron top and bottom to the cylinder block.

Twai again checked with his counter and, finding no evidence of any radiation, smiled broadly. X-ray inspection would show a normal block of cast iron where the engine should be, with all the attachments and pipes in position as normal. Any radiation monitoring would just detect standard background levels.

'You have done well, Professor,' Twai said. 'This machine will travel today, but you will stay in the barracks for a further week. Anything you require to make your stay enjoyable will be provided.'

'I welcome being your guest,' Rashid replied. 'But perhaps a Pakistan or English TV channel and a newspaper could be provided. And some whisky . . . ?'

A week later, Rashid boarded an Air China flight to Seoul. This time the NCTC failed to detect him.

# 29

## Mersin, Turkey

In the darkened smoke-filled bar the crewman raised his glass pulled the burning stub of a cigarette out of his mouth and muttered 'Serefe' in drunken Turkish although he pronounced each syllable slowly as 'Sher-if-feh'. The crewman then coughed and sprayed half a mouthful of cheap whisky over the bar towards his fellow crewman. Cursing, he wiped his eyes and nose with the back of his hand, snot streaking across over a weeks stubble. His colleague grinned back drunkenly through bloodshot eyes and offered back his salutations. The crew had been in the bar almost three hours since walking off the dock and planned to stay until they were thrown out or collapsed.

Kourosh Hussain and Mostafa Nakhjavani had been waiting two weeks for their arrival. Not them, actually. The vessel they crewed; the freighter '*Mehtap*' and its master, Huseyin Cakiroglu.

Grabbing the first crewman, Kourosh moved his face closer until the reek of whisky made him blanch. He said, 'Hey, where is your Captain? Where is Cakiroglu?'

Grinning insanely, the crewman smiled and answered, 'Who...who wants to know?'

Before Kourosh could reply, Mostafa grabbed the crewman by the throat, squeezed and flicked open a small flick-knife. As the sharpened point penetrated the crewman's cheek and pain registered, Mostafa said, 'We do. Now whether you keep your eyes in your head or I put them in your drink is up to you. Where is he?' as he pushed the blade tip deeper.

A trickle of blood ran down the crewman's cheek as he half-spat, 'Captain will be here soon. He's still aboard. He said he'd meet us later.'

Slowly removing the blade and relaxing his grip on the drunk's throat, Mostafa said, 'Thank you, my friend. Now enjoy the rest of your evening,' as he pushed him gently backward off the stool.

Kourosh slapped Mostafa on the shoulder and said, 'Let's visit the Captain and welcome him to Mersin,' as the drunk fell to the floor with a crash. Walking out the door to the shouted curses from the drunks, they turned and headed towards the dock.

Climbing the gangway, they could see the Captain on the bridge, smoking a cigar. He sauntered over to them and introduced himself.

'I am Captain Cakiroglu. What do you want here?'

'Captain, we have been waiting for you. We are going on a little voyage together.'

'Who are you? How do I know who you are?'

'Captain, I am Kourosh, my colleague here is Mostafa, and we will be bringing a package on board tomorrow morning before you sail. That is all you need to know. We will accompany you to the Canaries when we and our package will leave you. We will act like extra crew, but we will have the run of this rusting hulk. We will leave the operation and running of the *Mehtap* to you and your crew but you, in turn, will do what we say when we say. You are being well paid for this and Allah is on our side. You will not ask questions, and you will tell no one that we are on board. Is that clear?'

100

The Captain had been briefed in Morocco and had been expecting these two, but still, he had hoped they wouldn't arrive.

'When does your unloading finish?' Mostafa asked.

'We are already finished unloading,' the Captain replied. 'New loading starts at dawn, and we sail at noon. What will be in the package?'

Cleaning his fingernails with his flick-knife, Mostafa said, 'You do not need to know. If you value your life, you won't ask again. We will arrive at ten. Have a two-man cabin cleared for us and a lockable storage area. We will have the only keys. Do I make myself clear?'

Trembling, the Captain agreed and watched his new fellow travellers depart. If he hurried with his paperwork, he could get to the bar within half an hour. He needed to. He badly needed a drink.

# 30

**Mersin, Turkey**

The sun had only just started brightening the sky in the east when the old crane on the dockyard belched black smoke and burst into life. Within minutes, the first boxes and containers were swinging over the gunwales and disappearing deep within the hold. The *Mehtap* had been built in the twenties and the engine modernised from burning coal to diesel oil in the mid-sixties. Very little had changed since and she was still a sound vessel. The crew of eight consisted of the Captain, a cook, four general crew, the engineer and his young assistant. The general crew and the engineer's assistant would regularly rub down the all-pervasive rust and daub paint on what remained, but even that couldn't hide the fact that she was a very old lady. But the engineer and his assistant worked wonders, and the Lithgow 6-cylinder 3,000HP engine still throbbed to a beat as regular as a heart, pushing all 170 feet of her along at a little over twelve knots. She'd managed over fifteen in her sprightly youth, but age had taken its toll, and twelve was all that could now be reasonably expected of her.

By ten o'clock, the loading was well underway. The *Mehtap*'s cargo hold was separated into three sections. The front hold was kept for dirty items such as engines, cement or wood. The middle was left for clean items such as clothes and electrical goods, while the rear, actually nearer the middle of the ship, was kept for fresh and dried foods – dates, olives, flour, maize, tins and packets – whatever was needed. Her ports of call were those along the northern coast of the Mediterranean – ports in Cyprus, Lebanon, Egypt, Libya, Tunisia, Algeria, Morocco, and the Canaries. Whatever needed trading, she would carry. She had been traversing the same waters for so long, she was invisible.

Kourosh and Mostafa arrived at ten by van. They had four large canvas holdalls and a large wooden crate. They carried two each of the holdalls onto the *Mehtap* but struggled with getting the crate out of the van. The two crew members from the bar the previous night looked at them with contempt. Captain Cakiroglu shouted at them to lend a hand, but they just ignored him and continued staring. Two others from the crew offered to help, but Kourosh shooed them away, cursing. The crane placed the wooden crate into the middle hold and Kourosh and Mostafa manhandled it inside the lockable section of the hold, the area where Captain Cakiroglu normally stored items of value.

Kourosh and Mostafa then took their holdalls to their cabin and remained there until the Captain ordered the lines cast off and the heartbeat of the big Lithgow increased and moved them underway.

As they cleared the harbour, Kourosh and Mostafa joined Cakiroglu on the bridge.

'You keep to your regular trip. You do nothing to raise any concern. You do nothing to raise suspicion. These are your orders. Do you understand?' Mostafa said, leaving no room for doubt.

Cakiroglu was quite a large person. Almost five foot eleven and solidly built. His skin was weather-beaten and suntanned, and he had numerous scars and marks. He'd been the successful winner in many a bar fight and his crew feared him, but even he was intimidated being in the same room as these two.

103

'I understand,' he replied. 'I shall inform the crew. You will have no problems.'

The trouble started in Casablanca.

# 31

## Seoul

The change in engine note indicated a move to descent before the pilot announced it. *"Ladies and gentlemen,'* the announcement system said, *'we will shortly be starting our descent into Seoul Gimpo International..."*

Saif stretched, arched his back and yawned. There was no direct flight from Tehran, so he'd flown via Beijing, but it still took almost fourteen hours. The flight attendant offered him a final coffee, but he declined, preferring to wait until he arrived at the hotel. As expected, he had no issue with immigration, and within twenty minutes of landing, he was in the back of the hotel limousine.

Thirty minutes later showered and shaved he called Rashid and instructed him to come to his room. He opened the door at once on Rashid's knock and closed it quickly behind him.

'Welcome, my friend,' he said. 'You have been enjoying yourself since Shanghai?'

'Well, the whisky is good, the TV channels are American, and the girls are pretty. So yes, I have been enjoying myself,' Rashid said.

'Tomorrow we fly to Hawaii, and your work starts again,' Saif said. 'Our flight leaves at 21:00, but we travel separately. We do not speak with each other or communicate in any way at all. I have a new passport for you. You are an Indian, your name is Professor Ashok Patel, and you are a university lecturer in Mechanical Engineering here in Seoul. You are attending a conference in Los Angeles but visiting friends in Honolulu on your way through. Your return ticket was booked through a Seoul travel agent, and your onward flight goes via Los Angeles back to here. You will be carrying almost one thousand dollars cash, and have credit cards and a driver's licence in your new name,' he said, passing a padded envelope over to Rashid.

He continued, 'The envelope contains everything you need, including the Honolulu address of your friends and your 'background'. You need to read and remember all of this and then burn this paperwork and flush the ashes down the lavatory. Do you understand?'

'Yes, yes, I do,' Rashid replied, 'but why this level of secrecy?'

'This leg of getting you to Hawaii is crucial, but America has extensive surveillance. It pays not to underestimate the efficiency of the US Customs and Border Patrol Agency. They always seem to be staffed by people who are overweight and chewing gum, but they have extensive training and excellent intelligence support. After you have done your work, you will change your ticket to fly straight back here claiming an illness in the family. Once back here, the money will be transferred into your account, and you will be free to join your family. The passport and cards are all genuine, and there is a Professor Ashok Patel at the University. He is taking a short vacation at the moment and cannot be reached,' Saif said. 'Tomorrow evening, after you check-out, put your current passport, credit cards and every other form of identification in the envelope and give it to your driver. When you arrive at the airport, you will be Professor Ashok Patel, and you must have nothing on you saying different. When you return here, the same driver will meet you and give you back all your original documents. Do you understand?'

Mumbling his agreement, Rashid took the envelope.

<><><>

Saif arrived early at the airport where he could keep an eye on Rashid's arrival and check-in. Although not used to acting a double life, Rashid seemed to be coping well. Saif had already received an SMS text from the driver confirming the swapping of passports, and he watched from a distance to ensure Rashid checked in without trouble.

They were both sat in the business lounge but away from each other. Making eye contact once, Saif smiled to reassure Rashid he was doing well. The next time he would make eye contact would be after passing through US Immigration.

The flight took almost nine hours and, being an overnight flight with little turbulence, both managed to sleep. Saif was travelling on a forged US passport under a new name and cleared Customs quickly. Rashid was questioned, but his 'legend' stood up to questioning, and he was soon through and picking up his luggage. Met by a Chinese looking limousine driver, Rashid exited the airport complex and joined the Queen Liliuokalani Freeway before heading West and North.

After about an hour travelling with the sea on his left side, the driver turned off the main highway before following a smaller road that then transformed into a track. At the end was a large house set in secluded gardens. Saif was stood on the porch waiting for his guest's arrival.

'Good, everything went according to plan. The shipment is due to arrive overnight, and we start work tomorrow. You will be taken to the workshop tomorrow, but you will stay here until the work is finished,' Saif said, allowing no argument.

# 32

## Honolulu, Hawaii

The Chinese cargo ship, the Tim Pu Zhedang, was en route from Shanghai to Rio de Janeiro, via Honolulu, Los Angeles, Mexico, Guatemala, El Salvador and the Panama Canal. It was only destined to stop in Honolulu for nine hours, just time to disembark and load cargoes. Time spent in port is wasted time and expense, so these larger ships spend over ninety-five per cent of their life at sea.

The cargo drop was quite small. There were one-hundred-and-thirty large containers, and sixty-three small containers to remove, with just seventy-four new ones to load. The paperwork for one of the large 3-axle semi low-loader trailers arriving showed the contents as a 1941 Caterpillar D6-4R Bulldozer.

All the cargo passed through regular screening. First, conventional X-ray's to determine there was nothing in a package that shouldn't be there and secondly, since 9/11, a gamma spectrometer surveillance and monitoring device, designed and built in California.

The overall shape of the bulldozer passed on X-ray and nothing out of the ordinary with the bulldozer was detected. As to radiation testing, the cast-iron and lead-lining protection operated exactly as designed. Radiation levels were again within the normal background 'scatter' levels detectable virtually everywhere. Within minutes, the trailer was cleared for delivery to the customer.

Fifteen minutes later, the trailer was attached to a truck with all paperwork stamped and handed over, and a Chinese driver drove it slowly out of the port.

The pick-up truck had been stolen earlier that day with false license plates, and fake company logos added.

Driving to one of the industrial areas of Pearl City, the driver turned sharply off into a run-down warehouse area. Behind it were a number of car body workshops, but none of them invited your average driver to visit. One of the larger workshops in the rear specialised in the illegal body chop business behind the front façade of tyres and exhausts. Pulling into the warehouse workshop named The Yellow Lotus, the doors were speedily closed. Two armed Chinese stood guard. The stolen truck would have the false company logo graphics and license plates removed, be wiped clean of fingerprints and returned to the owner by morning.

Saif felt a wave of relief. It was here. And he had fooled Homeland Security.

Turning, Saif motioned for Huang Fu, the workshop owner to come over.

'Huang Fu,' he said. 'Your men ready?'

Within moments four small Chinese men clad in jeans, t-shirts and overalls emerged, ready for work.

Over the next few hours, Rashid instructed the men to grind off or un-weld and remove the cast iron protection and to take out the weapons components.

Laying them on a bench, Rashid checked, re-checked and triple checked every item to ensure nothing was missing, and no damage had occurred.

Satisfied everything was complete, Rashid began the slower process of re-assembly. This was partly hampered by the need to wear thick gloves and overalls for protection against the uranium, but working diligently he finished within nine hours. He also connected, tested and fitted the timer and trigger card to the system's electronics. Happy that all was working, he began placing the components into a locally purchased Pelicase.

Unknown to Rashid, this model was marginally larger, almost 1mm wider, than the model he'd used in Deira, but the dimensions he had emailed through for the thin lead sheeting to screen the inside were still accurate enough.

Free of the protective casing, the final weapon was approximately four-foot-long by one-and-a-half-foot wide by a little over one-foot deep and weighed almost three-hundred pounds.

Huang Fu had already received details of the fibreglass housing to be built and had instructed one of his workers, Xin Du, to do so. When Xin Du had questioned its purpose, he had received a severe beating. Huang Fu was not a man to be questioned.

Rashid turned to Saif and said, 'She is ready to be armed. You can set the time and date up to two years in advance, accurate to within a second. Once the code has been entered and the time set, it is ready. You can set the code yourself, up to sixteen digits, but once armed only the code will de-activate it. You only get three attempts, each one with a longer delay between retry. On the third and final wrong attempt, you are locked out permanently. Even disconnecting the timer battery won't help as the processor card has a built-in battery. Cutting any of the wires or pulling cables out will likely cause immediate detonation. The original electronics are very sophisticated, and all I have done is override the old altimeter final arming with a timer.'

Saif smiled and thanked Allah. He set a unique sixteen-digit code and then set the timer to 06:00, 11th September. Locking the lid, he turned back to Rashid and said, 'Get them to put it in the housing.'

Huang Fu called two more workers to assist, and they and Xin Du wrapped the Pelicase first in heavy-duty waterproof sheeting, then in a lighter outer plastic sheeting before manhandling the fibreglass cage around it.

Rashid's design had been a two-piece construction in metal-ridged fibreglass, with an interlocking lip at the joint. The joint was also protected by a neoprene 'O' ring that fitted and expanded into a groove cut into the other section. Expanded foam stopped the contents moving, and twenty stainless steel bolts held both sections together. The waterproof sheeting around the Pelicase would stop any internal moisture build-up, while the screws and the neoprene 'O' ring on the fibreglass container would clamp the joints tightly and prevent any water ingress. Outside had four large 'D' Rings fitted for attaching tie-downs.

Due to the size and weight, Xin Du was positioned under the Pelicase as he guided it into the fibreglass container. The design Rashid had produced had allowed little room for manoeuvre, and in fitting this millimetre wider case into the container, it snagged and compressed the neoprene rubber, pulling it out of its groove and stretching it. Xin Du saw this happen but aware of the beating he had received before and the fact no one else could see thought it wiser to keep quiet. He quickly pushed the neoprene back into place, and the Pelicase finally slid snuggly into the fibreglass shell.

The fractional larger width of the Pelicase also very slightly distorted the fibreglass container causing two of the lower stainless steel bolts to cross-thread and not fully tighten. Again, Xin Du thought silence was the wiser option to save a beating. Anyway, eighteen bolts would surely be enough, he thought.

With the Pelicase fitted and the timer set, the device had already started its countdown. Three of them lifted the unit on the bench, and Saif called for the chains and anchors. He checked each of the four Danforth style anchors had thirty feet of galvanised chain attached and suitable shackles and straps to connect to the D rings.

Having satisfied himself everything was ready, he spoke briefly to Huang Fu. 'You have arranged for delivery?' he said.

'Yes, Master. My cousin operates a fishing boat. For the sum agreed he will deliver the device and place it where you have requested in two weeks. It will be done. And we will be on high ground on the twelfth.'

'Excellent,' Saif said. 'And you will take care of the trailer and the remains of the bulldozer?'

'Yes, Master. They will be disposed of.'

Turning slightly, he quickly pulled a suppressed pistol from the small of his back, aimed and fired. The 9mm round entered Rashid's head slightly behind his left ear, spraying blood and brain matter over the wall.

'Put him with it as well,' he said.

# 33

## The Marshall Islands

In the warm waters just south of the Marshall Islands in the mid-Pacific, the last few days had been warmer than usual. The locals didn't care - they were used to the warm weather. This extra heat, however, made the sea surface warmer than normal and, in turn, evaporate a little more quickly than usual. The ensuing evaporation of that water turning into clouds and rising produced a slightly lower-than-normal low-pressure area, causing cooler, higher-pressure air to the outside to pull in.

The rotation of the Earth causes all weather to be affected by what is known as the Coriolis Effect. Here, the effect was to make the approaching cooler winds gently swirl counter-clockwise around the low-pressure area and form the very early beginnings of what is known as an eye. The extra friction of the now gently swirling winds pulled over the surface of the sea caused the sea to warm up even fractionally more, including the already warming low-pressure area in the centre.

This extra warming of the sea surface caused the evaporation rate to increase slightly, making more water vapour condense into clouds faster, increasing the heat in the clouds and making the low-pressure area even lower and thereby pulling more swirling outside air in. And so it continued repeating itself and a few days of extra sunshine enjoyed by the locals were also the early beginnings of a tropical depression.

# 34

## Hawaii

The archipelago known as Hawaii is actually made up of over one hundred small islands. There are eight main islands of which seven are populated with the largest also known as the Big Island giving its name to the archipelago. Oahu is the third-largest island with the point of entry for most people being the airport at Honolulu. Like many Western countries, Hawaii has an underlying drug culture. Although drugs can be found anywhere, it is more prevalent in the towns of Pearl City and the smaller west coast towns of Makakilo City, Nanakuli, Waianae and Makaha. Overall, crime was higher here too, to pay for the drug habits.

Detective Third Grade Akoni Kamaka was known as 'Koni' to his colleagues. Based at the Alapa'i Police Headquarters in downtown Honolulu, Koni had seen most things Hawaii could throw at him.

Recently there had been an upturn in car thefts, and the suspicion was they were ending up in chop shops. Cars that are cut apart and then welded back together could become death traps if involved in an accident as the structural integrity would be missing, as had happened last week on the Kamehameha Highway on the east coast. Three cars had been involved in an average 'bump and shunt', but the rear car had folded in on itself, trapping the passenger and killing the driver. The car had recently been bought from a used car lot in Halawa and Koni had already spoken with the lot owners. They claimed they bought some cars from some workshops in Pearl City, so that was where he was headed today.

At none of the workshops was he given a warm welcome, but at one it was positively hostile. At The Sleeping Dragon, he could see a number of vehicles covered by canvas. The owner was Chinese and claimed not to understand English. His body language was aggressive, and he and the mechanics made it obvious Koni was not welcome. They refused to answer any questions and demanded a search warrant before they would even allow him inside. Knowing the Chinese ran many of the larger drug cartels and were also heavily into people smuggling, Koni planned to return the following day with a greater force including translators and warrants.

Information spreads quickly throughout the area, and Huang Fu was alerted to possible police raids occurring soon. The device was not meant to be moved yet and deployed until September 9th, over two weeks away, as per Admiral Zhang's orders, but this detective and his raids could mean trouble. Grabbing his cell phone, Huang Fu called his cousin, Tao Pui Dong, and master of the fishing boat, Li Rong. After much cursing and shouting, it was finally agreed that the device would be delivered to the fishing boat tonight and kept on board until needed. Xin Du and three other workmen would deliver it that evening under cover of darkness.

At midnight, a grey coloured truck left the warehouse of The Yellow Lotus and drove down to the fishing docks at Main Basin, Honolulu. The Li Rong was at her normal berth, and the truck pulled up close to the gangway. There was always some overnight activity in the dockyard due to on-going maintenance, so a truck arriving and loading or unloading wasn't unusual. After checking that the dockyard security guard had already completed his hourly inspection and was probably back in his hut with his feet up watching TV, the four of them unloaded the fibreglass container and carried it on to the rear deck of the Li Rong. Tao was waiting with two of his crew and, between them, they moved it down to the forward hold. It was also agreed that Xin Du would stay guard until the mission was completed.

# 35

## Cyprus

British Army sergeant Bill Thompson was halfway through his afternoon/evening duty when he intercepted a call that aroused his suspicion. Although intercepts were often interesting, most were in standard languages or popular dialects easy to understand. What made this intercept noticeable was that it was the second time recently he had heard this particular very localised Pashto dialect which had many words and phrases too difficult for him to identify. Checking his notes, he found a previous entry over four weeks before with his reference to the word 'jaws'. Again, this same word was spoken, but as part of a longer series of phrases. He wasn't sure but thought some of the words might mean 'mouth' as well as 'Allah' but in the local dialect. If correct, the phrase might mean 'mouth of Allah' or 'jaws of Allah', but this didn't seem to make sense.

Still, he reasoned, his was not to reason why. He raised it to his superior officer who transmitted it onward to GCHQ for full translation.

Within the hour of arriving at GCHQ, it had been designated and forwarded as 'Flash Traffic' and was on its way to the National Security Agency in Fort Meade, Maryland, marked for the attention of a number of individuals including Lieutenant Stringer.

# 36

## Honolulu, Hawaii

Tao Pui Dong knew what was planned was bad. If this device was found on his boat, he was aware that he faced a lifetime in prison after an undetermined period in Guantanamo. Americans were soft, but they were not fools. Huang Fu had insisted he take this device over two weeks ahead of schedule because he was worried about police raids on his workshop. But keeping the device here was even riskier. True, it was unlikely he would have the Police or Customs come on board, but accidents happen. He'd received personal messages from Admiral Zhang's representatives and knew what was expected of him. He also knew that if he valued his life, he wouldn't disobey Zhang but Zhang wasn't here under the constant eyes of the damned Americans. He was also terrified in case it went off early. Sitting on top of a nuclear device is not good for your health, he decided.

Checking his charts, he decided to act. The exact location of where to place this device had been very clearly given to him. It had to be placed on the rock face approximately a half-mile offshore at a depth of exactly three-hundred-and-fifty feet by the south-east of the Big Island, Hawaii, in the shadow of the Kilauea volcano. The rectangular fibreglass case was waterproof and had 'D' rings where straps, chain and anchors were attached. The plan was to gently lower the device by rope with the four anchors already extended. The seabed had a steep slope there and was covered in loose rocks and scree. The anchors would bite in and stop the device from sliding further down. When in place, the pull of a slip knot would enable the rope to be removed. The water depth was almost a thousand feet deep here and even deeper just a little further offshore, so the placement at three-hundred-and-fifty feet against the rock face was crucial.

Zhang's orders had been to place this device on the 8th or 9th of September, but now, Tao realised, it meant having this devil device on his boat for far too long.

The following morning, after a sleepless night, Tao had finally decided. They would place the device today. It was self-contained and already armed. Once the device was planted, and the rope removed, no one could move it. He wouldn't tell Huang Fu or his other masters, but smiling to himself, Tao felt he had come up with the perfect plan.

# 37

## The Pentagon, Washington

Mitch reviewed his e-mail inbox. He had requested updates directly from NCTC, NSA, CIA and Shane in Dubai on anything concerning the Middle East. Anytime increased radio, telephone, or data traffic in the Middle East occurred, it made the hairs on the back of his neck bristle. Unusual Pashto words and conversations spoken in some form of code also fired up his suspicion, and to have intercepts with the phrase 'mouth of Allah' or 'jaws of Allah' just added fuel to the fire, he thought.

To make matters worse, Shane had reported yesterday there was an unsubstantiated report that the extra security in Pakistan was because their Special Plans Division, the very people responsible for guarding and transporting their nukes around the country, had gone and lost not one, but two. How the fuck does someone lose two nukes, Mitch thought. Highly likely some asshole has not filed the correct paperwork, and they'd turn up somewhere safe, but he began to think of the shit-storm that must be happening over there if they've lost two nukes.

And what about this dead Professor guy? Maybe 'mouth' or 'jaws of Allah' referred to an insurgent attempt to kidnap him which went wrong. He'd supposedly been found dead, shot in the mouth, or jaw. Perhaps that was what it meant. It was also possible that the person detected entering Dubai twice was just similar looking to the Professor, as the facial detection software had only given a 75 per cent probability, but what if the Professor had turned rogue and was offering his services elsewhere.

And if this Professor was alive, could he have anything to do with the mislaid nukes? Could the SPD be working in cahoots with him? To what aim?

It was well known that Iran was trying to gain nuclear weapons, he thought. They have been following a program to enrich uranium for years. Mitch had read recent reports that centrifuges at the bunker-like Fordo facility near Iran's holy city of Qom have already been churning out uranium enriched to 20 per cent. Technically, Mitch knew, enriching uranium from 20 per cent purity to the required grade for weapons use of 80 per cent plus, was far easier and quicker than getting it from 0.7 per cent to 20 per cent.

Mitch also knew that Mossad, the intelligence agency of Israel, had carried out various covert operations against Iran in the last two years, including the killing of four Iranian nuclear scientists, as well as mysterious explosions at nuclear facilities. Perhaps Mossad had learned of Professor Rashid's intention to defect and offer his services to Iran and eliminated him – that would account for his 'death' being hushed up by ISI, but not for him reappearing in Dubai twice. No, he thought. If Mossad had known, then Rashid would definitely have been eliminated, and if Pakistan had known they would have arrested him. Relationships between Pakistan and Iran were quite good, but not enough to share nuclear secrets. No, the only situation that made sense was that Rashid had faked his own death for some reason, assuming the persons entering Dubai were actually Rashid.

And if that were the case, were these two nukes just mislaid or had they been taken? And if taken, by whom

... and for what? And was this Rashid part of it or is it just a coincidence?

Moving on to the next part of the puzzle, Mitch sat thinking about the phrase 'jaws of Allah'. That one would also have to go on the back-burner for now, he thought.

# 38

## Honolulu, Hawaii

The Li Rong dropped her mooring ropes and motored out of the main basin, her powerful diesel engines spewing black smoke into the morning still air. They planned to be off fishing for five days, their regular time away. Do nothing different to raise suspicion, Tao had been told.

They were heading towards the fishing grounds three-hundred miles offshore. Their heading took them south-east, passed the islands of Molokai, Lanai, Kahoolawe and Maui and close to the big island, Hawaii.

Even from a distance of over fifty miles, the mighty Mauna Loa volcano on the big island was visible, drawing them towards it like a magnetic beacon. Steam rose from its top. It was one of the world's highest and most active volcanos, and it gently simmered all day. Occasionally, with a snort and a cough, a few more tonnes of earth would be thrown in the air, and the land would shake and vibrate. But Mauna Loa blocked the view of Kilauea – smaller, but currently the most violent volcano in this region.

Radioing the US Coast Guard, Tao said in poor English, 'Coast Guard, Coast Guard, this is fishing craft, Li Rong. You receive? Over'

'Fishing craft Li Rong, US Coast Guard. Receiving. Over.'

'US Coast Guard, Li Rong. We have engine problem and will anchor by big island to fix. Over.'

'Li Rong, Coast Guard. Understood. Do you require assistance? Over.'

'Coast Guard, Li Rong. Negative. Only small problem. We have it fixed soon and advise. Over.'

'Li Rong, Coast Guard. Understood. Out.'

That, thought Tao, takes care of anyone contacting the Coast Guard about them being in close to shore or at anchor.

Using GPS, he positioned the Li Rong close inshore under the southern shadow of Kilauea. The engineer began to dismantle part of the generator to support their story if anyone official approached. Two ropes were attached to the device, one to take the weight and one as a slip rope, and it was hoisted overboard. They relaxed a little as soon as it was under the surface. The overall depth below the keel was a little over nine hundred feet, and it took only minutes to winch the device down into place at three hundred and thirty feet. The chains and grappling anchors were hanging approximately fifteen feet lower. As the anchors touched the slope, the flukes grabbed at and embedded in the loose rocks. Tao allowed the Li Rong to drift slightly offshore to stretch the anchors and then lowered again until the anchors were supporting the entire weight of the device and it rested against the rock face at the required depth of three hundred and fifty feet precisely. At that stage, the slip rope was pulled taut, and the main supporting rope broke free.

Within minutes, the lines had been winched back on board, and the Li Rong set off back on her fishing course. Tao radioed the Coast Guard to inform them he was underway again as he pushed the throttles to the maximum. We are still playing your game, he thought.

As the ropes were released and the seabed sediment slowly cleared, fish swam past their new visitor. Only two of the anchors had gripped the slope properly and were supporting the weight stopping the container slipping further down the rock face, but in doing so, had distorted the interlocking lip between the fibreglass halves even more. The weight and pressure of three-hundred-and-fifty feet of water pressed heavily on the fibreglass housing, further slightly distorting it. Within seconds, the first drop of seawater had eased past the two crossed-threaded screws.

<><><>

Detective Kamaka was already in a bad mood. He'd overslept, gotten delayed in traffic and then couldn't find a parking place outside his office. He also had a hangover. Even his usual daily Starbucks 'fix' would do nothing to brighten his day.

'Koni, in here,' the Lieutenant shouted, 'got another one for you. Someone's stolen an old bulldozer on a flatbed. It arrived three days ago at the port, cleared Customs and was signed for and driven off. Customs clearance was sent to Hawaii Heavy Diggers over in Waipahu, but it seems the 'dozer never arrived. Someone drove off with it. Now, what kinda dumb schmuck steals a fifty-year-old broken 'dozer? Look into it, will you?'

Realising the day had just gone from bad to worse, Koni took the paperwork and tossed it on his desk.

'Sure, Lieutenant, when I get around to it. I'm still chasing down all the paperwork on the chop shop bust,' Koni said.

The raid on The Sleeping Dragon had been successful. They had busted in the early morning, and shots had been fired. Various cars in pieces had been found as well as sales paperwork to used car lots throughout Oahu. This trade had been going on for months and was taking quite a lot of footwork to track all the vehicles down. Processing the arrests and completing the paperwork was taking far longer than Koni expected.

Walking up to the Lieutenant's office, Koni said, 'Lieutenant, I'll put a BOLO out on the bulldozer truck and see what happens. Will give it a few days and see what comes up. I expect it was just delivered to the wrong company.'

Getting the Lieutenant's agreement, Koni filled in the paperwork for a BOLO and got back to his main task for the day.

# 39

## La Palma, Canary Islands

Fawaz Al Farah walked up through the undergrowth to the old farmhouse. He had been here for almost four weeks and had explored the area carefully. He had spoken to the few locals in fluent Spanish and had used a modified cover name of Manuel Diego, but these were hill people farmers mostly and they would keep themselves to themselves. He'd explained that he was a writer and looking for solace and inspiration – that would cover any sightings they had of him exploring or wandering the hills. He'd also been buying and stocking up on provisions. Just a little a day so as not to arouse suspicion.

Sitting down, he opened up the maps and diary he had taken off Rachel Sanchez over two years before. He could never understand how easy it was to pick up western women. Just smile, say some things they want to hear. Pretend to be interested in the same things they are, and they become doe-eyed with emotion, he'd thought. He'd used the same technique many times.

She'd been totally focussed on her thesis about the possibility of terrorists triggering man-made disasters. She'd done extensive research work and was quite convinced it was feasible. She'd even uncovered old maps and diaries and claimed to have discovered some secret caves and tunnels under one of the main trigger points. He'd stolen all her work and passed it back to his masters as instructed; but although initially suggested by his Imam to remove her and leave no trace, on reflection the Iman had instructed him not to hurt her. He had felt

# 40

## Hawaii

In the waters off Hawaii at a depth of three-hundred-and-fifty feet, the rate of the water entering the container increased. The amount of water pressure at that depth, along with the weight of the container hanging on the anchors had made the casing twist and distort slightly more, resulting in a fine mist escaping past the damaged neoprene 'O' ring.

# 41

## Mediterranean Coast

The *Mehtap*'s engine beat with a constant rhythm. Once up to its usual speed of twelve knots, the engine note just became part of her. The crew had regular maintenance to keep them busy, but for Kourosh and Mostafa, along with Saif, who had joined the ship in Tunis, the days and nights had become boring. Saif had wanted to double-check the steel tool chest container was surrounded by lead ball-bearings inside the wooden outer crate. The US Navy, along with the British stationed in Gibraltar, monitored vessels entering or leaving the Mediterranean. They used a smaller modified version of SOSUS, the US Sound Surveillance System, placed on the seabed to listen for the engine sounds of surface and sub-surface vessels. Also, this modified version also contained radiation sensing Dosimeters to detect any nuclear-powered submarines transiting the Straits of Gibraltar. The *Mehtap* was a sea-kindly vessel, not rocking or corkscrewing in the short choppy seas close along the coast; and although their engine noise was detected, along with the sounds from dozens of other vessels each day, no radiation was detected emanating from her hold.

They had last stopped in Rabat, Morocco; Tangier before that, and the routine had become mundane. The crew had gone ashore in Tangier, but Captain Cakiroglu had warned his men not to speak of the three extra crew, and the night had passed drunkenly, but peacefully. The crew still ignored them but had quickly realised they were dangerous men. None of them wanted to cause a fight against people who trained and exercised on the deck most days. Twice, they had thrown bags of rubbish overboard and then fired AK-47s at them until they sank.

Saif's arrival had caused a small issue in that the only spare cabin was already being used by Kourosh and Mostafa. It was easily fixed, though. Captain Cakiroglu had gone below to find his belongings thrown out into the corridor and had been instructed to use his day cabin for the remainder of the journey.

Arriving in Casablanca, the vessel was subjected to a random complete search by Moroccan Customs. Saif was worried about the crates discovery but it was well hidden beneath legitimate food supplies. Even bribing the officials didn't work this time and the crew were subjected to a detailed search and confiscation of their porn magazines and films as well as large quantities of cigarettes and tobacco.

That evening was an overnight stop, and the crew, to a man, headed to the nearest bar to cool off.

The beer and whisky flowed, and the atmosphere soon went downhill. The crew, angered by losing so much tobacco, decided it was all the fault of the three 'guests'. Sober, they wouldn't have started, but drunk they egged each other on until finally one of the crew had begun shouting. Complaining to the other bar members that the *Mehtap* was carrying a secret cargo of gold and diamonds and it was being guarded by Special Forces soon raised an unwelcome interest. Within the hour a gang of over twenty drunk and semi-drunk crew from various ships all approached the *Mehtap* wanting to see its cargo. Kourosh and Mostafa quickly jumped down onto the dockside to break up the gang, but the drunks had been planning this. Pulling out crowbars and knives, the crowd began to taunt them.

It didn't take long. Kourosh and Mostafa were well trained. Within moments, a number of the crowd had fallen to kicks and beatings with their own weapons. Two fell to stab wounds, and gradually the crowd thinned. Mostafa grabbed the drunk crewman trying to board the *Mehtap* and judo punched him in the head. Falling awkwardly, most in the crowd could hear the snap of his neck just before they heard the sirens of the Customs and dockyard police arriving.

Corruption in most North African countries is rife with officials open to bribes. Here was no exception and the ship and crew were allowed to leave but not before a considerable amount of dollars had been paid over by Saif.

As they eventually left port Captain Cakiroglu looked a worried man, and the rumours ashore grew stronger that her cargo was worth killing for.

# 42

## Marshall Islands

The tropical depression continued to strengthen and began to move north-west slowly. The US National Oceanic and Atmospheric Administration, in conjunction with the US National Weather Service, issued an early alert of a tropical depression that had increased to a tropical storm in the mid-south Pacific with the potential to increase to a full typhoon.

The Joint Typhoon Weather Centre (JTWC), a joint US Navy and US Airforce command located in Pearl Harbour also received the warning. Tasked with the issuing of tropical cyclone warnings in the North West Pacific Ocean, South Pacific Ocean and Indian Ocean for all branches of the US Department of Defense and other US government agencies, a Tropical Storm Formation Alert warning was distributed to all naval departments and shipping currently stationed within the middle Pacific rim.

# 43

## Hawaii

Detective Kamaka snatched up his ringing phone.

'Koni,' he said.

'Detective, Sergeant Hensen over in traffic. Your BOLO has just come in. Two of my men have spotted a flatbed over in Makaha inside the swamp reserve. The number on it ties up with your missing one, so I guess it's just been dumped. You gonna attend?'

'Sure, be there in an hour,' Koni answered. 'Your guys be on scene?'

'Yeah, I'll get them there,' the Sergeant answered.

Koni arrived just before noon and was guided to the location by a uniform traffic cop. The low-loader had an old faded yellow bulldozer strapped to it. Koni had not seen one that old before, but looking more closely, they saw someone had been tampering with the engine area. The engine block had marks on it where welding had taken place, and the top cylinder head and sump were missing. It also looked like it had been doused with something and set on fire – probably to remove fingerprints, Koni thought. Looking around, there was no evidence of powder or resin, but he guessed something like drugs had been smuggled in. If so, he estimated it would have been a big haul to have filled up the hollowed out engine block. Druggies are getting sophisticated, Koni thought. Not a lot he could do here, so he would write it up and pass it onto narcotics. It looked like someone had been trying to drive the trailer to the wet swamp area and then sink it. Dumb shit had driven the wheels off the edge of the blacktop onto mud and gotten it stuck, he thought, then just panicked and left it.

As a standard procedure, Koni instructed the uniforms to conduct a 360-degree search out to two hundred yards. Taking some photos and making notes, Koni was about to call his Lieutenant when a call went up.

'Detective, you'd better come and check this out.'

Clambering over the low-loader and pushing aside the overgrowth, Koni headed to where the uniforms were waiting. There was what looked to be a shallow grave with loose soil on top. Local animals had been scavenging and had dug down and pulled something out. Koni realised with a sinking feeling he was looking at the gnawed fingers of someone's left hand.

# 44

## Mediterranean Coast

One day from Agadir, Morocco, the main bearing on the generator on the *Mehtap* seized. They could continue to run on engine power and use the batteries to run the electrics, but a days' worth would be all they could expect. Captain Cakiroglu radioed ahead and arranged a replacement, but it would delay his departure twenty-four hours. While waiting for the repair, the crew continued their regular duties and unloaded and loaded the cargo. After that, there was nothing to do until the generator bearing was replaced early the following day. As normal, the crew headed for the bars, but the atmosphere was different now. Since Casablanca and the death on the dockside, the crews' feelings towards the three strangers had grown colder. To make matters worse Kourosh and Mostafa were with them now to make sure no more trouble came their way.

The underground telegraph system between ports and dockyard workers would put the CIA to shame. Within an hour of arriving at the bars, rumours were again being raised that the ship was carrying something special. Under the glaring stares of Kourosh and Mostafa no fights actually started and they escorted the crew back to the *Mehtap* when the bars finally closed.

The following morning as they got underway after the generator had been repaired, Kourosh and Mostafa sat with Saif in his cabin and reviewed their plans.

# 45

## Hawaii

To the fish swimming near the strange looking device, everything seemed calm. The weight of water pressure, along with the added weight of more water now inside the container had made the casing twist and distort even more putting further pressure on the already damaged neoprene 'O' ring.

With a slight 'pop' which alarmed two fish swimming close-by, a minute section of the 'O' ring gave way, and the rate of the water entering the container increased from a mist to a fine high-pressure jet with the cutting power of a small laser. It took only moments for the water to cut a hole through the protective outer waterproof plastic layer around the Pelicase. The heavier duty inner waterproof layer would take longer, but it began to distort under the relentless high-pressure jet.

# 46

## Mediterranean Coast

Palmas de Gran Canaria was the last westward-bound port the *Mehtap* called at. After unloading and reloading, the standard practice would have been for the crew to enjoy the fruits of the bars and local ladies of the island, but Saif had called them all together and made them a collective offer. He had shown them the money and had offered each crew member two thousand US dollars if they stayed on board that evening. To a man, they all agreed. Saif also said that he and his two colleagues would be leaving the ship soon after they left port the following day and would be picked up by a fishing boat offshore. The crew began to smile, even planning on returning to port the next evening to spend some of the extra money.

The following day Saif spent time with the Captain giving him a course to steer to intercept the fishing boat. As they neared thirty miles offshore, Captain Cakiroglu checked the radar then turned to Saif and asked him what was going on as there was no other vessel in sight. Pulling his suppressed pistol from the small of his back, he aimed at the Captain's forehead. As he put pressure on the trigger, the last sounds Captain Cakiroglu heard was the rhythmic chattering of AK-47's as Kourosh and Mostafa murdered his men.

Leaving his men to attach chains to the bodies to stop them floating before dumping them in the hold, Saif altered course towards the island of La Palma.

<><><>

Sixteen hours later in the early hours of the morning, they approached El Remo on the western coast of La Palma. The small harbour was unlit at this time of night, and the *Mehtap* crept in until a flashlight flashed three long, one short, and two long flashes. The signal that all was clear.

Anchoring three hundred yards offshore, an inflatable with an outboard approached them. All three had their weapons at the ready until out of the gloom the smiling face of Fawaz Aziz Al Farah appeared.

'Salaam alaikum, brothers,' Fawaz called, 'Allahu Akbar.'

'Wa alaikum as salaam,' Saif replied. 'I am relieved that we are here, Insha'Allah!'

'It is good to see you, brothers. Everything is running to plan. Let me help you with the cargo.'

# 47

Cabo Galeno Jiminez had been in the Guardia Civil for four years and was hoping for a promotion soon. He was eager, attentive, and wanted this promotion more than anything, if for no other reason than to prove to his mother that he was right to join the Guardia Civil straight from college. His mother had wanted him to go to university, to learn a proper job, but Galeno had always liked watching US cop shows, and that was where his career was heading.

He was driving back to the local station after his routine evening inspection of the villages. He'd been on the lookout for underage drinking and drug use but being it was three in the morning mid-week, and with gentle rain falling, he hadn't seen any sign of life and was now looking forward to coffee, an early breakfast, and a couple of hours of sleep. As he turned the wheel to head his car back up the hill towards Puerto de Naos, his headlights reflected off something shining out at sea.

The standing instructions his sergeant had drilled into him were to call in anything suspicious and then wait for back-up. But Jiminez was fed up with his rank as Cabo and was keen to show he could handle anything. His mind raced. There seemed to be a vessel just off the breakwater. It wasn't showing lights but looked anchored, which meant possibly it was up to no good. Perhaps this was his chance to show how good he was, he thought. In his mind's eye, he could already see the Comandante shaking his hand and promoting him, to the accompanying applause of his colleagues. Turning off his headlights and engine, he quietly free-wheeled and positioned his car near the breakwater and watched. A while later he saw a darkened grey inflatable slowly coming ashore with four men on board.

This was it. This was his promotion just waiting. He could imagine the proud look from his mother as the photographers took his picture. He could almost feel the handshake from his bosses.

Quietly exiting his car, he crept along the darkened breakwater until he was just above where the dinghy was approaching. Until he had crept closer, he hadn't noticed the darkened van on the breakwater as well. Creeping around the back, he was about to draw his weapon and to shout at them to halt when a hand snaked around his throat. Before he could emit a cry, his chin was pulled up exposing his neck, and he felt a stinging sensation on his skin. His chest heaved as he tried to breath, but all he could do was gurgle. Held firmly, he slowly felt his energy drain from his limbs, and he then slid down to the cold stone.

# 48

Mostafa stepped away from the body. He had seen the Police car parked and watched the person creeping along the breakwater. Slipping silently over the side of the dingy, he'd swum to the iron railings set in the wall and quietly climbed them, coming up behind the intruder. After confirming he was alone, it had been simple to slit his throat, the razor-sharp knife cutting through the jugular and windpipe. The guy had never stood a chance.

They had already removed the steel tool chest container from the wooden crate as well as the six-inch protective layer of lead shot surrounding it, placed there to defeat radiation detection. It now only took two of them to lift the chest into the van. Saif ordered Kourosh and Mostafa to put the body in the dinghy and take it back to the ship. They were to raise anchor and set her steaming due west, with the seacocks open. She would sink within the hour and, as the depths became very deep close inshore, she'd never be found. The bodies were weighted and wouldn't float. Then they would come back ashore with the four canvas holdalls and meet at the beach further south. In the meantime, he and Fawaz would find somewhere to dump the Police car.

Leaving quickly, within the hour they had met again. The *Mehtap* was last seen riding low in the water and heading off to a watery grave in almost a thousand feet of water. Saif was driving the van and had followed Fawaz in the Police car up into the hills. They had driven the Police car off a cliff into trees on a deserted road, but

143

unlike in Hollywood, it didn't explode in a fireball. It just rested there almost entirely obscured from the road. If it were found it would be assumed the Guardia officer had tried to crawl to safety.

Fawaz was driving now and led them up through narrow lanes to the remote farmhouse. Taking the steel chest indoors, Saif posted Kourosh and Mostafa as guards. But no alarms had been raised, and no one showed the slightest interest in the farmhouse.

Saif had been sat reciting the words of the Qur'an for the last thirty minutes: *Muster against them all the men and cavalry at your disposal so that you can strike terror into the enemies of Allah.*

Over and over he recited this, almost in a trance. Finally, he said 'Brothers, now we sleep. Tomorrow we finish our plans, Insha'Allah.'

The quiet chanting began, '*Allahu Akbar, Allahu Akbar.*'

# 49

## Hawaii

Deep below the surface, the remaining 'O' ring seal on the container eventually succumbed to the weight and pressure of water. The outer and inner waterproof layers surrounding the Pelicase, damaged by the high-pressure jet, failed to protect it and seawater quickly washed around it. Never designed to be waterproof at that depth the rubber seals on the Pelicase also failed and seawater flooded inside.

The effect of Uranium 235 on the seawater surrounding it was the very slight heating of the water. Not enough to feel by hand, even measuring equipment would only notice a one-tenth of a degree rise, but the water was now radioactive. To the fish swimming close by, they failed to feel the effects of swimming in highly radioactive water.

The US National Oceanic and Atmospheric Administration, in conjunction with the US National Weather Service, increased the alert status of the tropical storm in the mid-south Pacific, to a severe tropical storm with potential to increase to a full typhoon.

The JTWC distributed to all naval departments and shipping currently stationed or operating within the Pacific rim its upgrading of the tropical storm formation alert to severe tropical storm warning status.

# 50

Not all areas of Hawaii are rich from tourism. Kalapana, on the Big Island, was an area of low income and poor quality housing. Many families were out of work and living on benefit. Two local boys went shore fishing each day after school, partly for fun but also to help bring food home. They would have liked to skip school and just fish all day, but their parents were strict they attend. On this particular day, they noticed fish floating on the surface. Usually, this happened if the fish had been attacked or had been dumped from a passing fishing boat, but when they swam out and pulled these in, they looked fine. Pink snapper and sea bass - they were still alive but were feeble. Perhaps they were just tired the boys laughed as they put them in their catch basket. Kona crabs were rare and expensive. Walking around the water's edge, they could see them in the depths. Kona's never came this close inshore usually, the boys thought, but who cared. Mum will love these, they decided as they stripped off and dived into the waters. That night, and for the rest of the week, both families dined like royalty.

# 51

The attending doctor at the Hilo Medical Centre, Doctor Chase Lampton, had not seen a case like this before. Eight people had all turned up together complaining of nausea and vomiting. The two mothers and two eldest boys also seemed to have a strange rash or burns on their hands. He'd first assumed they had food poisoning and he had them admitted and put on antibiotics. But they didn't seem to be getting any better. None of them could keep any food down – typical with food poisoning, but they also had blood in their diarrhoea and vomit, and the burns on the hands were not reacting to treatment.

He decided he would increase their antibiotics and review the situation again in twenty-four hours.

# 52

Detective Kamaka's phone was ringing as he reached his desk. Snatching it up, he answered, 'Yeah, Koni here,'

'Hey, Koni. Thought you'd never answer. Get your butt down here. Got some news for you,' Dr Kate Bannerman said.

'Can't you tell me on the phone?' Koni asked.

'Nope, I like surprises,' she said.

Arriving at her office in the adjoining building, Koni said, 'OK, gorgeous girl. Whatcha got for me?'

'Your victim was killed by the intrusion of a metal object between the left occipital and temporal lobes. Death would have been instantaneous,' she said.

'In English, the first part I mean.'

'Shot behind the left ear with a 9mm,' she said. 'But that's not why I got you down here.

'No I.D. or distinguishing marks,' she continued, 'middle Asian appearance – Indian or Pakistan I guess, so I ran his prints. Nothing. Nada. So I think maybe he's a visitor to our beautiful shores, so I ran them by Immigration. Bingo.'

'Bingo?'

'Bingo. Came back from US-VISIT that he is Professor Ashok Patel from Seoul. Arrived last week in Honolulu visiting friends here, en-route to LA. So could be the victim of a mugging.'

'So was that the surprise?' Koni said.

'Nope! Because I hadn't got a hit with his prints, I'd used facial recognition to all the standard databases.

Earlier this morning I got a call from Homeland Security. They are alerting the CIA, the FBI and the Department of Defense. The surprise is that this guy is also Professor Yousef Rashid, a nuclear weapons scientist from Pakistan, who was pronounced dead over a month ago at a crime scene in Pakistan.'

# 53

Dr Chase Lampton was re-examining his patients' charts. Although they had been on strong antibiotics and increased painkillers for over twenty-four hours, their symptoms were not improving. The rash on their hands had worsened too. The rash appeared similar to severe sunburn, but the rest of their skin wasn't affected. They still had nausea and vomiting, and one boy had started bleeding from the mouth and nose. Worried that they were all suffering from some form of infectious disease, he ordered them moved to isolation wards and for further tests to be performed.

By lunchtime, the elder of the two worst affected boys had been in a coma for almost twelve hours. Twice his heart had stopped, and he'd been defibrillated, brought back from the edge of death, to again just lay unconscious. At two-seventeen, his life finally ran out. He again suffered a heart attack and this time even repeated attempts with chest massage and defibrillations failed to bring him back. By now, the other boy was also slipping in and out of a coma.

The test results were also indicating a far higher white blood cell count than normal, high enough to usually suggest Leukaemia. However, families and neighbours don't all suddenly contract Leukaemia at once. Referring to the Chief of Staff on duty for advice, they jointly agreed the only diagnosis that made sense was some form of radiation sickness caused by exposure to sources unknown.

Following standard procedure, the hospital then initiated a 'suspected contamination' lockdown and alerted the Hawaiian Department of Health (HDOH) as to its nature.

The HDOH, in turn, informed the FBI, the Department of Homeland Security, and the Department of Defense.

# 54

Later that afternoon, Dr Chase Lampton, along with nurses, an FBI agent and a Homeland Security officer, all wearing protective clothing started interviewing both mothers. Neither knew of anything different happening within the last two weeks apart from the boys had brought home some extra fish they'd caught recently. The mothers had prepared it, and both families had eaten it. It had tasted fine, they said.

'And no one has given you anything else? Anything metal?' he asked.

'What sort of thing do you mean, Doctor?'

'Well, anything they'd found or anything unusual?'

'No, Doctor, nothing at all. The boys have been at school all week and just fishing in the evenings,' she said.

Moving to the isolation ward containing the semi-comatose boy, Lampton instructed the nurse to add adrenaline to his drip. Shortly afterwards, his eyes flickered open.

'Tommy, I'm Dr Lampton. Those fish you caught have made you ill. Where did you catch them?'

'We din't really catch 'em, Sir. They was floating, like. On the surface. Just floating and waiting to be taken,' Tommy replied.

'And where was this, Tommy? Where, exactly, were they floating?'

'Off the point. Along the bay and off the point,' came the reply.

<><><>

Within the hour, agents and inspectors were combing the beach and the headland. Homeland Security had also brought in the Domestic Nuclear Detection Office (DNDO) who were carrying out further analysis. They had already examined the families' homes and checked the fridge for additional fish. Sure enough, the radiation readings had been off the scale. This also explained the burns on their hands from the boys handling the fish as they caught them to both mothers handling the fish to clean and cook them. More dead or dying fish could be seen floating a little way offshore. The Hawaii Police Dept sent a small launch to collect samples. Nearer the headland, samples of mussels and anemones were taken; but although these fish were also highly radioactive, no obvious source of the contamination could be found.

# 55

## Islamabad

The draft email was in code, and Shane's heart raced as he decoded it. The sender was requesting an urgent meeting the following morning.

Shane communicated with his informants through Hotmail accounts. Each informant had a specific account which only they and Shane knew the password to. Instead of actually sending an email, which could be monitored or hacked and even if later deleted would usually remain on a server somewhere, all they did was compose an email but not send it. Written in code and saved in the 'Draft' folder it would remain until the other party logged in and read the draft message. As it hadn't actually been sent, there was nothing to intercept and, having not been sent, once deleted was permanently erased from the system. On reading the 'draft' message, the reader would delete the original, add his reply and again save it as 'draft'. This system has become foolproof as nothing is actually ever sent therefore no data is able to be recorded, and no email addresses are ever exposed.

Arriving at Benazir Bhutto International Airport early the following morning, Shane walked out of the terminal, ignoring all the hawkers and drivers vying for his business. Walking down the length of the taxi rank he chose the sixth in the queue. It didn't really matter whether it was the fifth, sixth or seventh; he just wanted to select one at random. He'd travelled from Dubai that morning using a fake Canadian identity which showed his reason for visit as meeting with the Pakistan

Department of Agriculture in downtown Islamabad to discuss Canadian wheat.

The taxi dropped him at the corner of 9th Avenue and Charman Road. Exiting, he paid the driver and walked across the road to Service Road West. As he walked around the corner, another taxi pulled up, and he quickly jumped in. This one was operated by a CIA local, and it sped off changing direction multiple times to throw off any followers.

The email message Shane had received had come from his Pakistani Government informant, a quiet, unassuming physically small man who'd been easily corrupted for a sum of US$10,000. Shane had met him once before but usually relied on communication by Hotmail. The fact that he'd demanded to meet Shane urgently highlighted something, but Shane didn't know what.

The driver drove towards downtown Rawalpindi, finally stopping in a quiet alley close to the Purana Oila district, a densely populated old area of the city. Knowing this meeting could be a trap, Shane took a small handgun from the glove compartment and put it in his pocket. He exited the car and walked around the corner before entering the dark building through a broken and worn wooden door. Shane was also holding a small plastic transmitter in his right hand and kept his finger depressing the button. If he released it, four armed backup agents located in the shadows outside would be there in seconds.

Waiting for his eyes to become accustomed to the gloom he sensed another person in the corner.

'I am looking for the baker,' Shane said.

'He is not working today. There is no bread,' came the correct reply.

155

Finally able to relax Shane breathed out heavily and said, 'Ashok, it is good to see you again, my friend. Tell me, what is so urgent we had to meet?'

Ashok moved forward and shook Shane's outstretched hand. 'Mister Shane, I have some more information, but I need more money. Much more.'

'Hey pal, I've already paid you ten grand. What's the information?'

'One hundred thousand, Mister Shane. I want one hundred thousand, and I tell you.'

'A hundred grand? You gotta be joking. What the hell do you know that is worth a hundred grand? You're wasting my fucking time, pal.' and he moved towards the door.

'I know about the nuclear bombs, Mister Shane.'

Shane's blood froze as he slowly turned back around.

'OK, pal, you've got my attention. Now talk.'

'I want one hundred thousand US dollars, Mister Shane. Then I talk.'

'Now listen to me, pal. Don't fuck with me. I'm sure your bosses would love to know you've been passing information to another country. What do they do to traitors here? Huh? Now you tell me what the fuck's going on and, if it's good information, I'll pay you twenty thousand.'

'Ninety thousand, Mister Shane. My information is very good. Very important.'

'Forty thousand and that's my final offer. Now spill it!'

At that, Ashok shook hands with Shane and started talking.

Twenty minutes later a visibly shaken Shane got back in the taxi and said to the driver, 'The Embassy. Now!'

# 56

The US National Oceanic and Atmospheric Administration, in conjunction with the US National Weather Service, increased the alert status of the severe tropical storm in the mid-south Pacific, to an impending slow-moving full typhoon. Tracking its path and speed would show it pass directly over the Mariana Islands just as it reached full power in four to five days.

Early indications showed it could grow as large and powerful as Typhoon Pongsona which struck the Marianas' in 2002 and had produced winds in excess of 170 mph, leaving the islands without power for almost a week.

# 57

## The Pentagon, Washington

Mitch Stringer was still feeling uneasy. For the past weeks, he had tried everything he could think of, everyone he could squeeze for information, to find out what was going on. Counting off on his fingers so far he knew that a senior Pakistani nuclear weapons scientist had been robbed and mugged, and then ended up dead having been shot in the mouth. In all probability, that same person had then appeared in Dubai twice over a period of a few weeks using a different name and then the leads had gone cold. There had also been an increase in both radio and telephone traffic but only the word 'mouth of Allah', or possibly 'jaws of Allah' had been fully understood. Finally, there were reports from the Middle East of increased feelings of tension in the air.

Not getting anywhere, he turned to his computer as his e-mail inbox pinged. It was a copy of the regular 'Threat Level' daily briefings. By page two his blood had run cold. As he read page three, he murmured, 'Holy shit! Holy fucking shit!' as he reached for the phone.

# 58

## La Palma, Canary Islands

Saif Khan had had a sleepless night. The plan was almost complete but now was the part most crucial to its overall success. It was imperative they find the exact location underground; the professors had made it very clear where they needed to place the device for maximum effect.

They had each taken it in turns to stand a two-hour guard shift through the night, but everything had been quiet. Fawaz had done an excellent job in preparing the farmhouse as best he could. He had purchased simple camp beds and sleeping bags, torches and shovels and had stocked the kitchen with plenty of food and water. Before they'd settled down last night, Saif had made them check, strip down and clean all the weapons. Between them, they had enough to start a small war. There were six Kalashnikov automatic rifles, two grenade launchers, twelve launch grenades, twelve hand grenades, various automatic pistols, knives and over four thousand rounds of ammunition. They also had 4kg of C4 explosives, detonators, connecting cord and timers and two pairs of night-vision goggles. Alongside their clothes, they had protective vests, helmets and three First-Aid kits.

Fawaz had also brought webbing straps, similar to those used in the manufacture of seatbelts, to allow them to make a sling carrying harness for the chest.

Leaving Mostafa on guard at the farmhouse, Fawaz, Saif and Kourosh started up the steep climb to the hidden entrance, still almost invisible from more than a few feet away. Pulling aside the bushes and gorse Fawaz had used for camouflage, they could see the entrance before them. Fawaz had already spent time kicking the two skeletons aside and had spent two complete days in gradually widening the first part of the opening. Now they had room to walk in without stooping but also had a full view of the approach paths, making it easier to defend.

The loom of their torches reflected off the wet walls as they moved deeper and deeper in through the tunnel. The splashing of the water got louder as they approached a number of small caverns which had some small tunnels running off them. The larger tunnel continued downwards into the mountain, but breathing was difficult. Saif 's chest heaved, and his eyes watered as he tried to breathe in the thick, moisture-heavy air, rich with sulphur fumes. The water coming through the cracks in the walls and tunnel roof was pooling around their feet before disappearing through gaps in the floor. It was also extremely humid, almost like a Turkish bath, Saif thought wryly. Occasionally, steam vents erupted spraying near-boiling water towards them. Kourosh screamed in pain as a powerful scalding jet cut into his shoulder, the skin quickly reddening and peeling back into a third-degree burn, the muscles and tendons clearly showing. Ripping off his sleeve, he wrapped it around the raw flesh. There was little else they could do so headed further on.

Following the tunnel, the slope finally began to rise a little, and they came near the end. The walls were still damp, but no longer as sodden. The air was slightly drier too. But hotter.

At the very end, the tunnel walls were darker and made of a different type of rock. Tapping it with the butt of his pistol, Saif could hear a differing sound of an echo. This was more of a deep reply, something solid that didn't want to be moved.

'This is the place,' Fawaz said. 'This is where the two rocks meet. This is where we need to bring the chest.'

Looking around, Saif could understand the reasoning. They had travelled almost a mile into and under the mountain. The temperature had been steadily rising, and they were as far in as they could go. The entrance was easily defended, and they only had six days to go.

Having found what they were after, they exited to return to Mostafa and the device. As they turned the last bend, a low moan sounded from within the tunnel. Even in the heat of the air and water, their blood ran cold. It got louder and louder until it suddenly stopped. Feeling icy cold, Saif turned and pointed his torch towards the cavern roof.

'Brothers,' he said. 'It is nothing to worry about. It is where the steam is escaping from the walls. I think the mud is running and blocking the vents and then the steam pushes it clear again. It is nothing. Come on, we must be strong, Insha'Allah, and complete our mission.'

Trying to be reassured by what Saif had said, they continued to the exit. Reassured or not, all three of them were quietly reciting Allahu Akbar to themselves as they left the tunnels.

# 59

After further treating Kourosh's shoulder, they returned with Mostafa, the device and the shoulder webbing straps. It took them almost six hours of struggle to move it to where the rock faces met. The heat was crippling with the weight of the device on their shoulders, and there were many places where it had to be moved by hand, where the bends in the tunnel were too sharp to use the straps, but eventually, it was in place.

Instructing the others to move away and turn their backs, Saif unlocked the combination locks. Inside the timer display glowed as before, just waiting to be armed and set.

Quietly chanting Allahu Akbar to himself, Saif smiled and set a unique sixteen-digit code followed by setting the timer to 18:00, 11th September.

Pressing the 'arm' button, he closed and padlocked the Pelicase lid, and then the outer chest lid.

It was done. Nothing now could stop the two explosions, one in Hawaii and the other here, Insha'Allah, he thought.

'Brothers,' he said, 'this is a mighty day. The Qur'an says *"Muster against them all the men and cavalry at your disposal so that you can strike terror into the enemies of Allah"*. We have set this in place. The Sheik instructed us to *"Avenge the American wars on the Muslim world. Attack them, strike at them at random in their homelands and beyond"*. Brothers, today we have put the final piece to the plan, Insha'Allah. In six days' time, the Jaws of Allah will bite, and the mighty Satan will feel the teeth sink into their flesh. Allahu Akbar.'

His two colleagues joined him in chanting his rejoice to his God as they moved back towards the entrance.

Stopping in the tunnel mouth, Saif said, 'Brothers, I must leave you tomorrow, but you are tasked with a mighty role. The device will explode in six days, on 11th September at 18:00. That is already pre-programmed and cannot be changed. Until that time you must guard this entrance with your life,' he continued. 'At 16:00 on that day, you must leave quickly and get to the other side of the island. You will be safe there, and you will be able to leave the island to Africa in the chaos that follows. But if Allah wills it and the enemy arrive sooner, you must become Shaheed, Insha'Allah. Do you understand, brothers? You must not fail. You will be well rewarded in paradise, brothers,' he said. 'If the enemy comes you must fight them. If you need to you must set an explosion to block the entrance to this cave. There is to be one person on guard here at the entrance at all times. One person may sleep, the other stays on guard at the farm. You have eight-hour shifts. This tunnel is never to be left unguarded. Never. Do you understand?'

To a man, all three agreed and vowed to protect the cave at all odds.

They spent the remainder of the day making a number of defendable gun emplacements.

<><><>

The following morning Saif flew to Tehran via Marrakech and Abu Dhabi.

# 60

## GCHQ, Cheltenham, UK

Department 17 was always busy. It dealt with the translation of intercepts from around the Middle East. In particular, it dealt with the translation of intercepts in the Arabic, Farsi and Pashto languages or variants thereof. Today a young female junior, a British-born Pakistani with excellent language skills was on duty. Born in Bradford, UK, a city densely populated by Pakistanis, Arabs and Turks, she'd become fluent in English, Urdu, Punjabi, Sindhi, Arabic, Farsi and Pashto, with a further number of Pashto dialects due to her grandparents having lived in the north of Pakistan.

Her tasks today were numerous including full translation of a stack of messages recorded a number of weeks previously at various listening stations. The first eight sets of messages were relatively mundane and even boring, but as she listened through her headphones to the start of the ninth, her ears pricked up. She hadn't heard this particular unusual Pashto dialect since she'd last spoken to her grandmother. It was such a rarely used dialect that she'd never heard it spoken elsewhere apart from at her grandparent's home.

With rising excitement, she played the recording over and over while she typed up the English translation. The message clearly stated 'Great Satan will soon feel the mighty bite of the jaws of Allah'. Re-reading the earlier intercept notes, she realised it had been previously mistranslated. She immediately raised this to her superior officer who marked it as 'RED - Flash Traffic' and transmitted it onward to GCHQ.

Within minutes, it had been forwarded as 'RED - Flash' and was on its way to the National Security Agency in Fort Meade, Maryland, marked for the urgent attention of Lieutenant Stringer.

# 61

## Honolulu, Hawaii

Detective Kamaka was waiting for the Lieutenant to get off the phone. The Lieutenant usually left his door open – an 'open door' policy he'd always said. But, that also meant when it was shut, you didn't disturb him. After what seemed an age, the Lieutenant placed the handset down and beckoned Koni to enter.

The Lieutenant sighed and said, 'Jeez, just when you think it can't get any worse.'

'What's up, Lieutenant?'

'Just been speaking with Admiral Carter, Chief of Naval Operations in DC. How the hell he knew, I dunno, but it seems we have two families admitted to Hilo on the Big Island with radiation sickness, and we've been asked to assist. Second point, where is the bulldozer right now?'

'In the vehicle pound with Forensics.'

Grabbing his jacket, the Lieutenant said, 'C'mon, let's go. You get Bannerman. I'll meet you at the pound,' as he ran towards the door.

Racing in through the door, Koni sought out Kate Bannerman. 'Kate. Who's running forensics on the 'dozer?'

'Two of my team. Why?'

'Doc, it might be radioactive. You've got to warn them.'

Grabbing a box from a cabinet while she was speed dialling, she said, 'C'mon. You drive.'

By the time they had reached Koni's car, Dr Bannerman was speaking with her lead technician, 'Guys, get away from the 'dozer. It might be radioactive. Get away right now. I'm on my way with a counter.'

<><><>

With the siren blaring and lights flashing, Koni was enjoying the drive. It wasn't often he got to drive this fast. If it hadn't been for what they might find, he might have almost smiled.

'We're lucky,' Bannerman said. 'We brought the trailer to the vehicle pound because of its size. It was due to go off to Hawaii Heavy Diggers tomorrow.'

Smoke streamed from his tyres as Koni exited the highway and skidded through a ninety-degree turn in through the entrance of the Police car pound. The Lieutenant's call to the security people had already caused them to evacuate the buildings, and two marked Crown Vic's were already in attendance, their uniformed officers helping escort the few office staff safely away.

Helping Bannerman carry her equipment the two of them walked over to the warehouse containing the 'dozer. Bannerman stopped, put down her cases, and pulled out a portable Geiger counter. Turning the volume up, it was evident something in that building was causing a reading.

'That's far enough,' Bannerman said. 'No one gets any closer without my say-so. Clear?'

'Sure. I don't mind dealing with things I can see trying to kill me, but not this.'

Changing into protective gear, Bannerman picked up her cases and walked into the building. From outside, Koni could see her examine the digger scoop, the support arms and the cab. It was clear from the noise of the Geiger Counter whatever was causing the high radiation count was coming from the engine area.

Turning the counter's screeching down to an acceptable level, Bannerman climbed up onto the engine block and looked down through into the bay. After a few minutes, she exited out and approached Koni.

'Find out if anybody else has touched this' she asked.

Walking over to the head mechanic Koni discovered three workers, as well as the head mechanic, had been involved in bringing it here and unloading it but due to Forensics being called in no one had started work on it yet. Calling them over Bannerman checked them all with her Geiger counter and found they had higher-than-normal levels of radiation. Calling her two technicians over, both had higher-than-safe levels. Both also said their hands were burning.

While Koni had been waiting on Bannerman to complete her tests, two more security vehicles had arrived. The driver of the lead vehicle climbed out and called, 'Hey, looking for Detective Kamaka and Dr Bannerman.'

'I'm Kamaka. And you are?'

'Eric Staples. Senior weapons inspector at NEST.'

'NEST? Nuclear?'

'Yeah, we're the Nuclear Emergency Support Team. Your Lieutenant called us.'

'But we don't have a bomb here, do we?'

'No, Detective, But our people know what they are doing around radiation.' With that, Bannerman was instructed to keep away from the 'dozer and NEST people would continue the examination.

Staples shouted some orders to his team who'd already begun unpacking and setting up emergency showers. Anyone who had entered the building that day was instructed to strip off and shower, most radiation detected on people being attributed to dust landing on skin and hair. The three workers and head mechanic along with the two Forensic technicians were stripped and showered by NEST nurses, their clothes placed in bags to be incinerated. All six were given Potassium Iodide injections. The Forensic technicians' hands were then dressed with aloe vera, and they were hospitalised for treatment. By this time, the Lieutenant and the Assistant Chief of Police had arrived and taken control of the scene. The bulldozer would remain, and the warehouse it had been in would need full decontamination measures applied. It was to be locked with no access allowed. Any car pound employee's showing signs of sickness from vomiting to diarrhoea were to call a specific number immediately. Finally, all the employees were called together where the Assistant Chief of Police warned everyone that this was highly classified under national security, and absolutely no one was to discuss this in future.

# 62

## The Pentagon, Washington

The meeting in the conference room in the Pentagon was delayed almost two hours under the orders of Admiral Carter until everyone had arrived. It seemed like representatives from half the US Intelligence Services were there. Sitting around the conference table were Mitch Stringer; Admiral Douglas Carter – Chief of Naval Operations; the Chairman of the National Intelligence Council; the Director of National Intelligence; the newly-appointed Director of the CIA; representatives from Homeland Security and the FBI; and the Head of Special Operations Command.

The Director of National Intelligence opened up the meeting. 'Gentlemen, I think we all know each other here, so introductions are unnecessary,' he said, looking at Carter. 'We have a situation over in the Middle East and Hawaii, so let me pass over to Admiral Carter. Admiral ….'

'Thank you. Actually, I'm going to pass this over to one of my researchers, O2 Mitchell Stringer. Mitch?'

Although Mitch had held presentations before, it was always nerve-racking when in front of so many senior figures. He began, 'Sirs'. Gentlemen. As you know from this morning's reports Shane Walker in Dubai has received information from one of his trusted sources in the Pakistan government that two nuclear bombs were stolen from one of their unmarked SPD trucks over eight weeks' ago. We don't know who has them and they could be anywhere by now.

To make matters worse, Professor Yousef Rashid, their top nuclear weapons specialist also went missing around the same time. It was reported by their intelligence agency, ISI, that he had died in a mugging that had gone wrong, and his body was supposedly fully identified, having been shot in the head and also in the mouth. Since then he has possibly shown up at least twice entering Dubai under a different name, but the facial recognition software only scored a 75 per cent probability, which we put down to similar features. Last wee—.'

'So was he identified or not?' one of the audience interrupted.

'We believe so, sir. The facial recognition software throws out a probability rating. Anything less than 85 per cent is rated suspect. Had he been entering the US, a 75 per cent 'hit' would normally have been enough to question him, but this was in Dubai, and we have no jurisdiction. So last week it appears he did actually enter the US in Hawaii. He came in on a flight from Seoul, but he had altered his appearance, changed his hair length and colour and was also wearing glasses. Facial recognition failed to detect him, and he came in under a different name again, a Professor Ashok Patel, a university lecturer in Mechanical Engineering from Seoul. He claimed he was visiting friends on his way to attending a conference in LA. His tickets and passport were all in order, so he wasn't flagged. Where he then went we don't know. We also don't know why he was coming to Hawaii or whether it was his last planned stop, but he turned up dead a couple of days ago, alongside a bulldozer that was sent, again with all the correct paperwork, from China to a town outside Honolulu for repair.

'Police initially thought the 'dozer had been used for drug smuggling – the engine compartment had been carved out—.'

'Son, cut to the chase, what have we got?' the DNI asked.

'What we have, sir is two missing nukes, a missing nuclear weapons specialist found dead here in Hawaii, an imported bulldozer oozing weapons-grade highly enriched Uranium 235, and yesterday NCTC and GCHQ in the UK translated the message 'Great Satan will soon feel the mighty bite of the jaws of Allah'.

The silence lasted less than two seconds before the room descended into frenzied shouting and arguing.

It took almost ten minutes before any resemblance of order could be restored. Eventually, Admiral Carter's presence calmed the room enough. 'Lieutenant Mitchel hasn't completely finished yet. Mitch, please continue...'

'The bulldozer engine compartment had been hollowed out, and U-235 had been packed in there, with lead around it to reduce radiation. By the looks, they refitted the sump and top panels so that it would pass unnoticed. We also have two families ill with radiation poisoning from over on one of the other islands. NEST think the high levels of U-235 have come from a dismantled bomb potentially hidden in the engine compartment. This guy Rashid had the skills to dismantle and re-assemble a nuke, so we have to assume currently that we have a rogue nuke somewhere in Hawaii or even en-route to the mainland. It could even be here now.'

'But this Rashid is dead?' the DNI asked.

'Yes, sir,' Mitch continued. 'Someone whacked him with a 9 mil behind the ear. Until he was identified the local police assumed it was a drug deal gone bad. It was after they got a hit from US-Visit and Homeland which was flagged to us, I put two and two together and alerted

172

their Forensics about the possibility of radiation. They checked it and called in NEST who confirmed the amount and type.'

The Chairman of the National Intelligence Committee raised his hand for quiet amidst the uproar now beginning. 'Gentlemen. GENTLEMEN! Keep order. Lieutenant, you seem to have made a good guess, but it seems to me to be just that, merely a guess. What else have you assumed?'

Mitch had sat down after he had finished speaking but now quickly rose again. 'Sirs, with the information I have I think there is a high probability of a terrorist organisation as yet identity unknown having control of a fully armed rogue Pakistani nuke somewhere in Hawaii. What we don't know yet is their intended target. Gaining access to the islands, as with any US port, would not be easy. Getting terrorists to Hawaii would actually be harder than to mainland US, so they may consider exploding a nuke in Honolulu worth it, but Honolulu has never been designated a strategic target. Los Angeles or New York are far bigger. Now they may be shipping it to the West Coast, but personally, I don't think so. They could have used that ruse to get it through LA had they wanted it there directly. My worry is instead of targeting civilians, they may be aiming at our military. Honolulu might not be the target... it could be Pearl and Hickham.

'The final point, gentlemen, is that the reference in the phrase to 'Jaws of Allah' indicates more than one and jaws usually signify biting from both sides. I think we should consider all our major naval bases as targets, namely Pearl, San Diego and Norfolk —.'

This time there was no way Admiral Carter or the DNI could contain the uproar.

173

# 63

The United States Navy is the largest navy in the world and comprises of over 320,000 personnel and almost 300 ships in active service. Critics sometimes complain it is too cumbersome, too slow to react. But not today.

Within twenty minutes of the meeting finishing the Chairman of the Joint Chiefs of Staff had placed Pearl Harbour on DEFCON 4 condition meaning 'Increased intelligence watch and strengthened security measures'. Within the hour all US Naval Military bases worldwide had also had their status raised from the normal DEFCON 5 to DEFCON 4 along with a suitable Public Relations message being released of this being merely an exercise.

Along with the naval bases having their status raised, US Navy SEALs bases at Little Creek, Virginia, and Coronado, California, also had their readiness status increased, with leave being cancelled and training being postponed. SEAL Delivery Vehicle Team 1, usually based in Pearl Harbour, but currently completing deep sea training in Guam, were instructed to return urgently to their home base.

Lieutenant Deacon and his team in Coronado had completed ninety-five per cent of their retraining programme. The HALO (High Altitude Low Opening) parachute training had gone without a hitch, but the LALO (Low Altitude Low Opening) had claimed a few casualties, as expected. You couldn't leap out of an aircraft at four hundred feet and two hundred knots and expect to land without incident. Luckily, none of the injuries had been major, just sprained ankles and a broken wrist but still, it had taken its toll. Deacon had been a lucky one – he'd suffered a slight sprain to his ankle early on by landing heavily, but nothing strapping it up hadn't cured, and he was a hundred per cent fit again now.

Due to re-deploy to Afghanistan within the next three days, Deacon and his team were placed on high alert.

# 64

After liaising with DNDO Hawaii, Homeland Security Hawaii, and the Hawaii Police Department, Mitch made a case to Admiral Carter for naval help in examining the waters off the south-eastern coast of the main island, Hawaii. Meeting with the Admiral, Mitch said, 'Sir, although the bulldozer was found just outside Pearl, this was where the radiation contamination affecting the families has been suspected. Nothing has been found, and its location is too far away from Pearl to cause damage, but I think we should assist with the investigation.'

'Mitch, I've got Pearl on alert. I've got every man and his dog out checking, and I've got the NNSA flying in two of their radiation detecting 'copters on a C5 Galaxy from Andrews due to land within hours. If Pearl's the target, why should I deploy personnel to check out somewhere almost two hundred miles away?'

'Sir, it's just I have a nasty feeling. I want to cover all my bases and, so far, Pearl or Honolulu seem the natural choices. But that doesn't explain why those families are sick with radiation poisoning over there and why fish are dying.'

Over the next fifteen minutes, Mitch argued his point, and eventually, Admiral Carter agreed to re-deploy USS Anvil an Avenger-class minesweeper currently en-route from a refit in San Diego to Japan. It would arrive in Hawaii early the following morning.

<><><>

At 05:30 Hawaii-Aleutian Standard Time (HAST), the USS Anvil approached Hawaii from the east. The Captain's orders were to offer assistance to search local sea area, take radiation measurements and provide side-scan sonar inspection if required. It was expected this temporary stopover would take no more than one day out of the Anvil's schedule.

Based on tides and prevailing winds, it was determined that anything affecting the sea life around the big island would have to be within a ten-mile radius. On the first pass heading south-west close into the south-eastern shore of the big island, the crew took various water samples. The readings came back at high radiation levels, but only within a small area. The water depth along this coast is extremely deep, so the Captain agreed to launch the high-resolution synthetic aperture sonar transducer and repeat his course, covering the underwater rock face. This system makes a 3-dimensional picture of its target in high resolution and found the target easily on its second pass. The image came back as an object lying against the rock face at an angle of 160 degrees, held in place by two anchors and chain, with two more anchors hanging below it. Its size was a little over four foot by two foot by one foot. The sonar also detected a shape within the container, but couldn't see it clearly due to the casing. It looked like it had been purposely placed in position and only come to rest due to the anchors holding it. It was designated 'Target 1'.

A tethered submersible with cameras and lights was despatched, although the photographs showed little more definition than the sonar had. The depth of three-hundred-and-fifty feet was deemed too deep for

177

conventional Navy divers, coupled with the strong currents and radiation levels.

Within 30 minutes, the call went out to SEAL Delivery Vehicle Team 1 for position status. However, the typhoon by now at full power and slowly moving across the Northern Mariana Islands would realistically block them from leaving Guam for at least a further twenty-four hours.

Fifteen minutes later the call went out to Coronado for Deacon and his team to re-deploy urgently to Hawaii.

Thirty minutes after the message had been received, Deacon and his team were racing out to the waiting US Air Force C130 at NAS North Island, San Diego. They barely had time to load before the loadmaster hit the button to raise the ramp, and the pilot began to move the grey craft towards the taxiway. Priority clearance for take-off was issued and moments later, engines screaming at maximum thrust, they began rolling down the runway, next stop Hickham.

Deacon sat reviewing the latest sonar images while his men checked and re-checked their equipment. They would then spend the flight sleeping and relaxing before going through a complete team briefing ninety minutes before they were due to land. Sat there looking at the images, Deacon thought that diving to over three hundred feet would be tough. Diving to that depth in cross currents and wearing radiation protection was going to be damn near impossible, he thought, but hey, the only easy day was yesterday.

# 65

## Helmand Province, Afghanistan – 5th September

Major Patrick Hythe was not having a good day. He already had a headache and was hot and dusty, as were his men. Sat in the front passenger seat of the lead Humvee, the sun beat in relentlessly through the sand-scratched windscreen. They were heading back from a routine six-hour patrol – another chance to 'win the hearts and minds', he thought. The problem was, most of the locals didn't want to have their hearts and minds 'won'. What they wanted was to kill every foreigner and get them out of their country. American or British; it made no difference. Just kill as many as possible and drive the rest of them out.

Suddenly the crown shape of a man's head showed momentarily above a low wall up to their right. The driver had also seen it, and before Hythe could shout a warning, the driver's training kicked in, and he immediately slowed the vehicle. Moments later, an enormous blast lifted the front of the Humvee and slammed it back down. Maybe through nerves or inexperience, this Taliban fighter had moved and exposed himself, thereby alerting Hythe and his men. Firing the IED blind, with the Humvee slowing down unexpectedly meant the blast had lifted and damaged the front of the leading armoured car, but not caused any direct casualties. The windscreen was further pockmarked from shrapnel and, as the vehicle bounced down onto its chassis, one tyre shredded, but it could be repaired and would live to fight another day.

So would he and his men. The blast had been a big one, too, he thought. Had it been timed right, Mrs Hythe would be missing a son, and at least one more soldier would be going home in a casket, he thought. But this was where training and discipline paid off. Within seconds, the top gunner in the second Humvee was providing covering fire while shouting 'Action right, Action right,' while Hythe and his men evac'd the damaged vehicle, which was when the round nicked his battledress sleeve.

There were fifteen insurgents – normal odds heavily in their favour for the three or four British Army soldiers they'd expected from the second Humvee. But the odds were against them now as eight angry SAS soldiers returned a fusillade of withering accurate fire. Well trained and battle-hardened, the SAS quickly deployed out into their standard formation, offering pinpoint covering support fire, immediately followed by four high explosive fragmentation grenades lobbed behind the insurgent's low-lying fortifications.

Running towards a small wall for cover, Hythe could feel the blood running down his arm and over his watch. It wasn't painful yet and would likely only become a burning or stinging sensation when his adrenaline lowered, but for now, he was just pissed off.

Quickly appraising the scene, Hythe issued brief commands to his men through his helmet radio. As a man, the SAS attacked. Most insurgents died where they lay. Five had already fallen to the grenades, and within seconds the accurate fire of the attacking SAS claimed another four. Two were wounded, one seriously, and the remaining four tried to escape. They were cut down within moments by the SAS.

Taking defensive positions, they checked the dead and injured and quickly scouted the area. Now the risk was reduced, Hythe stood up and congratulated his men. Apart from some small cuts from flying debris, and a new paint job and tyre for the Humvee, Hythe's battledress was the worst injury the SAS team suffered that day.

The dead Afghanistan's were checked for weapons, booby-traps and anything of interest to the military. This IED had also been one of the newer, enlarged versions that had claimed so many coalition forces personnel and Hythe was determined to find out where they came from. Of the two injured insurgents, one was young, maybe 15 or 16, Hythe thought. This was the one who had exposed himself, probably through nerves, Hythe thought. The other was older and more severely injured and wouldn't last long.

It is often said the British play by 'Marquess of Queensberry rules', Hythe thought. And that we always fight under the rules of the Geneva Convention. Well, only when the other side also fights to the same standards, he said to himself.

The older, more severely injured insurgent only had moments to live. His injuries were too severe to waste time on. Dragging him by the collar, Hythe moved him out of eyesight of the younger boy. Smashing the butt of his Hechler & Koch down into the sand close to the dying insurgent's head, Hythe cursed him in Pashto and shouted at him to talk. Threatening to kill him, the boy could see Hythe kick and gun butt slam what he thought was his Taliban colleague. Finally, the boy saw Hythe turn his gun on the injured Afghan and fire three quick shots while spitting on his body.

What the boy couldn't see what the quick stage-managed scene Hythe had set up. The badly injured Taliban was already near death before he'd been moved.

The gun butt slamming, the firing and spitting were all into the ground next to the near-dead terrorist. It was all done for the effect it would have on the younger, nervous boy.

The Afghan boy looked on in terror, realising his fate as Hythe came towards him. 'Your next, fucker,' he said. 'And when I cut your dick and balls off, you're not gonna be much use to those seventy-two virgins,' he said.

Trembling, the Afghan's bladder relaxed, and the smell of warm piss clouded the area. In broken English, he said, 'I prisoner of war. You not must hurt me.'

Looking down at him, Hythe smiled in a cold way and said, 'Out here, pal, your mine. Live or die is your choice. You tell me what I want to know and you might live. You don't, and you'll suffer the same fate as your pal here. You're unclean. Do you understand? You'll never get to paradise now.' Bending down, Hythe pushed his two fingers into one of the bullet holes in the Afghan's shoulder and began to twist. His screams echoed back off the rocks and his back arched but still, Hythe's fingers dug deeper. Just as he began to pass out, Hythe slapped him hard across the face, and the process started again.

He was a tough kid, Hythe thought. Eight times Hythe asked about the bomb; where did it come from? Who was the bomb-maker? Where was he hiding? Eight times Hythe dug deeper and twisted, and eight times the Afghan almost passed out, needing Hythe to slap him back awake. But, gradually his will was being broken.

'Where did you get the bomb from? Who is the bomb-maker? Where is he hiding?' Hythe kept repeating.

Eventually, broken and crying like the boy he was instead of the man he tried to be, the Afghan gave over information. He gave the location for the bomb-maker and the name of 'Saif'. Hythe rounded on the boy, his eyes shining with excitement. This was not the first time Saif had been named.

'Who is Saif? Who is he? Tell me,' he demanded, pushing his fingers towards the boy's injuries again.

'Palestinian. He Palestinian. He very clever man. He say he made bomb and shields,' the boy gasped out before the fingers were pushed into his flesh again. 'And jaws of Allah,' he added, as Hythe's fingers found his flesh again. 'For him, we take bombs to border,' he said, before finally collapsing into unconsciousness.

Returning to Bastion with the prisoner in the relief convoy, Hythe handed over the injured boy to the medics and security. He would be treated and then interrogated, but in the days that followed he would fail to pass on anything else of significance.

In the meantime, Hythe ensured the information about Saif would be passed up the channels, while he and his men organised a raid on the bomb-maker.

# 66

## Hawaii – Thursday 6th September

Forty minutes from touchdown the pilot came back to check on his passengers. The flight had been uneventful, and the mid-air refuelling with the KC-10 Extender had gone off perfectly. The men were tense and ready, with a mixture of apprehension and excitement. They'd all spent the past eight weeks training and retraining. Simulations were good but going into a live situation was always different. They all knew this mission was going to be tough, but not from an armed combatant this time. Someone had stolen a nuke. Something was leaking radiation. The men all knew it was their job to find and neutralise it.

With practised ease, the pilot landed the C130 with barely a jolt. There is always a rivalry between the various armed forces, in particular between Navy and Air Force pilots as to who flies the smoothest, but even Deacon admitted their flight had been pretty good.

Two Sea Hawk MH-60S helicopters were sat waiting on the taxiway, their twin turboshaft engines running at idle, as the C130 approached. As the loadmaster lowered the ramp, their engines began to spin up. Within minutes, Deacon and his men had loaded their gear, and the two Sea Hawks were lifting off, heading south-east.

Looking out at the beaches and high rise hotels and apartments along Waikiki beach, Deacon felt serene remembering the last time he'd been there. The whole archipelago of islands always amazed him. SEALs often trained there for jungle experience – the mountains and hillsides were equal in undergrowth and danger to many regions in Asia, apart from the lacking of snakes and killer bugs. Deacon had never liked insects, and poisonous snakes actually worried him, but like most warriors, he locked that fear away in the dark recesses of his mind. The extinct volcano on Diamond Head passed by the port side of the 'copter and Deacon remembered the early morning race he and Bryant had run, the last time he was there. They had run up the steep path and the two sets of steps to the summit at 760 feet. The bet had been last to the summit would buy that evening's dinner, and Bryant had started running while Deacon was still paying the taxi. Laughing and joking, they had both bustled for first place, both wanting to win, but neither caring if they didn't. Finally, Bryant had beaten Deacon by mere inches, and they had sat looking out over the morning sunrise. Good times, Deacon thought.

Coming in close to the mountain, both helicopters approached the USS Anvil that was holding station a mile or so off the southern coast of Hawaii Island. Entering a hover pattern one aircraft at a time, Deacon and his men quickly rappelled with their equipment down to the deck.

The waiting XO led Deacon to the Captain's cabin.

Extending a hand, the Captain said, 'Lieutenant, Captain Ross. You've met the XO. Let me introduce you to Eric Staples - senior weapons inspector at NEST.'

'Sirs. Mr Staples. Tell me, what is the latest update?'

'Lieutenant,' Staples began, 'nothing has changed since the briefing pack was completed. The device, origin unknown, is lying tethered to the rock face at approximately three hundred and fifty feet depth. It seems to be held to the rock face by two or three small anchors that you can see here on the sonar. The levels of radiation in the sea around here are very high, and this device seems to be leaking radiation. The crew have all taken doses of Potassium Iodide tablets, and the medical bay has made them available for you and your men. That should shield you against the worst aspects of radiation. At this stage, we don't know if it is a weapon but have to assume it is. We also have to assume it's both armed and active. Our role is to deactivate it, but we need it on the surface to do that. You and your team's role is to bring it to us without triggering it.'

'Do we know when it's set to explode if indeed it is a bomb?'

'No, Lieutenant, we don't. We don't actually know it is a bomb but have to assume it is until we learn differently. We also don't know who planted it here or how they did so. But if it is a bomb, as I think likely, this is an active act of aggression towards the US.'

'Captain. Your thoughts?'

'As Mr Staples says, Lieutenant. Plan for the worst, pray for the best. Our usual choice would be to bring in a submersible, but the nearest is over thirty-six hours away. We don't know what this is and we can't afford to wait. My crew will offer any assistance they can. We have two cranes on board, either should be man enough for the job of lifting it, but none of my divers are certified to that depth.'

'One other concern, Lieutenant,' the Captain continued. 'This is an active volcanic region, and we have already had two small underwater eruptions overnight. The last one just before you landed caused some lava flow and loose rocks to slide. One falling boulder took away the camera. You and your men will have to go in blind.'

186

# 67

## USS Anvil

Deacon and his five men changed into Demron full-body radiation-protection suits, before donning conventional SEAL dry suits over. They also equipped themselves with helmets with two-way radios, gloves, torches and fins. They carried various tools, with each two-man teams' being duplicated, each team carrying a set of bolt cutters, two Helium gas containers and a set of attachable inflatable flotation bags, should the device need buoyancy added to it. Finally, due to the depths required, they attached their triple air cylinder tanks, this time filled with a modified variant of Trimix, made up of oxygen, helium and nitrogen. They each also carried their standard-issue divers knife, but no other weapons.

After a final briefing and equipment check, Deacon and his men entered the blue waters of Hawaii. It was important to keep all areas of skin dry to minimise any radiation. The Demron suits would protect them, coupled with the Potassium Iodide pills to protect their thyroids, should any contamination occur.

With a last look around to check everyone, Deacon flipped his head down and kicked with powerful strokes into the depths and followed the tagline. Easing the pressure building in his ears, Deacon performed a brief radio check. The radio clarity underwater was never brilliant, more like listening to the old analogue radio after being used to the cleanness of FM, but it was clear enough and understandable. All five colleagues reported back to him, as did the control room on the Anvil. The radio system also automatically altered the voice modulation to reduce the helium in the breathing tanks making them sound like Donald Duck.

Each clipping their harness 'D' rings to the tagline to counter the pull of the current, they stopped at a little over a hundred-foot depth and checked each other, equalised their ear pressure yet again, and then let their body weight sink them further.

Gently sliding down the tagline the light penetrating the waters became less and less. The underwater sides of the volcano were steep with loose shale and rocks being easily dislodged. When this happened silt and dirt clouded their vision – at this depth the current had less effect in keeping the waters clean. Knowing what they had to do, each SEAL was focussed on the job in hand. Random chatter over the radio was not needed, nor expected. This was as dangerous as anything Deacon had ever done previously. At this depth and pressure, there was no leeway for mistakes.

Approaching three hundred and forty-foot depth, it was clear to see this wasn't going to be easy. Visibility was poor – daylight was very dim here only allowing lichen and moss to grow. The Trimix in their tanks would only allow them twelve minutes at this depth, and already they would need multiple hours of decompression stops before reaching the surface. The immense water pressure – over 170 pounds per square inch – made breathing harsh and laboured, their chests struggling to inhale through the pressure equalised regulator. Unclipping themselves from the tagline, Deacon ordered them to fan out and swim gently towards the rock face.

Through the murky water, the loom from their torches reflected back off the grey shale, but the target could not be seen. Realising they had drifted a little downstream as they had descended, Deacon ordered his men to swim against the current, parallel to the rock face at five-foot depth intervals. This should ensure at least one of them should find the target.

Within minutes, Petty Officer First Class Jose Ramirez saw something looming out of the darkness. Pressing his PTT, he said, 'Lieutenant. Up ahead at three degrees rise. I think we have it, Sir.'

Collectively, the group pointed their torches in the chosen direction, and slowly a grey/brown shape came into view. As they approached Deacon could see two chains rising up behind it, still attached to anchors embedded in the rock face, while the two other chains hung down into the depths, their anchors tracing a line towards the murky black of the ocean floor.

Looking carefully from a number of different directions, Deacon relayed the information to the USS Anvil. 'Anvil, this is Team Alpha. Target in site. Position precarious. Looks to be a rectangular container, outer case probably of fibreglass measuring approximately four foot by two foot by one foot. It looks like two halves joined together around a darker coloured inner container. Two of the tethering anchors seem to have come adrift, leaving only two holding its support. Will attempt to connect flotation bags to it.'

Deacon stayed back while his men attached four of the flotation bags to it, one to each 'D' ring coupling. Slowly inflating each bag with the Helium, as the bags expanded and took the weight, the centre of gravity shifted slightly. As they continued to gently inflate them, another SEAL was holding on to the supporting anchors and could feel their tension being slowly released from them. 'Gently guys, she beginning to float,' he said. With a little more helium added, the device rose slightly, and the remaining anchor chains fell slack. Using the bolt cutters to cut through each chain was slow progress due to its thickness, but slowly three came free, the chains quickly disappearing into the depths like long snakes. The fourth chain though was more troublesome. The neutral buoyancy of the device had caused the anchor to slip slowly further down the rock face, and the weight was now all in one corner and in danger of unbalancing the free-floating device. Petty Officer Ramirez could see what was going to happen so quickly grabbed his pair of bolt cutters and swam underneath the device, close into the rock face.

Setting the jaws of his bolt cutters either side of the chain he flexed his forearm muscles and squeezed, but Newton's Third Law of Motion, which states 'For every action there is an equal and opposite reaction' came into play. Without the added mass his teammates had enjoyed of being in a group, as the jaws bit through, he caromed backwards into the rock face, his tanks and fins digging into the loose shale and rocks. Struggling to free himself the domino effect took over. As rocks and shale fell free, more slid from higher up to fill its place with dirt and silt quickly obscuring everyone's view.

The downwards rush of rocks caused a water surge effect and pushed the device and the divers away from the rock face. But not Petty Officer First Class Ramirez.

Caught by the bulk of his divers' gear Ramirez was caught in the avalanche. The more he struggled, the deeper entombed he became. The razor sharp shale sliced through his protective suits cutting into skin and bone. Rocks and small boulders crashed onto his helmet breaking the radio as he tumbled downwards amongst them.

Gradually the mini-landslide subsided having slid almost two hundred feet deeper. The water was obscured by silt which gradually cleared in the ever-present gentle

190

current at these depths. Had Ramirez been able, he might have seen against the lighter backdrop of the surface the small shapes and figures of his colleagues over two hundred feet higher than him, their weak torches probing down to the depths. Had he been able to hear, he would have heard the distorted shouts in his radio earpiece from his colleagues.

But he was drifting slowly deeper, face down, towards the top of the Papua Seamount at almost three thousand feet depth, his back broken and his air tanks ripped from his body.

# 68

Deacon had seen what was about to happen in slow motion. He could see Ramirez using his bolt cutters to try to cut the chain and saw him jerk backwards as the jaws snapped shut. He managed to shout, 'Watch ou--' before the rockslide had started, but then everything turned upside down. The surge from the falling rocks had caused the device to almost turn over and swamp the flotation balloon, and the men had all bounced around in the flow, but gradually things subsided, and the water cleared, and Ramirez was gone.

At this depth, even the torches only lit the water for twelve to fifteen feet. Shining them down into the abyss was just darkness. Ramirez's radio was dead too.

SEALs will never leave a fallen comrade – living or dead. It's as simple as that. It's not in their ethos. But sometimes the mission is more important. Reluctantly, Deacon issued orders to return to duty.

Allowing more air into the flotation bags increased its buoyancy, and it slowly rose. After they had ascended fifty feet, Deacon called a halt for the first decompression stop of five minutes. During this time, they attached the device to the waiting crane cable and tray hanging down from the USS Anvil.

They then ascended slowly while the crane winched the device to the surface, quickly leaving Deacon and his team to spend many hours slowly decompressing before they were also finally allowed back to the surface.

Breaking the surface hours later, Deacon felt the sun on his face. The last decompression stop had been at just ten feet for almost thirty minutes – tantalisingly close. SEALs, by the nature of their role, are superb swimmers, often feeling more at ease underwater than on land, but even they were pleased to be back on the surface. The decompression hours had dragged by. In tank decompression exercises, the men would often have music piped through to them to ease their boredom, but nobody on the Anvil had done that for them today, a rogue nuke holding more interest.

In the meantime, Staples had waited until members of the crew, all wearing protective gear had brought the wire basket on-board. Quickly examining the device, he could see clearly that it contained a further case of some sort. Using a portable X-ray machine, he tried to examine the inner case, but the lead shielding prevented it. Using ultrasound had the same effect. Staples then carefully drilled a 2mm pilot hole, before trying to insert the end of a flexible endoscope with a lens and light attached. Water ran out of the hole, so he then drilled a second small hole through the fibreglass bottom to allow the trapped water to escape. The water dripping from the container was showing high levels of radiation on his Geiger Counter, but after the water had cleared, the ambient radiation was much lower. Checking the image from the endoscope as he carefully manoeuvred it around within the container, Staples couldn't see any evidence of wires or triggers, but there was little space available to manoeuvre.

What he did see, though, was a green slime covering the inner case.

# 69

The live feed from the endoscope was uploaded to various secure locations by satellite, including NEST headquarters in Nevada, as well as SEAL HQ in Coronado and the conference room at the Pentagon. It was also relayed live to the White House Situation Room, a 5,000 square-foot intelligence centre housed below the West Wing of the White House.

Along with the President was Admiral Carter; the Chairman of the Joint Chiefs of Staff; the Chairman of the National Intelligence Council; and the Directors' of National Intelligence, the CIA, Homeland Security, the FBI; and the Head of Special Operations Command.

In Nevada, other senior members of NEST were watching.

Slowly unscrewing the twenty stainless steel screws, Staples commented, 'Two of these seem cross-threaded and were not done up as tight as the others. The remainder were all firm, as expected, but these two were definitely loose.'

Putting all twenty screws in a container, he then carefully examined the joint between the two halves. Water was still dripping from the joint and Staples correctly guessed that water had ingressed the casing through the joint. Sliding a thin plastic blade along the joint, he felt the resistance lessen around where the screws had been cross-threaded.

With two men on each half, they managed to gently prise the outer casing apart, more seawater escaping as the two halves separated, exposing a grey/black Pelicase with two lockable handles.

Repeated attempts to examine the contents using X-rays or ultrasound failed, so after a brief situation report back to the experts in Nevada, Staples decided to drill the case.

As the bit began to chew into the polycarbonate, Stales was filled with dread that there could be various anti-tampering devices fitted which would cause the device to trigger. If there were an ultra-violet detection system, then daylight would activate it. If infrared, then any heat source could become the trigger, and air pressure sensing could trigger activation as soon as the drill bit cut through the case. Holding his breath, he pushed the drill deeper as it slowed against the lead lining until the sudden lack of resistance made him gasp.

He hadn't thought any form of air pressure sensor would be fitted, due to the depth it had been placed, but he also knew the old rule of not to assume ... .

Fitting the endoscope with the lamps turned off allowed him to look for any light source within the case, but there was none. His next heart-stopping moment was in switching on the infrared lamp. He held his breath and flicked the switch.

Nothing.

Finally, he switched to white light, again silently saying his prayers.

The crew of the Anvil had placed a sun cover over the rear deck where Staples and his men were working, but although the temperature was in the mid-eighties, Staples blood was ice in his veins.

Manhandling the endoscope to the rear of the locked handles, Staples said to his waiting audience, 'There appear to be two wires into the back of each handle. I'm going to have to check whether there is power applied,' as he called for a different endoscope to be fitted.

This one had two small retractable needle tip points in the head that he manipulated into place before extending the tips and pushing them into the wire.

Not detecting any current flow or standing voltage, he decided to short both wires together as he drilled through the handle locks.

With both locks drilled, he removed the endoscope, counted to three and gently opened the case.

The bomb components were laid out as Rashid had left them. The clicking from the Geiger Counter rapidly increased as he moved it over the contents, and the acrid smell of chlorine filled his nostrils. The electronics were complete, but the display was blank. Checking back to the battery he quickly snipped the cables and removed the plugged-in electronic boards. Placing the now isolated timer board in a tray of rice to absorb moisture, he disconnected the remaining circuit cards from deeper inside the device.

Turning to the camera, he sighed, 'Mr President. Gentlemen. We were goddamn lucky. From my first inspection, this looks to be a fully active and armed nuke. I can't be exact on yield without further study, but I guess it to be in the fifteen-to-thirty kiloton range. It looks to be of Pakistan origin from some writing I can see and seems to have some additional electronic boards added.'

Shouting erupted in the White House Situation Room until the President held up his hands for silence. 'Mr Staples, please continue and please explain why we are 'lucky'?'

'Mr President. This device should still be working. Everything looks to be connected, and there is a timer here that should still be working. There's also anti-tamper mechanisms, but none of them went off. No one would

196

have placed it at that depth to retrieve it later, so it must have been armed. Luckily for us, seawater got in. That's what caused the radiation around here – not the actual device, but that seawater entered and then got pushed out by a mixture of chlorine and hydrogen gas produced when seawater covered the batteries. I'm guessing here that further examination will show it got in by the two screws that were cross-threaded. We were lucky whoever placed this here a) did a sloppy job of closing the case, and b) it was in the sea and not a freshwater lake.'

'Why lucky it was the sea?' the President asked.

'Freshwater wouldn't have caused the problem, Mr President. Luckily for us, the salt in the seawater caused the copper wires on the battery to corrode and the electronics to fail. It also caused the battery to give off the gases. Without that pressure of the gases pushing the water out and the battery contacts being corroded, we'd have known nothing about this until it went off as planned. As soon as this timer has dried, I'll connect it to a power source.'

# 70

## USS Anvil, Hawaii

Eric Staples was joined by Deacon and his men on the rear deck. Having ensured everything was safe and after removing the Uranium sphere and placing it in a lead-lined container Staples and his men had continued examining the bomb.

Being only 9 countries officially have nuclear weapons - UK, China, France, India, Pakistan, Russia, USA, North Korea, and Israel, Staples began looking for any markings or evidence of country of manufacture. The components needed to make nuclear weapons are quite exact and will usually contain some sort of product or serial number, usually written in the language of the country of manufacture. It didn't take Staples long to find evidence in both Urdu and English.

Everything Deacon and his men had brought up from the sea would be transported back to NEST headquarters for further detailed forensic analysis, but Staples and his men felt they had examined it enough to make an initial report.

The rice had absorbed all the moisture on the timer board, so after finding a fresh battery, Staples connected it to the timer. The display flickered to life, and he began pressing buttons.

'Holy shit,' Staples said, 'Holy fucking shit.'

Liaising with Admiral Carter, the live video link was set-up again.

'Mr President, Gentlemen. Having examined this device closely, we can now be certain beyond any reasonable doubt that this device is of Pakistan origin. It is, we believe, the pieces from one of the three warheads designed to fit the Shaheen-III intermediate-range ballistic missiles currently being built in Pakistan.

'It has been stripped down, and only the required components are here. The altimeter fuse usually feeds into some fairly sophisticated electronics. In this case, the altimeter fuse has been replaced with a simple timer, again feeding into the same electronics board. This is not simple work. You cannot just plug any old timer in, but someone with enough skill has connected it all together and altered the programming to suit. They have also laid out the components to best effect and to maximise blast.'

'Is this something Professor Rashid would have had the skills to accomplish?' one of the voices in the Pentagon asked.

'Most certainly,' Staples replied. 'I never met Professor Rashid personally, but I know he was very highly skilled. He, or any of his people working for him, would likely have had the skills.'

'But why was it planted there? I thought Pearl was the target,' the President asked.

'Mr President. I cannot answer that for you. All I can tell you is this bomb was planned to detonate at 06:00 on Tuesday 11th September and, had it not been for the ingress of saltwater that corroded the battery and stopped the electronics from working, it would have detonated as planned. In five days' time on the anniversary of 9/11.'

# 71

## The Pentagon – the same evening

Mitch walked back to his desk, sat down heavily and pushed some of the paperwork out of the way to make room for his coffee cup. Since the video call earlier and the subsequent meetings with Admiral Carter, he'd not stopped working. He'd called Helen earlier and explained he was going to be pulling an 'all-nighter' and was relying on the regular caffeine fixes to keep himself going.

Something still didn't add up, Mitch thought. Why go to all that trouble to steal a nuke, transport it halfway around the world and then bury it in the sea where it couldn't cause much harm? No, he was missing something major here, he thought.

Picking up a blank notepad he had just begun to note what he knew or strongly suspected when his e-mail chimed. Reading the e-mail both helped and hindered. So now he was aware that Saif was Palestinian and responsible for the improved IED design and also the camouflage blankets the insurgents were using. He also knew that Saif had been instrumental in moving the bomb across the border. Was this the same bomb that had ended up in Hawaii?

Reading further down the e-mail, Mitch was just about to log-off when he read the footnote that a Major Hythe from the British SAS had carried out the interrogation of an Afghan prisoner and obtained this information.

Checking his watch, Mitch decided to try to call Major Hythe directly. It wasn't easy tracking him down, but Mitch had the necessary clearance and, after a thirty-minute or so wait, he and the Major were finally connected by secure radio link.

'Major? Lieutenant Mitchell Stringer – US Navy. I worked for Admiral Carter – Chief of Naval Operations here in the Pentagon.'

'Lieutenant. It must be something pretty important for you to call all the way from Washington. What can I do for you?'

'Major, I have a copy of a report you logged yesterday. It's about an interrogation you performed on an Afghan prisoner. You mention in it the 'Jaws of Allah'.'

'Correct, Lieutenant. The prisoner was captured after a failed attack on myself and my men. They detonated an IED too early, and we managed to capture two of them, although the other prisoner died before he could be questioned. We were particularly interested in where they are obtaining a new improved type of IED from that is causing us concern. It's more powerful than normal and negates the bomb deflection shields fitted to the underside of our vehicles. Over the past two months,' these IED's have claimed over twenty lives. The prisoner eventually gave up the name of the bomb-maker and his location. We raided it late yesterday afternoon. Unfortunately, there was nobody there, but we gathered a lot of intel that is now with Intelligence, and have placed a watch on the location.'

'Major, what about the 'Jaws of Allah?'

'We'd assumed it was the name they were using for the new IED's they are using. Something like jaws clamping shut on us, but it appears we were wrong. The prisoner eventually admitted the same person responsible for these IED's and camouflage blankets had also organised the transport of bombs across the border. The 'Jaws of Allah' refers to this bomb, but that is when he refused to talk anymore, despite repeated incentives to do so,' Hythe said.

Mitch felt his sweat go icy cold on his arms. 'Major, I believe the 'Jaws of Allah' refers to something far larger and worrying. Can you remember his exact words? Did he say bomb or bombs?'

'Lieutenant, this interrogation didn't take place in a nice cosy air-conditioned room. We were still under sporadic fire, two Apache 'copters were approaching, and his speech wasn't the clearest, but if I had to put money on it, I would say he said bombs. Plural. What's the significance?'

'Major,' Mitch said, 'the significance is I firmly believe a terrorist organisation, identity so far unconfirmed, but now thought to be Hamas or Al-Qaeda, smuggled not one, but two nukes out of Pakistan. One has turned up in Hawaii, fully armed but luckily found in time. But it raises the question, *Where the fuck is the other?*'

# 72

## Washington - Friday

Rivalry still exists between the various services and branches in the US security arena. The CIA are considered the 'spooks', the FBI are the 'G' men, the NSA the geeks, and Homeland Security the 'newbies', all wanting to be the group that gets the praise. But, when the chips are down, inter-departmental worries are cast aside, and they all come together as one. Or that's the plan.

However, in practice politics and rivalry plays its part, especially in Washington, with each service still wanting to be seen as 'top dog', so although some data is shared, it's not as complete as the public would believe.

Working together in the conference room, the various teams analysed the data. Admiral Carter was present for some of the time but being the senior officer present assigned his protégé Mitch as group spokesman.

The FBI began tracking how the bomb had reached the shores of Hawaii and where it had come from, and who within Hawaii had helped. The CIA was trawling every intel source and archive trying to find a lead while Homeland was following up with NEST.

The ship the bulldozer had been transported on, the Tim Pu Zhedang, had already been identified, but it was already out of USA territorial waters. The cargo manifest had been checked, and all paperwork passed inspection. The company shipping the bulldozer was legitimate and had shipped other equipment with no issue so it was already thought likely any investigation would lead to a dead-end, especially if it was going to rely on assistance from the government of the People's Republic of China.

The tension between the two countries had been worsening, Mitch knew. There had been frequent small skirmishes between US and PRC naval ships and aircraft. China was flexing its oriental muscles, Mitch knew, and that could only lead to trouble. But, he wasn't convinced yet that China would actively assist a terrorist organisation launch an attack against the US. The US firepower and weapons systems were still many times stronger than anything China could raise. But China was growing fast and wanted their fair place in the world.

As part of their major naval expansion programme in early 2012, they had launched their first blue-water aircraft carrier, the Liaoning, a refit and improvement of the ex-Soviet carrier Varyag, equipped with the latest radars, sonars and weapons systems. The Liaoning was also equipped with the latest carrier-based fighter aircraft, the Shenyang J-15, a stealth version of the highly effective and proven Russian-designed Sukhoi Su-33.

They had also carved a vast cavern under a mountain on Hainan Island. The walls and roof were heavily reinforced and the entrances fortified and guarded by their latest anti-aircraft missiles and radar systems. The entrance being big enough to sail aircraft carriers through with the complete structure being heavily reinforced with multiple blast-proof doors. It was estimated the roof around the entrance would even withstand multiple hits from the American 'Bunker Buster' bombs used so effectively against underground bunkers in Iraq. They should be able to house up to thirty submarines in there as well as multiple aircraft carriers, all nicely hidden away from our satellites. Furthermore, with the water depth dropping to almost five-thousand metres within just a few miles of the harbour it's going to become damn near impossible to keep eyes on them, Mitch thought.

For years China had been a continuing thorn in the side of the American administration and had been involved in plenty of skirmishes against the US, but never directly with weapons before, always preferring to use deniable techniques such as the hacking of computer systems.

Mitch knew that the US administration strongly suspected Chinese sponsored hackers had tried loading software Trojans – small undetected software bugs – into the US power grid system computers. Something had gone wrong, and the software had accidentally tripped the network to close down in August 2003. It had become known as the Great North East Blackout and had affected almost 55 million people between Ontario and the North East of the US. It had taken the US administration several months to uncover who they believed the real culprit to be. For political reasons it had been decided at the highest levels to keep the real reason quiet, preferring to lay blame on a network overload during an unusually hot period in the month, rather than cause political and financial turmoil in publicly stating that China was responsible.

More recently China had been flexing its military muscle in the disputed Spratly Islands and Senkaku / Diaoyutai Islands just north of Taiwan. They had also caused disruption to a recent joint US and Taiwanese naval military exercise held in the Taiwanese Straits between China and Taiwan, as well as making an unannounced surprise arrival with one of their Song class submarines by surfacing undetected very close to the USS Kitty Hawk in 2007.

Certainly, China was letting the world know that the western region of the Pacific was China's backyard.

If Pearl Harbour were put out of action, then China would have an almost free rein in the area, with San Diego being the closest US Navy base. But, there was a significant difference between sabre-rattling and actually attacking or being part of an attack on the US, Mitch thought. Also, he'd like to know what Admiral Zhang of the PRC had been doing in Bandar Abbas. Zhang was well known for being radical right-wing and very anti-American.

In the meantime, the FBI and the local Hawaii police department were checking who might have been involved on Oahu, where the Tim Pu Zhedang had docked.

But what Mitch couldn't understand was if Pearl Harbour was the target or even Honolulu, why was the bomb underwater over two hundred miles away. Obviously, Pearl for the military impact but even Honolulu would be a good terrorist target being a large US city. But here we are on some outlying islands thousands of miles from the US mainland. Sure, it would be a coup for the terrorists and would badly affect tourism, but any attack there would not have the same impact as striking somewhere in the US heartland, Mitch reasoned.

No, there has to be more to it than that. He was missing something, and it annoyed him.

Re-reading his notes from his conversation with Major Hythe, Mitch considered the possibility of two bombs on Hawaii. Could the other one be placed nearer to Pearl, he wondered. But why waste the one they'd found on a different island? Especially one pretty sparsely populated? There was no military site there, and all the explosion would have done was damage the side of the volcano or maybe trigger an eruption ...

The old cliché that all the pieces of the jigsaw begin to fall into place really did happen to Mitch at that moment. He suddenly thought again what if the explosion of the bomb was planned to trigger the volcano? But what would be the expected result? What were they trying to achieve?

Leaving his colleagues to carry on their investigations he knocked and entered the Admiral's office before sitting down. 'Sir, I think I may have been looking at this the wrong way. What if Pearl wasn't the direct target? What if the mountain was?'

'Why the mountain? How would they benefit from that?' the Admiral answered.

'Not sure, Sir, but the team is all over every other possibility. So with your permission Sir, I'm going to look into this. In the meantime, perhaps the Anvil can examine the other coasts of Hawaii for the second device?'

'Granted. Find out whatever you can. I'll order the Anvil to resume searching, but that's a lot of coastlines to search. Keep me appraised. This has gone to the highest levels, and I don't want any surprises foisted on me. Understand?'

'Yessir,' Mitch answered. As he stood to leave the room, his mind was already far away, trying to retrieve something he had watched or read many months earlier.

# 73

Mitch's phone started ringing as he hurried back to his desk and snatching it up he saw the dialling number to be the UAE. Hitting the green button, he answered, 'Shane, how are you doing? What's up, man?'

'Mitch, I'm good. Listen, I've got some news. The tension in the air here is palpable. One of my local informants here overheard a conversation in a coffee shop. He is a waiter, and while serving a group they continued talking, and he heard them say two huge events are happening on Tuesday, it being the anniversary of 9/11. It seems there will be two significant events, not one, and they will affect the US directly, but they aren't the same as last time but are much larger, or at least, will cause more damage. They also said 'Americans will need to look both ways', but then he got shooed away.

'I don't have anything more than that, that's for you to decode, but whatever's going on is now all in place, it's big, and it's to do with the US directly, not here locally. I am typing up my report as we speak but wanted to give you the heads-up. If I hear anything more, I'll come straight back to you, pal.'

Thanking Shane for his call, Mitch hung up and grabbed a coffee. He was now more convinced than ever that he was on the right track.

Mitch had always considered that the human mind works a little like a Rolodex card system. Things you know and regularly use, such as driving, or your partner's name were always available, but things you heard or learned a while back and didn't need to use daily were stored in your mind like a card system. When you tried to recall them, the little card system in your brain would start running through the billions of pieces of data it had stored. Often, the best way was to leave it running in the background – that's why you would often suddenly wake in the night having remembered something 'special'. But today Mitch's Rolodex was working quicker. All the cards suddenly came together, and he remembered a report he'd seen on the Discovery Channel months ago. It was about the dangers of a landslide from a volcano.

Closing his eyes, he could 'see' the presenters face. And the name of the presenter was ... was ... was Gaddows, Patrick Gaddows of the USGS – US Geological Survey, in Menlo Park, California. Their chief scientist, Dr Patrick Gaddows, was presenting about the work being carried out by the National Earthquake Hazards Reduction Program.

Finding the number of USGS on Google took moments. Reception passed him to voice mail but speaking with their security people and convincing them of his need to reach Doctor Gaddows urgently took slightly longer, but within ten minutes he had Gaddows cell number.

Dialling the 650 area code, Mitch tried to collect his thoughts. It was lunchtime in California and Gaddows had left instructions not to be disturbed, but this couldn't wait. After six rings a deep voice answered, 'Gaddows. This has better be good.'

'Sir, Lieutenant Mitchel Stringer of Naval Intelligence in the Pentagon here. Sorry to trouble you at this time, but I need your help.'

'Lieutenant, it's my wedding anniversary today, and I am in the middle of a very pleasant lunch with my wife which you've now ruined. I won't hear the end of this for hours. Give me your number and department. I will call you back in five minutes.'

Passing the number to Gaddows and hanging up, Mitch smiled ruefully. If Gaddows' wife was anything like his Helen, it would be days, not hours.

Exactly eight minutes later, Mitch's desk phone rang.

'Lieutenant, Gaddows. Needed to check you are who you say you are. What can I do for you?'

'Sir, hypothetically, if Mount Kilauea volcano on Hawaii's big island suddenly erupted, what damage would it do?'

'Well, there's nothing hypothetical about it, Lieutenant. The Hawaiian Islands are a chain of eight major and multiple minor volcanic islands. Most of the volcanos are extinct except those on the big island Hawaii. The Mauna Loa volcano there is the largest shield volcano in the world, but it's relatively inactive. It blows and bellows a little every day but doesn't do anything particularly dangerous to mankind. Next door to it is Mount Kilauea. That one's a bitch. It's erupted over sixty times in the past two-hundred or so years – it's currently still the most active volcano on the planet. Its southern flank moves almost five inches a year towards the edge.

'Sometime soon in the next seventy to eighty years or so it will over balance and the entire southern flank, over twelve miles long and six miles wide, will slide down into the sea. There's no question of doubt. It won't stop there. The hundreds of millions of tonnes of rock will continue downward gaining speed and momentum. Moving at something like three hundred miles an hour, it will glance off the Papua Seamount ridge at a depth of three thousand feet and turn slightly more east. Here it will drop a further twelve thousand feet before levelling out on the seabed and continuing eastward for fifty or sixty miles before eventually coming to a stop, having spent all its energy. This energy, this weight of hundreds of millions of tonnes of rock travelling at hundreds of miles an hour, will transfer to the sea and the resultant wave will likely first peak at almost five hundred feet. Then it will subside down to a mere five or six-foot high surge travelling eastwards at over five hundred miles an hour.

'Once it subsides ships at sea will likely not even feel it, just a slightly bigger wave than usual, but water moves easily. The mass of this water will be transmitted eastwards with virtually no loss of power, before slowing as the sea bed rises, but extending in size. What had been a small five or six-foot wave in the depths of the ocean, will grow into a wave seventy- or eighty-foot in height as it approaches the shallow bays of San Diego, Los Angeles, San Francisco and Seattle a mere five hours later.'

'Holy shit.'

'That's as good a statement as any, son,' Gaddows said, guessing the approximate age of Stringer. 'Once it triggers, there's not a damned thing you or I can do to stop it. You know, this is already well known by the Government. One of our scientists wrote a paper on this years' back and submitted it to the DoD, but like most things, they've just sat their fat asses on it.

'The only good thing,' Gaddows continued, 'is that I will likely be long dead and buried by the time it happens.'

Stringer was busy making notes, stopped mid-scribble and asked, 'This mass of water. Would it also affect Pearl Harbour and Honolulu?'

'Lieutenant, it would affect everything on the West Coast and those Islands. Being physically 'behind' the landslip area would mean the waves there would be smaller, but Pearl would likely get hit by a thirty to forty-foot wave – it would sure cause a lot of damage. You want to speak to one of my colleagues, Rachel Sanchez. She got her Master's a couple of years' ago, but her thesis was on Mount Kilauea collapsing and also Cumbre Vieja in the Atlantic. The one on Cumbre Vieja is bigger. Much bigger. I've got her number here somewhere. Maybe give her a call when you've got a few minutes,' he said.

Writing down the number, Stringer thanked Gaddows and then asked a final question. 'Mr Gaddows, what would it take to trigger this flank collapse? I mean, could a bomb do it?'

'Certainly could, Lieutenant. Especially if it was big enough.'

'A nuke?'

'Sure could. In fact, that's why you want to speak with Rachel about her thesis.'

'Why's that, Sir?'

'Her thesis was on the ability of terrorism and terrorist activities to trigger natural disasters,' Gaddows said.

# 74

Stringer tried calling Rachel Sanchez every hour, on the hour. He also tried her office, leaving shorter and more urgent messages as time went on. Finally, at 19:30 local time on Friday evening, his phone rang, and he snatched it up.

'Lieutenant Stringer. Can I help you?'

'Uhh, hopefully. I am Rachel Sanchez, and you have left me over a dozen messages to call you.'

'Miss Sanchez, thank god you've called. Where have you been?' he shouted.

'Lieutenant, I don't know who the hell you are or what you want, but unless you want me to hang up on you right now, I suggest you alter your tone. If you must know, I have just got back less than thirty minutes ago from a field trip, and I found you had left fourteen of the fifteen messages on my answerphone.'

'But why didn't you answer your cell?' Stringer asked.

'Because it's somewhere up in the hills, that's why! It fell out of my pocket when I was climbing over some rocks, last seen bouncing down into a ravine. So why don't you cut the crap and tell me why it's so damned urgent we speak?'

'Miss Sanchez. I apologise for my tone, but I have been getting more and more frustrated in not being able to reach you. Professor Gaddows told me a little about your Master's thesis. Could you let me have some more information about it please?'

'OK Lieutenant, I don't know why this is so important suddenly, but here goes,' and she then spent the next hour explaining to a more and more worried Lieutenant in the Pentagon.

He put her on hold twice and came back on the line after keeping her waiting almost twenty minutes.

'Miss Sanchez, I apologise for the timing, but at 22:00 tonight a US Navy staff car will come to your house. A sergeant will then escort you to Moffat Airfield where a C-37 Gulfstream will be waiting to bring you here.'

'What? I'll do no such thing. I'm not going to Washington tomo —.'

'MISS SANCHEZ. Good, I have your attention. Miss Sanchez, you will come to Washington tomorrow. You will then present what you have just told me to the Joint Chiefs of Staff, and likely, the President. You will NOT speak of this to anyone. Do you understand? Do I make myself clear, Miss Sanchez?'

'Y..Yes, yes I do,' she answered, gulping back her nervousness.

'Good. Now go and do whatever you need to do and get a bag ready to be picked up at 22:00. You'll only be gone a few days. OK?' Stringer said. 'Oh, Miss Sanchez. Make sure you bring all your documentation and your computer with you.'

Disconnecting the call, Rachel sat down slowly. What the hell was going on, she thought. She had just over four hours' before the car would arrive, so she quickly had a shower, prepared a quick meal and gathered some clothes, before sorting through her paperwork to await the pick-up.

# 75

## The Pentagon - Saturday, September 8th

Arriving at the Pentagon early morning, Rachel was escorted through security. She smiled to herself thinking about the flight. She could certainly get used to the lifestyle of travelling by executive jet and being addressed as 'Ma'am'. After landing at Andrews AFB, a black limousine had pulled up right next to the aeroplane steps, her bags had been carried, and moments later she was in yet another soft leather chair. Oh, how the rich and important lived, she thought, I could get used to this.

After showing her driving licence, she passed through the X-ray and metal detector scans, while her handbag, overnight bag and laptop bags were all thoroughly searched. Presented with a 'Visitor – Escort At All Times' badge, she turned to find a young female Navy clerk waiting for her. With a simple, 'Follow me,' she was led along the marble polished floors to the first floor on one of the outer rings of the Pentagon sanctum. The clerk knocked, waited briefly for an answer, then opened the door and directed Rachel to enter.

Both men in the room stood and smiled. The tall, good-looking younger one offered his hand. 'Miss Sanchez, I am Lieutenant Mitchell Stringer. Please call me Mitch. I am sorry to insist you being flown across the country at almost a moment's notice.'

'Well, it was made clear I didn't have a choice. I just hope you feel it is worth it,' she replied, with a slight icy edge to her voice.

215

'It certainly will be. Let me introduce you to my Commanding Officer, Admiral Carter. He is the Chief of Naval Operations here at the Pentagon.'

The Admiral, a medium height grey-haired older man, extended his hand and smiled at her as he said, 'Miss Sanchez. It is a pleasure to make your acquaintance. It was on my insistence that you are here now. Please accept my apologies for inconveniencing you. Was your journey comfortable?'

Looking into his twinkling eyes, Rachel's iciness began to melt. 'Yes, yes, it was fine, thank you, and please, call me Rachel.'

'Rachel, before we continue I need you to sign this form,' Mitch said. 'What we are about to discuss is in the strictest confidence. You can never disclose anything about it without authority from the DoD.'

Reading through the form, Rachel signed and passed it back to him. Thanking her, he motioned for her to take a seat before saying, 'Rachel. We will shortly be going into a meeting room. I will introduce them to you, but basically, the attendees will be senior members of the Government. I need you to tell again, in as much detail as you can, what you said to me yesterday. Some of the group may ask questions, and, if they do, please answer them as clearly as possible. Some of the people you will recognise, certainly their names, but please don't be intimidated. Now, having just flown in, would you like a few minutes to freshen up?'

Feeling butterflies in her stomach, she accepted his offer, if nothing else than to brush her teeth and re-apply some make-up. She also asked for a glass of water. Mitch smiled and led her to the door where the female Navy clerk was waiting to take her to the bathroom.

Ten minutes later, as presentable as she was ever going to be, she arrived back at the Admiral's office and was led to a large meeting room.

About twenty pairs of eyes swung towards her as they entered, and the Admiral briefly introduced everyone around the table to her. She recognised some names and faces from television and nervously smiled back. Taking a seat next to Mitch, she waited while the Admiral spoke first. 'Gentlemen. We asked Miss Sanchez here because she has a story to tell which we believe to be of the highest importance. Lieutenant Stringer spoke with Miss Sanchez last evening, and I would ask him to now run through the story with Miss Sanchez. Mitch?'

Thanking the Admiral, Mitch turned to Rachel and said, 'Rachel. Just relax and tell us, from the beginning, what you told me yesterday. OK?'

Feeling nervous and wishing she had never returned his call yesterday, Rachel turned slightly in her chair to better face the audience. 'I don't even know how to address you. Is 'Gentlemen' OK?' she said.

Feeling the Admiral pat her on the arm, he said, 'Don't be nervous, Rachel. None of us will bite. We're just a bunch of old codgers eager to hear your story, and yes, 'Gentlemen' will do just fine,' to the light laughter that spread around the room. 'Please start when you are ready.'

'OK Gentlemen, well here goes. My name is Rachel Sanchez, and I am a Geologist working for the National Earthquake Hazards Reduction Program or NEHRP in Menlo, California. This is a joint venture between multiple agencies including FEMA, the Science Foundation, and the US Geological Survey Department. I obtained my double Master's Degrees' of Geology and Volcanology from the Carlos III University of Madrid, a little over two and a half years back. My thesis was on the possibility and ability of terrorism and terrorist activities to trigger natural disasters. In particular, my work was about the fact that there are pending natural disasters that scientists know all about but governments seem to have ignored.

'The largest one is a big volcano, called Cumbre Vieja, on La Palma in the Canary Islands that when it erupts will cause a gigantic tsunami that will engulf America's East Coast. It will kill tens of millions, but most scientific experts don't think it will erupt anytime soon so are ignoring it.'

'What do you mean, Rachel, can you please explain?' Mitch guided.

'Sure. First I should explain that coming from Phoenix Arizona originally, and of Spanish-American descendants, my parents were happy to sponsor me going to Madrid for my studies. The reason being a lot of the local history is only available in old documents and books held in churches and monasteries in and around Spain. Obviously being fluent in Spanish was essential in understanding all the documents. While there I met a local guy called Manuel Garibaldi although I am now sure that was not his proper name. At the time I didn't question it, but I will come on to that later. What I did find out was this volcano has erupted six times in the past five hundred years. It last erupted in 1949, and the whole western flank about the size of Long Island became detached from the main ridge and slid over ten feet down towards the sea. There it stopped and has been teetering on the edge ever since. The next time the volcano erupts could be deadly. It could be next week or not for a hundred years. Scientists think it likely to be nearer the hundred years, hence they are not worried yet about it. Actually, the volcano won't cause the problem directly, but the heat from the volcano and all the little earthquakes you get when it erupts will.'

# 76

Taking a breath, Rachel continued, 'You see this volcanic mountain is made up of two sorts of rocks. First, the outer ones which are completely waterlogged - absolutely full of water – but the inner core ones are solid and dry, and secondly the outer rocks are part of this one gigantic loose slab.'

'OK, go on,' Mitch said.

'Well, if there is a large solid central core of thick rock covered by more rock which is saturated with water, then the water reduces resistance holding it all together. On top of that, the heat from the volcano erupting would make the water in the rocks boil and turn it to superheated steam, so building up the pressure and making it swell. It's simple physics really, just like when a saucepan lid lifts off slightly when boiling. A little bit of vibration from the ground shaking when the volcano erupts, and the whole lot slides down.'

'So that might cause a tsunami, but would it be as bad as you say?' he asked.

'I don't think I am explaining myself very clearly,' she said. 'Firstly, the amount of land we are talking about here is in the region of 140 cubic miles. Absolute masses. Then you have to take the height and the depth into account. The height of the volcano is almost 6,000 feet above sea level and is steep-sided, so this mass of rock has a long way to slide down a very steep slope. Therefore it will pick up tremendous speed and momentum. Then to make matters worse, the mountain angle carries on directly down under the sea to a water depth of about the same 5-6,000 feet and then levels out. What this means is that the mass of earth will travel almost vertically down approximately 11,000 feet before levelling out westwards. By the time it hits bottom, it will be moving at about 250 miles an hour and will travel horizontally about 50 miles before finally stopping. That mass of land moving like that will displace so much water that the initial peak of water could be up to a 1,000 feet high and travelling at about 600 miles an hour towards America, but it will settle down to a smaller amount of about 15 - 18 feet high but still going at that speed. That's as fast as a jet aeroplane. Now think of all that depth of 5-6,000 feet pushing up the height of the surface wave as the seabed gets shallower nearer to the US, and now you can see how the final waves breaking on the shore could be up to 160 feet high. And it's not just an initial wave. Like ripples on a lake from a stone, you get the initial wave but then secondary and subsequent waves behind. These are smaller, but they just keep coming. If you also think of the wavelength or thickness as being a mile or so long, it wouldn't be just one wave like on a beach, but as if the whole sea had risen up by 160 feet.'

'My God, it would wreck everything. Everywhere it struck would be flattened,' someone said.

'Sure would. Not many buildings could withstand walls of water up to ten storeys high.'

'Now think of the tsunami that hit Japan almost two years' back. There were waves up to thirty foot in height that killed something like 30,000 people. Whole towns were wrecked. It also caused major damage to the Fukushima nuclear plant, almost producing a meltdown. This was all the result of the tsunami, which hadn't been planned for. You see everyone had planned for the earthquake, and all the buildings were as much

221

earthquake-proof as possible, but it was the tsunami that caused all the deaths and damage. This one I'm talking about could be up to ten times as large,' she continued.

'Now think of Hurricane Sandy last year. That was just a storm, albeit a very major one. Over forty billion dollars' worth of damage, over one hundred people dead, but luckily we had over seven days of notice to prepare, and it turned out to be mainly just rain and wind. The storm surge was only about ten foot.'

Taking a moment to pause and look around the room, Rachel could see all eyes were on her. Gulping a little nervously from a glass of water, she continued, 'You see, you can't usually stop natural disasters, but you can plan for them and limit their impact. That's what my department plans for. When Mount St. Helens erupted in 1980, because scientists knew it was going to happen, all the people living nearby were moved to safety. Although it was a stratovolcano – really massive – only fifty-seven people died instead of thousands. With Hurricane Sandy, most of the injured or killed were people who refused to leave their homes.'

Turning her computer screen around to show the group, she continued, 'But the reverse of that is if you don't plan, you can get caught short. My thesis was on imagining if terrorists had the knowledge to trigger these disasters or similar? Just think how many more could die. Now let's get back to the present and Cumbre Vieja. That slab of rock I mentioned before is massive. If that slips into the water, the corresponding tsunami will be about a hundred times more powerful than the Japanese one. It will be massive. Here, you can see computer modelling of where the damage is likely to occur,' she said as she showed them the screen.

The video simulation was a detailed and graphic representation of the damage the tsunami would likely cause. Great swathes of land down the East Coast from beyond the Canadian border to the coast of South America would be hit by a series of enormous waves.

'When this flank fails on La Palma, the mega-tsunami hitting America would be about one-hundred-and-sixty feet in height. Just imagine the damage it would do and the millions of people it would kill. Don't forget it's not just one wave, either. The wavelength is so long it would drive ashore up to forty miles, and there would be multiple waves. Cities such as Boston, New York, Washington, Norfolk, Jacksonville, and Miami, would all be completely wrecked. It would be one of the biggest disasters ever to hit mankind, let alone America,' she said. 'And the waters would hit within six to seven hours. No time for adequate warnings or evacuations, just sheer panic.'

'But Rachel, isn't that only if the volcano erupts? I mean, how could a terrorist do this?' Mitch asked.

'Correct. The effect of the volcano erupting, the heat and the associated earthquakes, might trigger the landslide. But my thesis was about what if that landslide could be triggered deliberately? Once it starts, it can't be stopped. From the moment it was triggered, there would be only six or seven hours' notice before the waves slammed into the US east coast. Even with seven hours' notice, imagine trying to evacuate New York, Boston, and Miami within that time? Impossible,' she said.

'Now I don't know much about explosives, but I do know that to knock old buildings down they plant explosives in holes they drill into the structure to focus the blast. Obviously, there is more power if the explosives are planted within a structure than on the surface. With this volcano and the two sorts of rock, one porous and saturated with water, and the other impermeable, the ideal place to detonate anything would be at the junction underground of the two rocks. That would likely cause the porous outer rock to start sliding.

'My thesis, based on scientific evidence, was on the possibility of a terrorist placing enough explosives, or a nuclear device, at that underground rock junction.'

# 77

Looking around the room, Mitch could see everyone was watching Rachel closely. He said, 'Rachel, before you finish with this one tell us about Hawaii. Tell the group what you said to me yesterday.'

'There is a similar situation on the big island of Hawaii. There is a mountain called Mount Kilauea. It is also slowly slipping towards the sea. It will cause a similar albeit smaller catastrophe to the west coast. The main difference being the trigger for this one would need to be under the ocean. The rock formation is much nearer the edge and not waterlogged, but the slope is very steep. A large explosion underwater that destroyed the underlying rock face would have the desired effect in making the landslide start. Again, once it starts no force on earth would be powerful enough to stop it. The tsunami from this one wouldn't be quite as large but still in the region of thirty to forty feet high in Honolulu and seventy to eighty feet high in Los Angeles and San Francisco.

Stopping for a moment to take another gulp of water, Rachel looked around before continuing, 'As to Cumbre Vieja, the explosion has to be inside the mountain, not undersea. My studies focussed on an old diary and some maps from a monastery. It was the actual story of a boy, and a Priest chased by pirates back in the 1600s into caves and tunnels under the volcano of Cumbre Vieja. They were trapped but eventually found a way out. Years later, the boy wrote about his escape and described the caves in some detail. He wrote about their locations and how to get to the rock junction. He also did some roughly drawn maps of the area.'

'And do you still have the diary, Miss Sanchez?' a voice asked from within the group.

Rachel hesitated for a moment before replying, 'No, I don't. Because it belonged to the church, I was only allowed a copy. The original should still be in existence but the man I knew as Manuel Garibaldi stole my copy along with all my research and my laptop. I never managed to find him again despite repeated efforts. I came back home and completed my thesis here in the US. What did become clear though was it is possible this Manuel Garibaldi was actually Arabic.'

It took less than three seconds for the importance of that last sentence to fully bed in before the room erupted in turmoil.

Eventually, amid the shouting, Admiral Carter's voice was heard. 'Quiet … QUIET, I say. Let's have some order here, gentlemen. Quiet!' Turning to face Rachel, Admiral Carter continued, 'Miss Sanchez. You have certainly gotten our attention. Now tell me, what makes you think he was Arabic?'

Looking slightly embarrassed and also shocked by the outbursts, Rachel replied, 'Manuel and I had become … close. He had moved into my apartment. After he'd left so suddenly I searched for anything of his to find out where he had gone. But he'd cleared out all his belongings, and nothing of his was remaining. All of my friends and I searched the University, but he wasn't anywhere. He'd said he was studying law, but we checked, and he wasn't even registered. I hadn't noticed it at the time, but he never wanted his photo taken although one of my friends did actually get a snap of him. However, no one at the Uni knew him. At the time, I never picked up on it, but he asked me lots of questions about how much damage would be inflicted on the US and how these events could be triggered. Anyway, it wasn't until about a month later when I was packing up to move back home that I moved a bookcase in my bedroom and found a set of 33 brown glass beads behind them. I didn't know what they were, but a colleague friend identified them as Arabic worry beads. That's why I think he may have been Arabic.

'I did go to the Embassy and spoke with someone there, especially about what I was working on, but I never heard anything back,' she said.

# 78

Rachel was surprised to hear her name being called over the background noise and conversation her last comment had initiated. Admiral Carter took control of the room and again requested silence. Hearing her voice called again by a voice she recognised, she answered, 'Yes, hello. This is Rachel.'

The screen on the wall flickered to life, and she saw the face along with hearing her name spoken. 'Miss Sanchez. I would like to personally thank you for coming here and providing your overview. I would like to ask you one question and then for fifteen minutes' to speak with my Government colleagues alone. You mention that the Hawaii bomb could be under the water, but the La Palma bomb would have to be inside the mountain?'

'That's correct Sir. Because of the shape of the hillside and slope angle, a bomb undersea even a nuclear bomb at La Palma would be unlikely to trigger the landslide. Or to do so, the explosion would have to be immense. Big enough to vaporise over half the island. But a much smaller explosion at that rock junction would almost certainly do the trick.'

Admiral Carter pressed a hidden button under his desk, and the door opened to admit the young Navy clerk again. She guided Rachel back to the Admiral's office and waited with her.

All the time Rachel was waiting she was tense with excitement. The face on the screen and the voice belonged to the President of the United States, and he had spoken to her directly. She wasn't a person easily ruffled but having the President address her personally and use her name had certainly made her nervous.

After what seemed an interminable length of time but in reality, was only just over thirty minutes, the Navy clerk's pager buzzed, and she was led back to the meeting room.

Admiral Carter led her to a large screen with a camera lens above. There waiting for her on the screen was the President. 'Miss Sanchez, I trust my team are looking after you and making you comfortable?' he asked.

'Ye ...Yes, Mr President. Perfectly.' She stammered in reply.

'Well, Miss Sanchez, you have been a great help to us. Firstly, I must emphasise that you can tell no one, no one at all, about this meeting and what you have discussed here and what I am about to tell you. It's a matter of national security – I cannot stress that enough.'

'No, Mr President. I mean, yes, Mr President, I mean …'

'It's ok, Miss Sanchez. Please don't be nervous. Remember you have been a great help here. Admiral Carter will answer any questions you have, but we now believe the East Coast of America to be under an imminent and deadly threat from a terrorist plan to explode a nuclear device on the mountain of Cumbre Vieja. We believe the person you knew as Manuel Garibaldi might have been working with other terrorists and has planned a two-prong attack against the USA from Cumbre Vieja and Mount Kilauea in Hawaii by detonating devices in both locations to cause the enormous tsunamis you have discussed. We believe detonation is set for Tuesday 11th to coincide with the 9/11 anniversary just three days from now.'

The President continued, 'The device in Hawaii has been uncovered and made safe, but we don't even know where to look in La Palma. As of fifteen minutes ago a special flight of US Navy SEALs who uncovered the Hawaii device and made it safe are flying to their base in California to gather more equipment. They will then immediately fly to our Naval Station in Rota, Spain. In the meantime, the SEAL team leader Lieutenant John Deacon is flying directly here by military jet. He will arrive in approximately seven hours. I would ask one more request of you. Or should I say your country asks one more request of you. I ask that you accompany Lieutenant Deacon to Madrid today, find the original of the diary and any notes you used before, and make this data available to the Lieutenant. Our embassy in Madrid will offer you any support and personnel you need. You know what data you found before, and you know what to look for, but we need to know the exact location of the entrance to the tunnels on Cumbre Vieja. You will never be able to speak of what you have done, but I as your President ask you to help. Will you?'

With tears beginning to run down her face Rachel nodded and then managed to say, 'Mr President I would be honoured,' as loud cheers broke out amongst the other members of the inner sanctum meeting room.

# 79

Deacon was always amazed how quickly things could be arranged when need be. Less than an hour ago he'd been awakened by a phone call putting him and his men on Full Alert – Standby, meaning be ready to move out within twenty minutes destination unknown. Thirty minutes after the call his team along with Eric Staples and two of his men were escorted aboard a Navy Gulfstream C-37A business jet en-route to Coronado. Their journey would take a little over four hours, where further equipment and weapons would be ready for collection. They would then fly with a fresh aircrew directly to Spain, a journey of a further nine hours, arriving at 08:00 local time on Sunday 9th.

Deacon, on the other hand, was aboard another Navy C-37A heading to Washington. There were only four people on board, two pilots, a female Navy clerk flight attendant, and himself. They would arrive at Andrews AFB where Rachel would be waiting before immediately setting off to Madrid, Spain, arriving at around 07:00 local time on Sunday.

Although the C-37A was equipped with every luxury a man could need, including a well-stocked bar, Deacon chose orange juice and steak and salad for his breakfast-cum-lunch meal. He knew his people would have followed similar suit – nobody drank alcohol before possible action. Had this flight been post-mission he would have relaxed and had a few beers, and maybe even tried to hit on the attendant but this was pre-mission, and things are different. Briefed as much as he could be he made himself comfortable and settled down to sleep awakening only to the changing sound of the twin Rolls-Royce turbofans as they came in on final approach at Andrews.

As they taxied to a stop, Deacon could see a Navy staff car approaching them and pulling up alongside. Stepping down onto the tarmac, Deacon saluted as Admiral Carter alighted the car, accompanied by an attractive young woman with dark, shoulder-length hair, green eyes and well-shaped legs.

'Lieutenant. Admiral Carter. We've not met, but Mitch speaks very highly of you, and I have been following your exploits with great interest. Let me introduce Miss Rachel Sanchez.'

'Miss Sanchez, a pleasure,' Deacon said as he shook her hand. 'Admiral, do you have the latest briefing?'

'Lieutenant, these are the most recent briefing notes and video for you. I have also asked Miss Sanchez to provide as much information as possible about what she remembers,' he said, handing over a thick envelope.

The Admiral thanked Rachel again and then asked her to go ahead on board and make herself comfortable. Turning to Deacon, he said, 'Lieutenant. I don't need to tell you the seriousness of this mission. If what we believe is correct, there is a nuclear device likely to detonate on Tuesday afternoon local time that will cause a tsunami the size of which no living person has ever seen. It will devastate the complete eastern seaboard, and potentially millions or even tens of millions of people will die. We have sent the USS Tallahassee, a Los-Angeles class submarine, to check the underwater coastline for any devices. It has some of the latest sonar, but it would appear the only viable place for the explosion is inside the mountain itself. We can't raise the alarm and start evacuating people because as soon as this hits the news, it will be bedlam and would also alert the terrorists. Likewise, if we flood the island with forces, the terrorists would likely detonate it immediately. This has to be a stealth mission, and you and your men have to succeed.'

Shaking Deacon's hand, the Admiral continued, 'The President has spoken with King Juan Carlos, and you and your men will be offered every aid. However, being La Palma is Spanish territory, the King has insisted that their Naval Special Warfare Force, the Fuerza de Guerra Naval Especial (FGNE), in Cadiz accompany you and your men. I believe you have already met some of their people and trained with them under their previous name, the Unidad de Operaciones Especiales?'

'Yes, sir. We completed a number of joint exercises in Iraq and at their training camp near Cadiz. Some of their people have also trained in Coronado. They are good men – disciplined and well-trained. It will be good to work with them.'

'Well, good luck, Lieutenant. We are relying on you and your team to get it done.'

'Admiral, you can count on us. Remember, sir, the only easy day was yesterday. Hooyah,' he said as he sprinted back up the aeroplane steps.

As the door was closed and the engines wound up again, Admiral Carter muttered quietly to himself, 'Hooyah indeed, Lieutenant. There won't be much left here to welcome you home if you fail.'

# 80

## Madrid - Sunday, September 9th

The flight to Madrid was uneventful. Deacon made small talk with Rachel before reading the latest reports and watching the video. He then asked Rachel to repeat to him her story she had told Mitch and the Admiral at the Pentagon.

Finishing the story, Deacon asked, 'So what made you a girl from Phoenix suddenly start to think about killing millions of people with a tsunami'?

'Well, actually America did,' she said. 'During World War 2 in 1944, US and Allied Forces were working in New Zealand and were trying to build a tsunami bomb. The project was called Project Seal, and it was hoped to be as successful as the atomic bomb project. They exploded hundreds of tonnes of explosives underwater trying to cause massive tidal waves. The plan was to force tidal waves onto Japanese-held islands to wreck all the enemy defences before the troops went ashore. You can look it up. All the information was released in 2000.'

'So what happened? Did it work?' Deacon asked.

'It worked, but not as well as they wanted and the explosives had to be set off reasonably close to where they wanted the wave to hit. If I remember, the report said the Manhattan Project became successful and was deemed a better solution, so the tsunami one was halted and I guess all forgotten about. I was still undecided at the time about what to base my thesis on and thought that if the US had planned to use natural elements and disasters in times of war, what if some terrorist had the same idea but against us. So it became my thesis.'

'But if it didn't work then why do you think this Cumbre Vieja will cause such a problem now?'

'Well I'm not a specialist, but I did research a lot concerning hydrology and water. A lot of it is to do with how the force is applied. Water absorbs explosive power quite easily, but if water is displaced the force doesn't get absorbed the same way. That's why a stone tossed into a pond makes ripples run right to the bank, or a boats' bow wave will travel for miles. Instead of an explosion, if you can displace the water by moving something solid in it or through it, you get a much higher reaction. The Japanese tsunami two years ago wasn't caused by the earthquake per se, it resulted from the earthquake lifting an enormous section of seabed. That, in turn, caused an almighty displacement of water. Once that water starts moving, it's an incredible force, and it just keeps going. The Banda Aceh tsunami in 2004 travelled all across the Indian Ocean and struck parts of East Africa almost at the same height as locally in Indonesia. A surge was even felt all the way across the Atlantic on the east coast of the US. Cumbre Vieja collapsing into the sea will cause an absolute massive displacement of water. It's likely the surge will travel 2 or 3 times around the world before it eventually dies,' she said.

Having given Deacon a few things to think about made him raise a few questions, and it helped him to know the seriousness of the situation. Deacon also reassured her that she would remain in Madrid, well away from any personal danger, while he and his team flew to La Palma. He was careful not to give her any operational details, and after a further thirty minutes or so of small talk, they both dozed while the aircraft cruised at almost 50,000 feet over the cold Atlantic far below.

Arriving at Madrid-Barajas Airport early Sunday morning, Rachel remembered she didn't have her passport with her – just over twenty-four hours ago she'd been in Menlo Park. Luckily, Mitch had thought of this and alerted the embassy in Madrid. US representatives were waiting for the flight to a touchdown and had brought a temporary VIP pass for Rachel. Immigration and Customs were a formality, and within ten minutes of landing, they were heading down the M-40 towards the embassy.

At that time of the morning on a Sunday, traffic was quite light, and they made good time. Driving directly into the underground garage, Deacon picked up and carried Rachel's overnight bag for her, and they were escorted to the Ambassador's private office.

The Ambassador greeted them warmly before ordering coffee and toast and invited them to sit. 'Miss Sanchez. Lieutenant. The President has briefed me on why you are here, and Admiral Carter and Lieutenant Stringer have helped fill in the blanks. You will have mine and our countries full support. So, Miss Sanchez, what is your first step?'

'Mr Ambassador. Thank you for your kind welcome. First things first, I would really like some time to shower and freshen up. I've been travelling it feels almost non-stop for two days. Then I'd like to go to the Church of San Nicolas de Bari on Plaza de San Nicolas. That's where I did my original research and investigations, and I think I should start again from there.'

The Ambassador smiled, put down his coffee cup and said, 'Miss Sanchez, sometimes I forget my manners. One of my staff will take you to your room and will arrange for any laundry. I imagine the Lieutenant would also welcome a chance to wash and change. When you are both ready, a car will be waiting to take you to the church.'

Thirty minutes later washed and refreshed Rachel and Deacon were driven to the church. Rachel was wearing a floral print dress and Deacon had changed out of his fatigues and was wearing deck shoes, chinos and a polo shirt – the last thing they needed was anyone wondering why someone in American uniform was interested in a churches archives.

It was still only just after nine in the morning when they arrived amidst the small queue of people waiting for Sunday Service. Looking around, Deacon sought out and approached one of the Priests. 'Father, my name is John Deacon. Can you help us please?'

Father Tomas smiled, his dark eyes clear and shining from his sun-browned wrinkled face, and said, ' Lo siento, no hablo Inglés.'

Gently moving Deacon aside, Rachel said in perfect Spanish, 'Father, my name is Rachel Sanchez, and this is my friend and colleague, John Deacon. We are both American, but I spent three years here in your wonderful city a few years ago while studying at the Carlos III University. In my studies, I researched over many weeks old papers stored here in your archives but I don't think we ever met.'

Smiling even more than before, Father Tomas replied in Spanish, 'Señorita, I am getting old I know, but I would never forget meeting someone as lovely as you. I expect you met with my predecessor, Father Guis, who unfortunately passed into Heaven over a year ago. What can I do for you?'

Having decided on their cover story while flying, Rachel answered, 'Father, a university in America, in Los Angeles, was so impressed with my work they are offering me a scholarship. But they need to see my

237

research papers and unfortunately, my home was robbed last year. With your permission, I would like to again find the information in your archives and make copies. That way I will be granted the scholarship. But time is of the essence. I need this information today.'

'My child, today is not possible. It is the Sabbath. It is a day of solemn rest, holy to the Lord.'

'Father. I understand and do not wish to cause any offence, but this is really important. Is there anything you can do, anything at all?' she said, with tears welling up in her eyes.

With the church now part of the Catholic Servite Order, and in common with all religious orders strictly so called, the Servites make solemn vows of poverty, chastity, and obedience. However, all men have hearts, and Father Tomas's was larger than most. Taking her hands in his, he looked into her eyes and said, 'My child, do not cry. You have a good heart, and I will allow you a concession, but you must promise me to take great care of our works. You must not take anything away and not damage any of the older pieces. But if you find what you are after you may photocopy what you require. Will you observe this rule?'

Quickly translating into English for Deacon, both said they would obey. Father Tomas even offered them the use of the photocopier in the rear office. 'We are the oldest church in Madrid. We have been here since the eleventh century, but even we have fax and computers now. Come with me,' he said and led them down to the catacombs.

# 81

The dim light bulbs failed in their effort to light up the room. The shadows bouncing off the walls and ceilings and the strands of cobwebs made the atmosphere complete. There was history here. History from generations of people who'd lived and died, laughed and smiled, and fought and loved.

Making sure they were comfortable and had access to anything they needed, Father Tomas said he would come back down in a few hours and then bid them goodbye.

Looking around it was clear there had not been any real form of cataloguing, and there were piles of books, parchment and old papers in bundles. They decided the only way would be to just start to look through everything while putting things in date order. Rachel said that what she had found originally had been a small brown diary roughly A5 in size and some old parchment sheets a little larger than A4 with one folded sheet two to three times larger.

Working quickly but carefully with the valuable artefacts, they had made three main piles within ninety minutes. The first pile consisted of books in date order where possible, and those with no date showing, stored alongside. The second pile was obviously maps, and the third pile consisted of all other forms of paper or parchment.

Rachel's eyes were irritated by the fine layers of dust kicked up, and they had both put covers over their mouths to save breathing in the fine particles and paper dust mites. Deacon had used a handkerchief and Rachel her scarf. Starting with the dated books, Rachel quickly scanned each one dated 1690 onwards through to 1730. She knew the author had written the diary around the turn of the century but couldn't remember the year. Deacon had started reviewing the maps, trying to isolate those that showed any outline similar to La Palma.

By five in the afternoon, they had completed their search but had still not found what they were looking for. With a feeling of despair, Rachel went back upstairs to speak with Father Tomas.

Finding him finishing that afternoon's service, she asked him, 'Father. We have been very careful with your old works but have still not found anything. Could anything be stored elsewhere?'

He stroked his chin and thought for a moment. 'My child, it is possible that Father Guis may have moved some paperwork. There is another room further into the catacombs. I haven't been inside it myself, but it is possible. Let me find the key, and I will open it for you.'

Eventually, after many frustrated minutes of waiting while Father Tomas searched his desk, he gave out an excited 'Here it is' and taking her hand led her down into the depths of the church again.

Taking a torch, Father Tomas led them further into the darkness until he approached an old solidly built oak door. It had defied the years and was still as solid as when built. Putting the key in the lock, the Father had trouble turning the key. Deacon stepped in to help, and a resultant deep-throated 'click' signalled it was now unlocked. Gently pushing the door open the dried and stiff hinges groaned and squeaked, but the hinges were no match for the strong, careful pushing from Deacon.

Leading them inside Father Tomas said, 'Father Guis spent some time here before he passed. Perhaps the paperwork you are after is here. If not I don't know where else to suggest. Again I would ask you to please be careful. Much of this paperwork is valuable beyond belief - not in a monetary sense, you understand although collectors will usually pay high prices for antiques like this - but in a clerical sense. Some of these papers are hundreds of years old.'

Looking around, Rachel could sense the history here. Most of the room was empty, and some parchments had rotted on the floor, now no more than dust held together. Any attempt at movement would shatter their powder skeletons for all time.

Carefully moving across the flagstones, the loom of her torch picked out a small shelf. Sat tidily on the shelf were some books and papers. With her heart racing, Rachel carefully examined the books. Third down was the diary she was after.

'This is it,' she exclaimed. 'This is the diary. The maps must be here as well somewhere. Let's carry all this carefully out into the other room where we can see them properly.'

Rachel laid the paperwork down on the desk where the light was better. It was easy to see what fragile condition much of the paperwork was in.

Deacon gently unfolded the maps and found two that both seemed of La Palma. Rachel opened the diary and found the small map drawings she'd last seen briefly over three years before.

'This is it, John,' she said. 'This is the diary I saw before. I'd not had chance to read all of it before my copies were stolen, but I remember the main facts. First, let me give you an overview of the island I know from general knowledge, and she began to recite from memory, 'Once known to the ancient Romans as the Fortunate Islands, the Canary Islands were named after the large

241

wild dogs (Canes) found living on the islands. Located off the north-western coast of Africa, the Canary Islands are now one of the most popular tourist destinations on the planet, especially with Europeans. But during the Middle Ages, it was a bit different. In 1495 the islands were incorporated into the Kingdom of Castile. Soon after that, the islands became stopping-off points for the Spanish conquerors, traders, and missionaries on their way to the New World. This trade route brought great prosperity, and the islands became quite wealthy and magnificent palaces, and churches were built on La Palma during this period. But with wealth comes thieves. The islands also attracted pirates wanting to steal the gold and treasures brought back from the New World and destined for mainland Spain. These pirates, or Barbary Corsairs, are often shown as heroes by Hollywood, but, in fact, they were usually just murdering thieves and rapists. The pirates would often anchor along the shore and attack small hamlets and villages for food etc. Then they would wait for the bigger ships, attack them, steal the treasure and then disappear off. This diary is about one such attack.'

'So all this is about an attack?' Deacon asked.

'Well, yes and no,' Rachel said, gently looking through the diary. 'Let me find the correct pages ... Ah, here it is. It's written is Spanish, but in an old-fashioned dialect so it will take me a while to translate. It's about a farmer, Jose Fernandez, and his family living in a small village near the west coast. They weren't the poorest, being they actually rented the land and they had some crops as well as some animals, but the ground was quite steep and very rocky. Not much would grow, so they definitely weren't rich. But one day in 1683, Pirates came and attacked the village. They raped and stole and killed about twenty villagers. This diary is actually written by the farmer's

242

son, Galeno. The mother was raped and killed, the father had been left for dead, but initially survived, and his sisters were kidnapped and likely sold into slavery. Galeno, his father and the local priest, ran and hid from the pirates and took shelter in a cave on the farmer's land. The farmer and Galeno had found the entrance to the cave by accident and explored it about three months before. It led right into the heart of the mountain and was very hot. Galeno says here how he was frightened by the 'Devil groans' they heard, and so they kept away from it. But when the pirates attacked, there was nowhere else to go. They hid in the cave but then the earth shook, and the roof collapsed and trapped them inside.'

'But they must have got out for the diary to be written,' Deacon said.

'Yeah, it seems the father died in the earthquake. He was hit by the falling roof, leaving just the priest and Galeno. They moved into the other parts of the cave, and eventually found a small crack and got out, about three days later, it says. They were close to collapse due to heat exhaustion but had drunk a lot of the water coming through the tunnel face, so managed to survive. Galeno didn't have any family left and was too young to look after himself, so the priest took him to the city of Santa Cruz, and the church took him in. He was brought up by the church, taught to read and write, and became a priest. From the date, it seems he wrote this diary and drew the maps when he was twenty-eight, about twenty or so years later. He stayed in the church, and I expect records will show he died in the church. But when he wrote about what happened and being trapped underground, he gave a detailed description of where the cave and tunnels led and also where the mouth of the tunnel had been before the roof collapse. He describes here how it seems the tunnels led right to the very heart of the mountain. He

243

refers to the hot water coming out of the rocks and the mud. Then a little later, he speaks of the air being very moist but the rock at the end of this part of the tunnel being very hard and dry. This will be the central core of very hard rock that the looser, water-soaked outer loose rock sits on. John, you told me that a nuclear explosion produces intense heat as well as the actual explosive blast. Correct?'

'That's right. Often the intense heat does more actual damage than the blast. Why?'

'Well, if you set off something with intense heat at the rock junction, all the water in the loose outer rock would turn to steam and expand, making it even looser. Any blast would likely produce enough vibration to make the whole lot slip into the sea, and there's your mega-tsunami, and it's goodbye to America's East Coast.'

They then spent some time looking closely at the old maps, matching them against satellite images they had brought with them and the data she had collected years before. After about an hour she finally said, 'I can place the cave mouth location down to about six places all fairly close together. The main problem is that the landscape has changed a little over the centuries and some of the identifying points have moved or disappeared. When Galeno wrote this diary, luckily for us, he visited the site again, instead of just writing from memory, but obviously, the landscape has still changed somewhat since then. Out of the six sites we found, I would say these two are the most likely,' she said, putting red crosses on the satellite laminates.

# 82

## Cumbre Vieja - Monday, September 10th

Within the hour, Deacon was climbing on board a CH-47D Chinook at the military area of Madrid-Torrejón Airport for the ninety-minute flight to Rota to meet up with his team. He'd left Rachel to sleep and then enjoy a few days of leisurely break around the shops, bars and restaurants of Madrid, courtesy of Uncle Sam.

It was past one in the morning when Deacon's flight landed. Having been awake almost non-stop for over thirty-six hours, he decided to sleep and plan the forthcoming action in the morning. He met his men at 06:00 Monday morning and spent the next two hours briefing them and the Spanish FGNE Special Forces about the six potential sites. All the sites were within a two-kilometre radius, which raised its own problems. The sites were close enough and visible to each other for any exploring to likely be detected. Deacon knew the bomb in Hawaii was set on timer only, but it was highly probable this one would have a manual override switch as well.

Joint operation between the two organisations was essential, so Deacon liaised with Captain Eduardo Delgado, the commander of the FGNE team assigned to work with him. There were a total of six SEALs, including Deacon, as well as twelve FGNE; therefore each site would have two FGNE and one SEAL. As for Deacon and Captain Delgado, they would each lead a team into the two most likely sites. Once the correct site was discovered and made safe, Eric Staples and his team would take over and actually disarm the device or devices.

Flying from Rota to Gando Air Base on Gran Canaria before arriving lunchtime on Monday took a little over two hours in a US Airforce C130 temporarily re-assigned from operations in Europe. Conversation on board between the three teams was muted. Each man knowing what they had to do and each praying for a safe outcome.

The two teams spent the remainder of the day and evening getting to know each other during joint exercises. Each team has their own unique way of operating together and trying to suddenly bring in other members of other groups, without allowing time to acclimatise, would be courting disaster. Deacon and Delgardo spent the remaining daylight hours working with the men and making sure everyone knew their role as all Special Forces groups like to prepare plan and exercise as much as possible in a 'real' situation. Unfortunately, in this instance, the teams would be going in almost blind with therefore a higher possibility of casualties.

The ideal plan would be to attack all six sites simultaneously by helicopter and rappel down, but Deacon and Delgardo both agreed that the noise of multiple helicopters would alert the terrorists and allow them to re-group. Therefore he and Delgardo devised a simultaneous ground attack plan. At dusk, they boarded the Chinook again for the forty-minute flight to the small naval base at Santa Cruz de La Palma and then stood the men down for a four-hour rest period.

Meeting with the Commander of the naval base, Deacon asked Delgardo to translate and ask the CO for news of any strange or unusual activities within the last few weeks. The CO replied, through Delgardo, that a Turkish-owned freighter, the *Mehtap*, had gone missing a week or so ago after leaving Palmas de Gran Canaria en-route to Casablanca. It had left on schedule but never arrived. Air-sea rescue services had been informed, but no trace of the ship had been found. There had been storms close into the African coast, so the searches had now been called off, fearing the ship had been lost with all hands. In local news, most things were normal. He'd received a report from La Palma that an officer of the Guardia Civil, Officer Cabo Jiminez, had gone missing also about a week or so ago but after he'd failed to turn up for work for two days a search party had found his crashed vehicle eventually. It was in a remote, wooded part of the island and it was assumed he'd fallen asleep while driving and crashed. His body wasn't in the wreck, but search teams were hoping he might still turn up merely injured. He also reported that petty crime levels were dropping again as holiday visitors finished their summer vacations and the islands got back to normal for this time of the year.

Thanking him, Deacon then contacted Mitch and Admiral Carter by secure telephone. Getting them both on the line, he began, 'Admiral. Mitch. We have the final coordinates and Captain Delgardo and I are putting the final touches to the plan. A freighter and a local police officer of the Guardia Civil have both gone missing around the same time. It could be totally random, but perhaps you can get our intelligence experts looking into whether there is a connection. I'll send you the details by secure email. Apart from that, we are still working on the assumptions of the six sites Miss Sanchez came up with. Do you have any updates for me?'

'Lieutenant, our intelligence has concluded that whoever has planned this most likely scheduled for both devices to detonate at the same time. The phrase 'Jaws of Allah' refer to, we believe, the same as an animal. Therefore, if the jaws are expected to close together, we think the device at your location to be primed to detonate at 18:00 local, the same actual time as the defused device in Hawaii. This would have had maximum physical and

247

psychological impact causing maximum terror to the public,' the Admiral said. 'Further, our investigations have uncovered that a person of Palestinian birth, named Saif, working closely with Hamas, is most probably the instigator of this. This means there will likely be terrorists willing to ensure success. By the time you deploy at 04:00, a KH-11 will be in position, and active voice and video comms will be up and running. There will be live feeds to the Pentagon and the White House situation room. Good hunting to you and your men.'

# 83

## Cumbre Vieja - Tuesday, September 11th

At 03:00 the six teams climbed into their respective 4-wheel drive vehicles, with Staples and his team taking a truck. Radio checks were completed between each team member and team-to-team. Travelling across the island on the LP-3 they then turned south on the LP-2. The two police outriders broke off and returned to base. As they approached the village of Jedey, the six teams split to each assigned target.

Teams one and two stopped and quietly observed. There was no movement at either location. Infrared binoculars showed only heat targets lying down, appearing asleep. The team members approached stealthily and, using an endoscope camera in through an open window, quickly realised target one comprised of an old couple and target two was a family. Two of the FGNE team removed their masks and weapons before knocking loudly on the doors. The family at target two were startled and on vacation and knew nothing. It took a number of knocks before the old man came to the door at the other target. Speaking quickly, the FGNE soldier asked if there were any strangers around, or if he had seen anything suspicious. To the surprise of the soldier, the old guy didn't seem taken aback at all by the sight of a six-foot-tall soldier, dressed in black, holding a full-face helmet, asking him questions at 4:00 o'clock in the morning. He said a new stranger was renting the old farmhouse a couple of valleys over, promptly shut the door while muttering 'Goodnight' and went back to bed.

In the meantime, teams' three and four had found their respective targets and reported them as safe. One was empty and showed no signs of anyone having been there for ages. The other was a working farm and the owner already starting work had seen the FGNE approaching and had grabbed his shotgun thinking they were thieves. Only the quick-witted action of one of the men in sprinting forward and tackling the farmer to the ground had stopped a possible exchange of gunfire. Handcuffed and dragged into the farm kitchen, the farmer cursed the soldiers, the government, the Police and finally his God before eventually quietening down. He too mentioned the new person in the other valley.

Deacon and his team were just approaching their target, the highest up the slope when they got word that team five had also come up empty.

Deacon was just deploying his two colleagues into position when the loud rhythmic chatter of an AK-47 opened up, and one of his team fell.

# 84

Mostafa had not slept well this evening. He'd awoken and taken a piss but still couldn't sleep. Stood near the side door, he was just about to light a cigarette when he heard a vehicle stop. Something made the hairs on his neck stand up. Four o'clock wasn't particularly early for a farmer to be moving about, but the vehicle door hadn't slammed; it was more the click when someone was trying to shut it quietly. Slipping back inside briefly, he grabbed his weapon, a set of night-vision goggles and two-way radio. In the side barn, he'd previously moved some straw bales into a perfect shooting position so while climbing into the nest he'd made he radioed Fawaz.

'Hey, something is going on down here. Get to the entrance. Let me check this out, and I will get back to you. Insha'Allah,' he whispered.

The reply was almost instant, 'Death to the infidels, brother'.

Mostafa scanned around and could see three ghostly green figures slowly approaching. He could see their body armour, helmets and weapons. He sighted on the closest and just as the figure came into full view, gently pulled the trigger. The four-shot burst stitched across the targets chest and up into his face. The body armour took the brunt of the first two shots but shot three found its mark in the soldier's throat shattering his spine in two and shot four entered his face just below his nose, exiting along with most of his brains just above his left ear.

With a cry of 'Allahu Akbar', Mostafa sighted on the other two, but they'd gone.

# 85

Deacon had hit the dirt the moment the first shot had registered. The remaining FGNE soldier also had quick reactions Deacon thought as they both scrambled for cover behind a wall.

'Bear Group, Team Six. Targets located. Man down,' he radioed, knowing the other teams would all proceed to his location.

With his FGNE colleague laying down suppressed covering fire, Deacon hastily scooted to his left to get a better position and also started returning fire. It's always the same, he thought - No plans survives the first contact with the enemy.

Mostafa was now effectively pinned down by accurate crossfire but could also keep Deacon and the other FGNE soldier at a distance.

'Brother, what is happening?' came over the radio.

'The infidels are here. There were three, but I got one. How have we been discovered?'

'I don't know but do not let them pass, brother. God the Almighty has decreed we stand and fight. Kill them and then join us. Allahu Akbar.'

Mostafa kept up sporadic gunfire but couldn't keep both men under watch. Deacon moved again to better cover further on his left and opened fire again on him. While Mostafa was pinned, the FGNE soldier crept forward, but Mostafa saw the movement and fired a quick burst. With bullets spraying around his feet, the FGNE soldier dived back undercover, but the two seconds Mostafa had been shooting allowed Deacon to get an accurate sighting and he loosed off a quick burst of three shots. One missed completely, but the second and third found their mark.

With his left elbow and shoulder smashed, Mostafa dropped his Kalashnikov and dived back through the farmhouse door. Deacon was already up and running, his M4 rifle and scope up to his face. The red laser danced across the door as Deacon fired another three-shot burst, destroying the lock. Kicking the door in Deacon ducked inside in time to see the terrorist pull the grenade pin. Firing as he turned Deacon saw at least one round hit the terrorist and the grenade dropped.

'Grenade,' he managed to shout as he dived back outside for cover.

The blast that close was deafening numbing his ears and the force blew the windows out. Deacon saw but couldn't hear the terrorist's body hit the doorframe just before the roof collapsed, and dust obscured his view.

Sitting up moments later, ears still ringing from the blast, he brushed the dust off his goggles and slowly climbed to his feet. A helping hand from his FGNE colleague helped him the last bit. Nodding his thanks he could begin to hear the radio chatter as his hearing slowly returned.

Teams one and two were arriving along with Captain Delgado and team five, and they set about examining the collapsed farmhouse. It was obvious this was the terrorist base, and they looked for anything of interest. Deacon walked into the courtyard and was giving an update by radio back to the Pentagon.

'Admiral,' Deacon said, 'we have one terrorist down and one man dow- INCOMING! TAKE COV-,' before the remains of the farmhouse were hit by an RPG.

The blast blew Deacon sideways, but he was far enough outside to miss most of the force. Those still inside never stood a chance. One SEAL and four FGNE, including Delgado, were killed instantly. Another SEAL and two FGNE were injured, but he couldn't see how badly. Sweeping his eyes around the hillside Deacon could see the RPG trail smoke slowly fading.

'Admiral, we have lost almost half our force, but we have a good idea as to where the tunnel entrance is. Will regroup and attack. Deacon out.'

# 86

Kourosh put the grenade launcher back down and smiled. 'God is with us today, brother,' he said. 'That's five infidels who will never fight again.'

'You're correct, brother, but I fear our troubles are not over yet. We need to hold the tunnels for over fourteen hours, Insha'Allah,' Fawaz said. 'Keep guard while I set the charges,' he said as he moved over to the entrance and disappeared back inside.

Kourosh checked the magazine in his Kalashnikov again then placed a spare loaded additional weapon next to him as well as over a dozen full magazines and four hand-grenades. Fawaz had equipped his gun placement in the same way, and they had further weapons back inside the entrance. Between them, they had almost a 170-degree view of the hillside dropping away in front of them down towards the still smoking farmhouse ruin. The morning sky was beginning to lighten behind them, keeping the tunnel entrance, them and their positions completely in the shade. Kourosh smiled as he thought about the attackers fighting uphill, heading into the soon to rise morning sun. Allah is with us, he thought.

Fawaz was soon back. 'It is done, brother,' he said. 'If we have to withdraw we can collapse the roof. It will take them a while to regroup - let's eat before the infidels climb here,' he said, passing food and drink to his colleague.

# 87

Deacon left two men securing the area while he looked at the maps with his remaining men. Teams three and four had joined him, and he now had a group of ten men left, down from the original eighteen. The injured SEAL was out for this battle with a broken leg, but one of the wounded FGNE had been strapped up and was able to continue.

'I want five two-man teams A through E,' Deacon said.

'Teams A to C will attack straight uphill, covering each other. We need to stay well separated. If they use an RPG again, I don't want the chance of more than one of us being a target. It's the best part of 900 yards to where they are firing from, all of it uphill and with minimal cover. The bastards have us cold firing downhill. Team's D and E you will go over to the next valley, D goes left, E goes right. Get above them and then approach from over this way,' he said, pointing to the map. 'You need to get above the entrance and provide covering fire for us. Any questions? No? Good. Grab your gear, we moved out in ten.'

He then unpacked and assembled his MK11 sniper's rifle and attached the Leopold 'scope.

The men split into their respective teams and began the journey uphill. Crouching low behind the drystone walls provided some cover as they moved slowly up and over the steep, rough ground.

Within moments the AK-47's had opened up again, and bullets began peppering the ground around them.

Deacon rested his rifle on a wall near a large boulder and slowly took aim, trying to find a target. The whole hillside and target area was in deep shadow, but the muzzle flashes pinpointed their firing positions. Five times Deacon gently squeezed the trigger, but each time his rounds failed to find flesh.

The hidden shooting positions of Fawaz and Kourosh provided clear shots for them while minimising their exposure. None of the incoming shots found targets. Theirs however aimed from protected shelters were harder to avoid. Ricochets and splintering rocks began to take their toll on Deacon's men. It was also too easy to lose footing amongst the shale and loose rocks while trying to race up the steep slope.

Deacon aimed and fired again, this time his round clipping Fawaz's Kalashnikov, causing it to spin from his hands.

'Quickly brother, fire another grenade over to the right towards that boulder,' he urged Kourosh, as he picked up another weapon.

Deacon saw the puff of smoke and dived for cover as the grenade snaked down the slope towards him. The force of the blast lifted him before slamming him back down, but luckily the boulder and wall had deflected the worst of the explosion away from him. The FGNE soldier to Deacon's right wasn't so lucky. Fragments of metal and shards of exploding boulder sliced into him, severing one leg at the knee and reducing his right arm to a pulp. Dragging his colleague into what little cover there was, Deacon tried to apply field dressings, but the arteries were shredded, and he watched helplessly as he quickly bled out.

His rifle had also been damaged in the blast so dropping it down he quickly snatched his M4 off his back and scrambled further left, thereby making maximum target separation between his men.

Over the next hour, it became a painful game of providing covering fire while making slow progress up the slope, while teams D and E moved into position. Twice more grenades were fired down on them, and some of the men suffered small flesh injuries.

Not to be taken by surprise Kourosh had been keeping an eye on the slopes behind and above them. As a trained fighter the first thing he had done when arriving was to look at how he would have carried out the attack and built his defences accordingly. Their shooting positions had some rear cover, allowing them to get back to the entrance safely. Estimating it would take an hour for anyone to get into position, he was about to call Fawaz to regroup when the first few rounds from the rear began to land close. Grabbing their weapons the two of them quickly moved back into the shelter of the tunnel.

Now the defending firepower had reduced, Deacon and his remaining men could approach quickly. Within ten minutes Deacon had the surrounding area under control with his men positioned just outside the field of fire from the tunnel mouth.

While appraising the situation and deciding on the next action, Deacon heard a heavier truck arrive at the smoking farmhouse ruins. Looking down the mountainside, he could see Eric Staples and his men dismount, grab rucksacks and holdalls and start climbing up towards him.

Over the next two hours, it remained a stalemate. There was a continuous stream of murderous fire from the two terrorists towards anyone who came into their field of view. Deacon's men also kept up constant harassing fire and fired tear-gas and smoke grenades into the entrance, but the terrorist's firepower didn't seem to weaken.

With time running out and no visible progress made, Deacon decided the only way forward was a do-or-die full-on frontal attack.

With his men supplying a sustained and concentrated field of covering fire, Deacon and two colleagues crouched as low as possible and ran forward while volley after volley of stun grenades, teargas and smoke grenades were fired into the entrance to try to disorientate the defenders.

One of the SEAL team members got to the opening seconds in front of Deacon and saw movement through the smoke. As he fired a prolonged burst, he was hit by return fire. The force of the multiple impacts to his ceramic body armour caused him to fall backwards into Deacon knocking them both to the floor, with one of the rounds hitting him in the small gap between chest and shoulder armour plates.

# 88

Fawaz and Kourosh had defended well. The gun positions had worked as planned giving them clear targets. Once back inside the mountain, they had easily managed to keep up continuous fire knowing the attackers wouldn't use high explosives because of the danger of roof collapse, but the attackers had also been lucky. Ricochets and exploding rock fragments had injured both of them. Kourosh had been hit multiple times with his protective body vest deflecting the worst, but he still bled from numerous small wounds. Fawaz was similarly injured having lost blood from a cheek wound when a rock fragment had passed clean through his right cheek and out through his left, taking three teeth with it.

Realising the condition both he and Kourosh were in, and knowing they wouldn't be able to defend the tunnel for much longer, Fawaz strapped a bandage around his face wounds and withdrew further into the tunnel. Kourosh was still nearer the entrance when the attackers increased their firing. With stun and smoke grenades exploding near his position Kourosh also began to retreat further into the tunnel when the smoky daylight from the tunnel entrance was obscured by the darker outline of a man.

Kourosh tried to raise his weapon in time. Had he not had so many small wounds, he might have managed it. The muscles in his arm, along with the loss of blood and the tightness of the skin on his shoulder caused by the previous steam burn all played their part.

The attackers' bullets tore into him from stomach to chest. His vest slowed their impact slightly but all of them passed through, and Kourosh felt his stomach burn and convulse. As he fell back, his arm muscles finally obeyed, and he pulled the trigger and never let go.

When the hammer eventually fell on the empty chamber and with the attack momentarily stalled, the sudden silence was deafening. Only the faint gasping sounds of Kourosh slowly reciting 'Allahu Akbar, Allahu Akbar' could be heard as he transited this world for the one where 72 virgins awaited him.

Fawaz retreated further along the tunnel, pulled the 10-second fuse on the explosives and dived for cover. Deacon, having finally pushed his injured colleague off himself, started running headlong further into the tunnel, closely followed by an FGNE soldier. Firing his M4 in short bursts, it finally clicked on empty. With no more spare magazines, Deacon tossed it aside and grabbed his Sig-Sauer. As they both ran forward, Deacon saw the flash momentarily before he felt the explosive blast pick him up and throw him against the tunnel wall. This was followed moments later by a deep rumble as the wet tunnel walls seemed to bulge, spraying him with warm water as a 14-foot section of the tunnel roof collapsed down on him with something striking his head and sending him into a deep black void.

# 89

Slowly Deacon became aware of pain throbbing in his head. He tried to open his eyes, but the left one seemed stuck closed. He tried to bring his left hand up towards his face, but that was also impossible. Gradually he realised he could make out a yellow glow from a lamp flickering across his one good eye as he tried to raise his head. Pain lanced through his temple as he felt himself sinking again.

'Hey Pig, wake up. PIG WAKE UP!' he heard.

Slowly opening his eye again, he could make out the shape of a person. As his vision partly cleared, he could see one of the terrorists sat leaning against the tunnel wall, face wrapped in a blood-stained cloth, aiming his own weapon at him.

'Pig, wake up. You ain't dead yet but soon will be,' the defender said between spitting out globules of blood.

Coming more fully awake Deacon realised he was lying down and could feel a heavy weight pinning his lower part of his body. His left ankle throbbed and he tried moving his legs, but couldn't. His left arm was partly covered by rubble, but he managed to pull it free. Moving his right hand up towards his face, he gingerly touched a golf ball-sized lump on his forehead and winced. He was lying partly covered in warm water and tried splashing some with his right hand over his face. His left eye slowly regained vision as the dried blood cleared.

Slowly moving his head to look around, his brain was coming back up to full speed. There had been an explosion, and some of the tunnel roof had collapsed. On the positive side, he was alive and lying on the tunnel floor face down covered by rubble up to his waist, but also quite wet. He could feel his legs, but not move them and was trapped. His head throbbed, and his forehead was cut quite deeply. There was also a large swelling on his forehead where something heavy had struck him. His eyes, nose and mouth were full of dust and dirt, but his eyesight was OK now that he'd washed the dried blood away.

On the not-so-good side, the person he was chasing was sat not ten feet from him aiming his own weapon at him, face wrapped in a makeshift bandage, bleeding, couldn't talk properly, and not looking in the best of moods. It was also quiet, apart from the sound of running water. He listened, but there wasn't any gunfire.

'Pig. How do you want to die? I can shoot you with your own gun, or I skin you like the pig dog you are.'

'What time is it, fuckhead?' Deacon said.

'What?'

'I said, what time is it? You do understand English, don't you?'

'Yeah, I understand English. And Arabic. And Spanish. And I also understand that I'm gonna kill you.'

'Well, before you try and do that, why don't you tell me what the time is and then I'll kill you, fuckhead?' Deacon said.

'You're a crazy fucker ... It's almost 2, and you're abou — .'

'And you are Manuel Garibaldi, or at least that's one of your names, fuckhead' Deacon said. 'And there's a stolen nuke somewhere back there in the tunnels that's meant to explode and cause a massive tsunami to engulf the east coast of America,' he continued.

'What? ... How the fu ... ?'

'The plans shot, fuckhead,' Deacon said. 'We know all about the Jaws of Allah. It won't work. Half of the jaws have already been defused, so it won't really be much of a bite, will it? And once I've killed you, my colleagues will defuse the bomb, and I will personally make sure you're buried in a pigskin. No eternal after-life for you! No waiting 72 virgins, I'm afraid.'

'Kill me? That's where you're wrong, pig. My name is Fawaz Aziz Al Farah. The bomb will explode in four hours, and it will be death to America.'

'So why will it be death to America, fuckhead?'

'A powerful wave, more powerful than a mere man like you can comprehend shall engulf America. Millions of your kind will die,' Fawaz said, almost as he was reading it from a book. 'Both shores of America will feel the bite of Allah. Allah is the greatest. Allahu Akbar.'

'Why in four hours, asshole?'

'For the bite to be most effective both jaws must bite as one, Insha'Allah,' he said, between spitting out blood.

'Is that what you've been told? So, fuckhead, today is the anniversary of the Twin Towers. Today is '9/11', yeah?' Deacon said. 'The Hawaii bomb was set to go off today, but we've defused it, so there ain't no jaws to bite. Do you get it? Someone's been lying to you. Setting you up to die, asshole,' Deacon continued, trying to rile Fawaz.

'You were never meant to get out of here alive. They've planned on you dying, fuckhead,' he said.

'To die for Allah is the greatest honour. Allahu Akbar,' Fawaz responded.

'Yeah, in battle,' Deacon said, 'but not from one of your brothers wanting you to die. Sounds like they just left you for dead, fuckhead.'

'You're the one going to die,' Fawaz said, raising the weapon and pointing it at Deacon's face.

'Gotta take the cowards way out, huh fuckhead? Can't even kill me like a man. Yeah, that'll really impress those virgins – shooting a trapped man,' Deacon said, before adding the word 'Jaban', Arabic for a coward.

Fawaz kept the gun pointing at Deacon's head for almost 10 seconds before standing and placing it in his belt. 'You're right,' he said. 'There are better ways to kill a pig. Maybe I will skin you alive?'

Deacon quietly breathed a sigh of relief. He had no chance against a bullet in the head but if he could rile the guy enough to come close ...'

Fawaz picked up his fallen rucksack and pulled out a six-inch ceramic blade. 'How do you know about my name of Garibaldi?' he asked.

'Do you remember a young lady called Rachel Sanchez? She remembers you, fuckhead,' Deacon said. 'She told me all about you, and all about your little dick. After she had left you, she found a proper man, an American. Somebody who could satisfy her. Someone who made her feel like a real woman,' he said.

'That Bitch!' Fawaz shouted. 'I should have killed her when I had the chance. I wanted to skin the bitch alive. Make her suffer. Teach her how a proper Muslim woman should behave. I would have sliced her skin off and laid it out in the sun to dry. I would have made the bitch beg me to kill her,' he screamed while running his finger along the blade. 'Just like I did with Rosa. She begged for her life, the slut ... . You know hundreds of years ago all of Spain was run by the Moors. The whole country was Muslim. Women were decent then. Knew their place. Then they became like all the other western whores,' he continued, almost talking to himself. 'But I showed her how to obey a proper Muslim man,' he said.

'Real big of you, Jaban,' Deacon said.

With a cry, Fawaz rushed towards Deacon, still lying trapped on the floor, with the knife raised high, ready to bury it in Deacon's back.

In an eye blink Deacon twisted at his hips to his left and, as the knife came down, praying it would cut clean, jammed the palm of his left hand straight onto the point of the blade. As the blade cut deep into his palm and the hilt pressed against his skin, his arm countered the forward motion of Fawaz to off-balance him. At the same time, Deacon's right hand struck Fawaz's left knee cap with all the force he could muster.

The force of his hand hitting the kneecap would likely have done some damage. The jagged 2lb rock in his hand definitely did. With a crack like a dry branch snapping, Fawaz's left patella shattered. Fawaz howled and let slip the now bloody blade handle collapsing on the floor next to Deacon as his leg gave out. Deacon quickly pulled the blade from his palm, hoping he wouldn't inflict more damage to his hand than had already been done, and plunged it three times in quick succession into Fawaz's groin. Dropping the blade Deacon deftly pulled his own Sig Sauer from Fawaz's waistband and promptly shot him twice in the head.

'Like I said, fuckhead. Once I've killed you, my colleagues will defuse the bomb.'

# 90

That, Deacon found, though might be harder to do. Pulling himself free from the rubble, he managed to slowly climb back to his feet. He'd been lucky inasmuch as the rocks trapping his legs hadn't appeared to do any serious damage to him. His legs were badly bruised, and his left ankle was sore, but it took his weight as he stumbled around. He retrieved his first-aid kit from his rucksack and cleaned and bound his damaged hand. Swallowing a couple of pain relief tablets he gingerly tried moving his fingers. He had trouble moving his first two fingers but then decided he had bigger things to worry about.

He looked around until he found his helmet. It had come off in the force of the explosion. Putting it back on, he could hear static in the earpieces.

'Team 1, Team 2, anyone. This is Deacon, over,' he said.

'Boss, where the fuck have you been?' was an excited answer almost immediately.

'Just hanging around shooting the breeze. Damn it's hot in here. What's the sitrep?'

'Six of us in total, boss. Three of us, including you and three FGNE. All got small wounds, but nothing too serious. Bad guys out here are dead. The tunnel looks blocked. We estimated about 15 feet of blockage which will take hours to remove. NEST crew are here. What's your sit?'

Deacon explained what had happened then asked to speak with Staples. 'Staples, it's set to explode at 18:00 local, that's less than four hours to defuse it. Talk me through what I can do.'

A few minutes later, grabbing the battery lantern Deacon explored further into the tunnel. It sloped downwards, gently at first, and narrowed at parts. The further he ventured, the hotter the water was seeping out of the walls and splashing to the floor. In some areas it pooled in others it disappeared through cracks. Coming to a number of caverns, Deacon remembered the diary he'd read with Rachel and just kept to the larger, central one. Eventually, after almost another half-mile into the tunnel, he could see a glow from around the next bend. Extinguishing his own lamp, he crept slowly towards the light pistol at the ready. Edging around the last bend and creeping up the final incline he could see a metal chest against the end wall. Realising there was nowhere for anyone to hide and that he was alone, he relaxed a little. This was it. This was the little bastard that could change the world, he thought.

Examining the chest, he was careful not to directly touch it. He'd lost all radio communication as he was too deep in the mountain, so not seeing any wires or booby traps he quickly photographed it on his phone and ran back to the entrance.

The team outside had moved as much rock as they could in the last hour, but the tunnel was still solidly blocked.

'Teams, this is Deacon. What progress?'

'Boss, we're moving as much as we can, but we need heavier tools. As we move some of it more roof collapses. We're about four foot in, but now it's bigger rocks, and it's too slow.'

Over the next hour, Deacon dug as much rubble away from his side while his team did the same outside. The body of the fallen FGNE soldier had been found and removed, and there was a small gap at roof level where daylight could be seen, but it was still far too narrow for Staples to climb through.

Getting Staples on the radio again, Deacon described the position of the chest, while Staples examined the photos Deacon had sent to him. To clear the tunnel enough to get through would take at least 3 more hours assuming no more roof collapsed. It would then take over 30 minutes to get to the bomb. The main problem being they were now down to just over eighty minutes until detonation.

Quickly devising a plan Deacon contacted the Admiral.

'Lieutenant, you've been smoking some serious shit, son,' he said. 'Are you goddamn serious? What the fuck do I tell the President?'

'Sir, with all due respect, sir, that's your job. Mine's to find a way to get this done.'

'Lieutenant, if the President tells the nation now, it will start an almighty panic, but some lives might get saved. But if he waits until when it detonates ... .'

'Sir, I'm doing my best to make sure it doesn't fucking detonate.'

'Son, you're trapped inside a tunnel with an active fucking nuke about to blow in less than an hour and a half, and the people who can defuse it are trapped outside. Correct?'

'Sir, gotta go. You've got my plan. You'll hear in about 75 minutes if it's worked or not. Deacon out.'

'Lieutenant, LIEUTENANT! Goddammit, you don't hang up on a fucking Admiral,' he said, but it was too late. Deacon had gone.

# 91

With the team working as fast as they could outside, and Deacon doing the same from the inside, they managed to remove another couple of feet of rubble away during the next 30 minutes. With Deacon lying on top of all the rocks, he could reach the small gap and gradually widened it until it was about the size of a basketball. Staples passed two rucksacks through, and Deacon grabbed them and ran as fast as he could manage back down the tunnel.

Stopping when the static in his earpiece began to fade, Deacon pulled a spare radio from one rucksack, switched it to 'Talk Thru' and placed it on the ground.

Twice more he had to stop and do the same before he eventually got to the device at 17:48 local time.

'Staples, can you hear me?' he radioed.

'Faint, but clear,' came the reply.

Deacon smiled. At least one thing had worked. Although their radios had good distance coverage outside, radio doesn't transmit well through rock. By placing other radios in 'Talk Thru' mode where the signal began to fade, he could now communicate again with his team.

'Staples. 12 minutes,' he said.

'OK. Get the unit out, connect the battery, switch it on and press the 'charge' button.'

Deacon opened the second rucksack and pulled out the plastic unit, connected the lithium battery pack and flicked the switch to 'charge'. The small meter showed a slow-moving red bar.

'Done. 10 minutes,' he said.

'John, this is where you have to take a chance,' Staples said. 'The other device was in a Pelicase inside a bigger outer case. That Pelicase was booby-trapped, but the outer casing wasn't. My hope and guess is that they've done the same here. The metal case might merely be to protect it bringing it into the tunnels. You need to open the metal case. Use the angle grinder to cut the padlocks off. Good luck.'

Deacon pulled out the battery angle grinder, pulled his goggles over his eyes, pressed the trigger and said a silent prayer as he placed the spinning grind wheel on the first padlock.

With a loud screech and a spray of sparks, the diamond-coated grind wheel cut into the hardened steel clasp. The metal glowed hot until with a final clang it fell off. Deacon quickly switched to the second lock which also succumbed.

'Eric locks off. 6 minutes,' he shouted.

'OK John, now slowly lift the lid. Try and look to see if there are any connecting wires. Hopefully, there aren't.'

Using his torch as a backlight, Deacon slowly opened the lid.

'Eric, lid's open. No wires. There is a Pelicase. 5 minutes,' he said.

'John, how's the charge on the unit? Can you get the Pelicase out?'

'Charge is about 70%. No, as to the Pelicase. It's placed at an angle with 2 padlocks locking it. It could be opened in situ, but obviously, I won't do that.'

'OK, place the unit and the battery inside the metal case with the red side of the unit against the Pelicase. Don't press the trigger yet. What's the charge showing?'

'It's showing 77%. Will do. 4 minutes. I hope they set their watches right when they set this,' he said.

'Wait until the charge is at least 90%. Then close your eyes, say a prayer and press the trigger,' Staples replied.

Deacon sat watching the second hand on his watch slowly tick away while also watching the charge dial calmly creep up past the 80%, then 81%...82%...83%...

'Eric, 86% and 3 minutes,' he said.

87%...88%...89%...90%

'Eric, 93% and one and half minutes. Here goes nothi —.'

With a squawk in his radio Staples lost all communication with Deacon.

# 92

Plunged into darkness Deacon didn't know what had happened. He'd expected something to happen when he pulled the trigger, maybe a loud buzz or a bang, but nothing. Apart from his radio momentarily screeching and then going dead just as the lamp went out, nothing seemed to happen.

He fumbled for his torch, but that was dead too. Looking at his wrist he could see the glow from the tritium on his watch hands, but they'd stopped as well. He wondered if he was dead and this was what it felt like, but standing he hit his head on the tunnel wall and thought well if I can feel pain I must be alive.

He stood there for 15-20 seconds just thinking and then it came to him. Slipping his own rucksack off, he reached in and pulled out some light sticks and broke one. The tunnel was immediately filled with a pale, eerie green glow, and he smiled.

Had he done enough? He sat back down and waited, counting off the seconds in his head. After 5 minutes, he relaxed a little. After 10 a bit more. By 20 he was positively laughing.

Breaking another light stick, he grasped the Pelicase handle and by upending the metal chest, slid it out. He grabbed the angle grinder, pressed the blade against the padlocks and pressed the trigger.

Nothing happened.

Deacon thought for a few seconds then decided he wasn't going to be defeated. After making sure the angle was correct, he placed his Sig close to a padlock and fired. With the bullet ricocheting off into the distance, the first padlock fell off. The second also succumbed to the same.

Opening the case, he could see all the parts of the bomb neatly laid out. Ripping as much of the wiring out as he could, he yanked the electronic boards out as well as the large battery and tossed them on the floor.

Lowering the lid, he thought how something so small would have caused so much damage. With nothing more that he could do, leaving everything else behind, he grabbed the remaining light sticks from his rucksack and started slowly walking towards the entrance.

It was harder going walking out due to the dim lighting from the light sticks. Twice he stumbled, dropping them on the wet floor. The first two radio systems he came to were also dead but the one nearest the entrance worked. Resetting it to standard mode, he pressed the transmit button.

'Teams, this is Deacon. Anyone receiving me?'

The near-instant reply was drowned by the cheers echoing down through the tunnels. As he neared the entrance, he could see daylight more clearly and the shapes of bodies climbing past the rubble.

After hugs from his team and back-slapping all around, Deacon found Staples waiting with a smile on his face.

'You did it! You crazy sonofabitch, you fucking did it!' Staples laughed.

'Nah. You've got to go and actually take it all apart. I just stopped it working,' Deacon said. 'But tell me, what did I actually do?'

'Three things are produced when an atomic bomb detonates. Enormous pressure or blast; incredible heat; and a massive electromagnetic pulse or EMP. The first two are fairly obvious. The pressure or blast, same as with any explosion, does most of the initial damage, but obviously, with a nuke, it's much more. The second, the heat, is incredible. Almost as hot as the sun but only for a very short period. That does all of the secondary damage. Anything not actually destroyed in the initial blast gets incinerated. It actually causes more damage than the initial blast,' Stables said.

'Yeah, I know that. It was the heat here that was likely to cause the main problem,' Deacon said.

'Exactly. Well, what a lot of people don't know about is the EMP, the electromagnetic pulse. This is similar to the heat blast. Where the heat blast is a short burst of extremely high temperature, the EMP is a pulse of extremely powerful electromagnetic energy. Everything electrical produces electromagnetic energy, from light bulbs to supercomputers. When electrons flow down a wire, they set up an electromagnetic force, or EMF, around them. Likewise, in reverse, EMF induces currents in wires. A radio antenna receives a signal because the EMF induces a current in it. That's normal. Some large electromagnetic pulses are natural as well. Lightning is one. That's why your radio will crackle in a lightning storm. But that's very low powered compared to one a nuke produces,' Staples continued. 'An EMP from a nuke produces such a massive pulse of energy it induces large currents in wires not designed for it. It basically fries electronics. If an airborne nuke were detonated somewhere over middle America now, every computer system, every radio, every mobile phone, every modern car, every landline phone, virtually everything electrical within a 1,000-mile radius would be completely fried.'

'Yeah, but the nuke didn't explode, did it?' Deacon said.

'Correct, 'cus you and I wouldn't be here now if it had. But that plastic unit you charged up was a portable EMP generator. When you pulled the trigger, you fired a massive blast of electromagnetic energy directly into the Pelicase. The reason it took so long to charge is it had to build up a charge in an enormous capacitor. 100% charge would have been better, but time was short, so I guessed anything over 90% would be enough. Luckily I was right. When you pulled the trigger, you 'induced' massive currents and voltages in all the wires and components inside the case. The electronics inside were not designed or built to withstand them, and I expect I will find everything just fried and fused when I examine them.'

'But wouldn't it have been built to withstand that on a battlefield?' Deacon asked.

'Possibly, but remember the nuke usually produces this when it explodes. It doesn't expect to be sat there having it happen to it. Also, the original metal shell casing had been discarded – it was just the explosive components, so that reduced any shielding. And finally, the new electronics added were commercial – I guessed the ones here would be the same or similar to the ones in Hawaii. They wouldn't have been built EMP 'safe'.'

'So that's why the radio went out, but what about the lamps and the grinder,' Deacon said.

'The voltages induced would have blown the bulbs, and the grinder has a motor. I expect that's also fried, or it would have contained a small processor to limit speed, etc. Either way, it will need to go in the trash now. Everything electronic you had on you or near you will have been ruined.'

'Why my watch? It's mechanical.'

'Battery operated mechanics with electronics inside. Afraid it's shit-canned,' Staples said.

'OK, understand all that, but why is everything out here working. Was the pulse not strong enough?'

'Correct. That unit produces a very high pulse but very localised. An antenna inside it actually focusses and directs the pulse. That's why you had to face it the right way. Also, rock blocks EMF. That's why you needed radio repeaters. This blast would have travelled along the tunnels but reducing in power the further it went.'

'Well I guess I should call the Admiral and tell him,' Deacon said, smiling.

'Being we're all still here, I think he knows,' Staples said.

# 93

Deacon looked out of the cabin window as the commercial jet came into land at Madrid – Barajas airport. After a long and detailed debrief with the Admiral by secure radio, while his hand was attended to by a medic, he'd asked if his flight home could be via Madrid.

There was a young lady there waiting, and he wanted to buy her a drink.

Over the coming weeks, the FBI and CIA got confirmation of the nationalities of the defenders as Palestinian and supporters of Hamas, and that the two al-Qaeda nukes had originally been stolen from Pakistan.

Although suspected, no confirmation of Iranian involvement was uncovered.

Huang Fu of The Yellow Lotus was arrested and imprisoned but refused to give evidence.

China refused to provide information concerning the shipping of the bulldozer.

The fishing boat Li Rong was never found.

In spite of extensive searches, no Palestinian with the name of Saif was identified.

# Fact File

Operation Neptune Spear is the code name of the US-led operation to capture or kill Osama bin Laden in Abbottabad, Pakistan, on May 2, 2011.

Details of the potential collapse and subsequent tsunami likely to occur from La Palma, Canary Islands, was first published by Stephen N Ward and Simon Day in June 2001.

Project Seal (also known as the Tsunami bomb) was a programme by the US Military, in conjunction with the New Zealand Military to develop a weapon that could create destructive tsunamis. This weapon was tested in Whangaparaoa off the coast of Auckland between 1944-1945.

# About the Author

I am the author of the John Deacon series of action-adventure novels. I make my online home at www.mikeboshier.com. You can connect with me on Twitter at Twitter, on Facebook at Facebook and you can send me an email at mike@mikeboshier.com if the mood strikes you.

Currently living in New Zealand, the books I enjoy reading are from great authors such as Andy McNab, David Baldacci, Brad Thor, Vince Flynn, Chris Ryan, etc. to name just a few. I've tried to write my books in a similar style. If you like adventure/thriller novels, and you like the same authors as I do, then I hope you find mine do them justice.

If you liked reading this book, please leave feedback on whatever system you purchased this from.

http://www.mikeboshier.com

# Books & Further Details

## Terror of the Innocent

Join US Navy SEAL John Deacon as he stumbles across an ISIS revenge plot using deadly weapons stolen from Saddam's regime. Masterminded by Deacon's old adversary, Saif the Palestinian, and too late to save the UK, Deacon and the world can only watch in horror as thousands suffer a terrible fate. Determined to stop the same outcome in the US, Deacon is in a race against time.

## High Seas Hijack - Short Story

Follow newly promoted US Navy SEAL John Deacon as he leads his team on preventing pirates attacking and seizing ships in and around the Horn of Africa in 2010. When a tanker carrying explosive gases is hijacked even Deacon and his team are pushed to the limit.

Check out my web page http://www.mikeboshier.com for details of latest books, offers and free stuff.

http://www.mikeboshier.com

# VIP Reader's Mailing List

To join our VIP Readers Mailing List and receive updates about new books and freebies, please click on this link below.

<u>Click Me!</u>

I value your trust. Your email address will stay safe and you will never receive spam from me. You can unsubscribe at any time.
Thank you.

Made in the USA
Middletown, DE
01 July 2023

34357870R00172